About the Author

Taryn Leigh is a South African born citizen, who spent her childhood with her nose buried in books. Her love for reading transpired into her ambition to become a writer. She first tried her hand at blogging, which eventually led to her writing her first novel. She lives in Pretoria, with her husband, son and two cocker spaniels.

Perfect Imperfections

Taryn Leigh

Perfect Imperfections

Olympia Publishers
London

www.olympiapublishers.com
OLYMPIA PAPERBACK EDITION

A CIP catalogue record for this title is
available from the British Library.

ISBN: 978-1-84897-845-4

This is a work of fiction.
Names, characters, places and incidents originate from the writer's
imagination. Any resemblance to actual persons, living or dead, is
purely coincidental.

First Published in 2017

Olympia Publishers
60 Cannon Street
London
EC4N 6NP

Printed in Great Britain

Dedication

For my Husband Shane, and my Son Luke.

Acknowledgments

To my publishers, Olympia Publishers, thank you for believing in my book and wanting to share it with the world. You are making my dream come true.

To my husband, who believed I could write, and pushed me to complete this, thank you for encouraging me to follow my dream and loving my imperfections perfectly. I appreciate you. Your character inspired me to write this.

To my son, you have shown me what true love is. I hope you feel my love for you every day, you are my joy and delight, the apple of my eye.

To my mom, the strongest woman I know, who taught me how important forgiveness is. This valuable lesson has made living life so much easier, and played a huge role in this story. Thank you.

To my 'sister', Cindy, thank you for sharing in my joy and excitement as I wrote each chapter of this book. Sister sister!

To family and friends who will find threads of our memories fictitiously embellished in the pages of this book, thank you for adding colour to my life.

Prologue

She bit her lip, clutching the giraffe she had placed on her lap tightly. It would be the only reminder she would carry of the life she was leaving behind. From the moment she saw it in the Heathrow Airport gift shop she just had to have it, no matter the cost.

She breathed in deeply as the plane took off. The thrill of lift off had always been her favourite feeling, but now it just weighed like lead deep in her stomach. She wasn't sure she was making the right choice in leaving her life in London to return to her birth place. All she wanted to do was to get as far away as possible from the memories haunting her. She'd try and start afresh in the place she'd once called home.

The cabin attendant came along pushing the trolley, looking sympathetically at her swollen eyes; it was obvious she had been crying. 'Can I give you something to drink, miss?' She spoke in a soft whisper, almost too afraid to disturb her.

'A strong cup of black coffee please,' she replied, conflicted by the emotions engulfing her.

She was on her way to see her best friend after almost ten years. She looked nervously down at the ring still on her ring finger, wishing she could erase the time. Time really did fly; it seemed as if she were a completely different person now. Would her friend even notice just how much life had changed her?

'Butter chicken or beef curry and rice?' the attendant interrupted her thoughts.

'Butter chicken, please, and could I get a bottle of still water?' she muttered. She looked away as she took the ring off and shoved it into her jeans pocket.

'Enjoy your dinner,' the attendant muttered with the cheerfulness that was required in her job description. She handed over the dinner tray and exchanged a knowing glance with the passenger next to her as she handed him his dinner.

'Is this your first time to South Africa?' a male voice drifted up questioningly. Her neighbour was a handsome man in his mid-thirties, with a kindness in his eyes.

'No, it's my birthplace. My family moved to London when I was eighteen; this is my first time back since we moved.' She spoke reluctantly, between staggered mouthfuls of food. She had no appetite but knew she needed to eat. Her clothes were already hanging on her thin frame and her once loved curves were starting to fade away. The stranger smiled at her, sensing that she really didn't want to talk, and decided to leave her be. He watched her play with her food, which she eventually managed to finish just as the attendant came to clear away their trays. He could only imagine what could be wrong with the beautiful woman whose light brown hair curled loosely over her pale cream sweater. Her striking blue eyes spoke of her despair.

She closed her eyes; she hadn't slept properly in three months and she wasn't sure she could sleep now. She wanted to try and sleep so she would look a little more rested when she saw her friend on arrival.

She had called Katy three days ago and asked if she could come and stay with her in Durban for a while. She knew she could rely on her; they were like sisters, and right now she was the only sister she had. Katy hadn't questioned why she needed to come. She knew her friend had faced great anguish, and despite her not knowing if that was her reason for moving, she knew that if she was leaving the life she had loved in London behind, there had to be a legitimate reason. For now she would just be there for her, no questions asked, for as long as she needed her. That's what friends did for each other, wasn't it?

Chapter One

'Good morning, sleepyhead. Good of you to finally join me.' Katy's face split into a delighted grin as she made the statement, knowing full well that her friend was exhausted from her twelve hour flight from London.

It was already eleven o'clock. Sarah had arrived in the early hours and had slept off her jet lag until now. She probably wouldn't have woken up if the smell of fresh scones baking hadn't wafted into her room.

'I thought I would make you your favourite,' Katy offered, speaking in bursts of excitement as she always had.

'Scones are definitely still my favourite. Thank God they weren't something I had to give up when we moved to London,' Sarah mused, thinking of the differences in food between South Africa and London.

She sat down at the kitchen table, clearly the heart of Katy's home. Her friend had always loved baking: an interest they shared. She watched as Katy moved fluidly around her rustic yet modern apartment. The style suited her personality, each room flowing with ease into the next. Huge seamless windows allowed maximum light and plush oversized furniture that, despite its size, created a sense of belonging. The kitchen had a charming intimacy, with bamboo counters and pristine white finishes which extended into the lounge and dining areas. She could see Katy's hand in each detail. Katy had a flair for design yet chose to study criminal law. It was a stark contradiction to the gentle and bubbly person she was, with her rosy cheeks, playful brown eyes and a jumble of black curls piled high on her head like mounds of candy floss. She exuded decisive energy, which gave her the edge in the court room.

'Here you go,' she said, setting the plates down on the table. Each scone was piled high with jam and cream. 'I cleared space for you in the wardrobe in your room so that you can unpack your clothes.'

'Oh, that won't be necessary. I plan on finding a place of my own in the next week or two. No sense getting too comfortable, I might never want to leave then,' Sarah teased, watching as Katy poured her a cup of Earl Grey tea, just the way she had always liked it: black with two teaspoons of sugar.

'Now listen here, young lady,' Katy scolded. 'This place will be your home for as long as you need it. I suggest we get your business up and running before you move out on your own. I could do with the company, you know; it's lonely living in this huge three bedroomed apartment all alone.'

'I can never win with you, can I?' Sarah chuckled, knowing too well not to fight her. Once she had an idea in mind, it was her way or the highway.

'Well, I suggest you unpack later and make yourself at home. Once you're nice and settled we will focus on starting your new life here.' Katy looked at Sarah through narrowed eyes, wondering if she would offer an explanation for why she wanted a new life. She could see Sarah wasn't willing to spill the beans just yet, so she decided not to pry.

'So, when am I going to meet the man who has stolen your heart?' Sarah asked with a sly smile. Katy had never been one to last long in any relationship but this mystery man seemed to have succeeded in taming her heart. They had already been together for two years, yet Katy never seemed to offer up too much information about him.

'You will meet him soon enough; I can't keep him a secret any longer if you are going to be living with me.'

Sarah watched as Katy poured her another cup of Earl Grey and for the first time she noticed the teal polka dot teapot with a gold rim. She looked around and realised that it didn't match any of the cups and saucers on the table. Each piece of crockery had a definite vintage feel to it, all beautiful with gold etching, but nothing matched. The cup she drank from bore a floral print of orange, red and white, while her saucer was a different floral print with more blue and gold hues. The strange thing was, although they were all unique and beautiful, they seemed to blend together in perfect harmony. Katy looked at Sarah, sensing her thoughts, and spoke quietly in a way that seemed to bear more meaning than her words did.

'I know they don't match. I've always been the queen of symmetry and everything had to be in identical balance, no matter how you looked at it. But I've realised that sometimes things can be a little different, almost vastly different, yet make perfect sense when they are brought together. Sometimes differences are what make things symmetrical.'

Sarah stared at her friend, seeing a more mature side to her than she had ever noticed before. Despite her reference to the tea set, it was almost as if she was sharing a part of her soul, a part Sarah was yet to discover. Even over Skype, as they had kept in touch over the years, she hadn't realised how Katy had also changed over time. She was not the only one life had steered into the heart of wisdom; Katy seemed to be walking that path too.

'So, are you up to going out today? I thought we could take a walk around the *I Heart Market* at the Moses Mabhida Stadium. It's filled with handmade goodies you will love,' Katy offered, attempting to change the subject.

'Sure, why not? It's been too long since I've seen Durban. I'm sure so much has changed since I left.' Sarah felt excited to begin her new adventure but exhausted by what she had left behind. She knew that the sooner she started on this journey, the more her old life would start to fade away. Or so she hoped.

'Things really have changed. We have a new beach promenade where I normally cycle or jog every morning. There were more tourist attractions created to boost tourism for the 2010 FIFA World Cup. We've really seen the benefits of the changes.'

'Oh yes, I recall that the World Cup was held here. Let me just finish my scone and I'll take a quick shower so we can be on our way.'

Sarah made a beeline for the shower as soon as the last crumb of scone had disappeared. The water felt so good dancing on her skin like massaging fingers. She could have stayed in there all day but she knew Katy was waiting and she was excited to see her old home town again. Throwing on a pair of light blue jeans with a coral tank top, she pulled her hair into a loose bun at the back of her head, allowing some stray pieces of hair to dangle loosely against her shoulders. Her movements were swift and assured, with a newfound sense of purpose; she was determined to make this life count. She decided to pass on make-up, enjoying the freedom of being anything she desired.

The stadium was breath-taking, an engineering masterpiece and a defining landmark to match others like the Eiffel Tower or the London Eye. It boasted what seemed to be an endless arch, with the base of the stadium being dubbed by the locals a "bird's nest", with a glass-fibre membrane which produced a translucent glow when the stadium was lit. Sarah stared in amazement at the change in the landscape it produced, a glow of white against the blue afternoon sky. The *I Heart Market* was held on the grass outside the stadium entrance every Saturday. Tent-like structures were strewn neatly in all directions. The locals strolled admiringly through the stalls, enjoying the sights and sounds.

Katy led Sarah to the first stall in the open on the grass. 'You have to try this lemonade; it's so refreshing,' she stated playfully. Sarah watched as they poured the freshly made lemonade and added a few sprigs of mint and a sliver of ginger, topping it off with just a splash of champagne. 'I don't usually have it with champagne but I figured you needed a little pick me up,' she giggled, handing Sarah her glass and pulling her along to the next stall. Sarah sipped merrily on her drink, enjoying the sea breeze and live jazz music that wafted into her ears. Katy handed her a macaroon and when she took a bite she could taste the distinctive melt–in-your-mouth flavour of pistachio nuts. The combination of the lemonade and macaroon surprisingly seemed to complement each other and added to the experience. Katy motioned to a patch of grass next to where the band was playing. Sarah sat down while Katy went to get them some *boerewors* rolls, the South African version of an American hot dog. They contained thick, meaty sausage filled with herbs and spices, grilled over a barbecue of hot burning coals. Each bite had a smoky taste which could only be created on an open flame.

They sat eating their boerewors rolls dripping with tomato sauce and mustard, watching people dancing on the grass to the music. The sun was shining but it was winter and Katy seemed to feel the cold and tugged tightly on her jacket. 'Aren't you feeling cold?' she asked, referring to Sarah's lack of warm clothing.

'You forget I'm a London girl now. Your winter is like our summer.'

They sat for a while enjoying the music and then decided to go and look at the rest of the flea market. Katy went to buy some scented homemade candles while Sarah looked around at the stalls. Each table had a distinctive modern African feel and consisted of everything that was locally produced – clothes, handbags, food, jewellery and more. Sarah's eye was caught by a hand carved wooden key ring in the shape of a giraffe. Without thinking she made her way to it, running her hand over the smooth finish of the wood and before she knew it, she had paid for it and walked away with the package.

'What did you buy?' Katy quizzed on her return, her eyes crinkling.

'Umm, it's just a wooden key ring,' Sarah responded, trying not to give away the significance it held. Katy scowled, clearly sensing there was more to the key ring but not wanting to push her if she wasn't willing to talk.

'Okay, you can keep your secrets for now, but sooner or later you will have to talk and I'll be here waiting to listen.'

They meandered through the crowd, looking at all the beautiful things on offer. Katy bought more macaroons and some olives and feta. Although Sarah saw many things she liked, she felt no compulsion to purchase anything more.

'Come along, I have something I want to show you,' Katy said quickly, hoping to distract Sarah from whatever seemed to have clouded her clear blue eyes. Linking arms with her, she led her to a sky car that whisked them to the top of the stadium arch, giving a breath-taking view of the city's skyline overlooking the ocean. Sarah stood there in awe, taken aback by the sheer beauty of it all. They watched the sun setting and making the sky magically change from bright blue to a dusty orange glow.

'This is the home I knew and loved,' she sighed as Katy put her arm around her and squeezed her tightly.

Katy was everything Sarah was not: she was full of life, bouncy and cheerful, always the go-getter, adventurous and spontaneous. Sarah was the opposite and, despite her secret desire to let herself loose, she was cautious in life, more serious and homebound. She would rather be curled up in bed reading a good book and living her life through its characters than venturing out into the great unknown world. Sarah admired Katy's ability to see the positive in every situation and, when things got really tough, she still managed to find humour somewhere and would laugh her way through it. Katy offered the adventure Sarah wanted and provided the reasoning Katy needed.

They arrived home when it was already dark, having walked around all afternoon, chatting about their days at school and the tree house they used to hide in at the back of Katy's yard. It had been their "girls-only zone", where they would sit eating their favourite hazelnut chocolate and reading romance novels, imagining how they would be whisked away by their knights in shining armour someday. If only life was a fairy tale, it would be so uncomplicated.

Sarah was exhausted by the time they got home and after dinner she excused herself to sink beneath the warm grey down duvet that wrapped around her. Even though she struggled to fall asleep, eventually the ramblings in her mind settled and she drifted into her dreams.

Chapter Two

Sarah inhaled deeply as she woke and stretched. A beam of sun was streaming in through the crack in the curtains. She recalled where she was and forced her eyes open. Only now, as she began to wind down, was she feeling the effects of the journey, but she felt the urge to get up and start her day anyway. She scanned the room, with its high ceilings and king size bed covered in grey Egyptian cotton linen. The white plush carpet was immaculate and there were bamboo tables on either side of the bed, dressed with silver and grey lamps. The curtains where heavily lined with textured white fabric. She looked up as the chandelier hanging over her bed caught the light streaming through the curtain and made patterns dance on the walls and ceiling.

There were two wingback chairs in the corner at the window, creating a perfect spot for reading. Climbing out of bed, she made her way on her tiptoes to the ottoman, where two books were placed neatly on top. Sinking into a wingback, she picked up the first book, *Long Walk to Freedom,* an autobiography by Nelson Mandela. She had wanted to read it for a while but had never got around to it. Perhaps being back in South Africa was the perfect reason to discover the rich history this country had to offer and the legacy Nelson Mandela left behind – a legacy which allowed all South Africans to live free from oppression. His ability to forgive was a lesson she needed to learn in order to rise above her circumstances.

The other book was called *Destined to Reign*, by Joseph Prince. Clearly these books were not here by accident and Sarah had a sneaking suspicion that her long time best friend had placed them there with the hope that she could take something from them.

Sarah pulled back the curtain and allowed the strong African sun to stream through the window. Even though it was the start of winter here, she could tell by the sunlight that it was probably around six thirty. Seeing her still packed suitcase on the carpet, she made a mental note to unpack it later.

Prising herself off the chair, she made her way to the bathroom. It had a white marble floor with silver finishes, an oversized bathtub flanked the wall as you entered, and there was a shower most would envy in the corner on the left. Katy had made sure to fully stock the bathroom with everything Sarah could desire, from bath salts to toothpaste and fluffy baby-soft bath towels that wrapped around you like a blanket.

Sarah decided to have a relaxing bubble bath. She opened the taps and allowed the water to fill the tub, with bursts of steam engulfing the room while she poured in some peach scented foam bath, enjoying the sweetness of its aroma. Slipping off the t-shirt she had slept in, she cautiously entered the water, forgetting she should have checked the temperature before turning off the taps.

The fat bubbles clung lightly to her tingling skin as she immersed herself in the water, allowing her hair to get wet and enjoying the silence that engulfed her.

By the time Sarah lazily made her way into the kitchen it was already eight o'clock and Katy had a big pot of coffee brewing in the machine.

'Good, you're up,' she remarked cheerfully. 'Just in time for you to get changed into some running gear and join me for a jog on the beach!'

'You have got to be kidding me?' Sarah gasped. 'You know I do not jog. The best I could do is drive to the end and wait for you when you cross the finish line.'

'Nonsense, I knew you would make some excuse, so I have a solution. Now run along and change into something more comfortable.'

Sarah returned in her gym clothes with her hair neatly tied up in a ponytail, anticipating the worst from the outdoor experience. She drank the coffee Katy poured her and soon enough was being dragged out of the front door.

'So, since you won't jog, I know you can cycle. We will hire you a bike here on the promenade and you can cycle alongside me as I jog.'

'I guess I have no say in this?' Sarah chuckled, knowing far too well that it was too late to back out now.

They hired a bike and Sarah began cycling along the brick-paved Golden Mile, with the sound of the waves crashing to her left in the Indian Ocean.

'So, how far are you going to jog? Remember, I haven't exercised in a while, so don't kill me on the first go.'

'Well, I usually jog the six kilometres from Suncoast Casino in the north to uShaka Marine World in the south and then back again. But since you're being such a wimp, we can go three kilometres there and three back again.'

'Okay, great,' Sarah replied, already struggling to catch her breath, feeling the burn in her thighs. 'It's beautiful here,' she whispered, looking at the wide stretch of golden sands, artificially separated by various piers. 'It's so different from what I remember.'

'Yes, it's completely different.' Katy smiled at her, thinking of how the beachfront property now consisted mainly of tourist hotels with remnants of art deco architecture and several popular restaurants and nightclubs overlooking the ocean. 'Most people come here to jog, cycle or walk their dogs. There are skateboard parks, water parks, aquariums and a dolphinarium as well.'

'I remember the old dolphinarium. Ooh, Christopher would have…' Sarah's voice trailed off as she realised what she was saying. Katy stopped jogging, went to Sarah and wrapped her arms around her.

'It's going to be okay,' she said, wiping the tears off Sarah's face. 'Come on, let's keep going. You'll feel better once the endorphins kick in,' she said in the most cheerful voice she could muster, knowing the pain Sarah must be feeling.

They moved along, as Sarah seemed to pedal harder and faster from the grief that gripped her. Katy jogged alongside her silently, allowing her company to be the comfort Sarah needed. Katy couldn't imagine how Sarah must have felt.

The morning seemed to go at a steady pace as they made their way back to the side of the beach where the car was parked, ready to go back home.

Sarah opened the door to Katy's apartment and shrieked with excitement. 'Edward!' she screamed, running to him and wrapping her arms around his neck. 'What on earth are you doing here? Katy didn't mention you were coming over!'

'Well, hello, Little Miss Princess,' he said, calling her by the nickname he had given her as a child when she had believed she was destined to marry a prince and become a princess. 'I'm glad my presence is so well received. How are you? You're looking as beautiful as ever,' he said, scanning the contours of her face. 'No wrinkles yet, I see,' he teased as he wrapped her in a warm hug.

'As if! I'm only thirty-two!' she exclaimed. 'You're thirty-five, going on forty.'

'Okay, okay, you two. Calm down before I need to separate you. It seems nothing can stop you from teasing each other,' Katy giggled, coming between them as she looked back and forth between her brother and her best friend. She knew Edward would be the ideal medicine Sarah needed; he had always had a knack somehow of brightening up her mood.

'So you still haven't told me what you are doing here?' Sarah quizzed.

'I came to see you, of course,' Edward quipped.

'Yeah right, there has to be some other reason.'

'Okay, I confess there is. My apartment is being renovated from tomorrow and I called Katy last night and asked her if I could come and crash here at her place. She obviously cannot refuse her older brother and I know there is more than enough space for all three of us to fit comfortably without killing each other.'

'I was never the one in danger of being killed; I think Katy has always been more in the firing line of your brotherly antics than I was.'

'Yes, Edward, you always were kinder to Sarah than to me. It's not fair. She should have received the same treatment as me since she is practically the sister we never had.'

'Hey, Sarah was never *my* sister, she is your "sister". At no point did *I* take an oath to include her into our family.' Edward winked at Sarah and smiled. 'Now, let me go and unpack my things, since I will be here for the next week or so.' Disappearing as suddenly as he had appeared, he went into the other spare room to unpack.

Katy took Sarah into the kitchen and poured her some pomegranate juice. 'I knew seeing Edward would cheer you up; he's always had a way of making you feel better.'

'Yes, I suppose he has,' Sarah replied reflectively.

'So, since he is here, I thought it would be the perfect time for you to meet John.'

'Is John the mystery man you have been hiding?'

'I haven't been hiding him,' Katy blushed. 'Just wanted to be certain before he met everyone. Anyway, what I thought is, John can come over tonight for supper and Edward is inviting his girlfriend, Jasmine, so we can all meet at once.'

'Somehow I am starting to feel like a third wheel here. I'm the only one without a partner,' Sarah protested. She was apprehensive about meeting two new people all at once; she had never been comfortable in crowds and now she had to do it alone, with no one at her side.

'We would never make you feel like a third wheel,' Edward chipped in, walking up to her and putting his arm fondly over her shoulder. 'And anyway, you and I are going to bake a cake for dessert so you will be the star of the show. Who can resist your cakes?'

'Let me guess: I will be doing all the baking and you will just watch me work, making it seem you are helping, yet all you are doing is getting in my way?'

Edward laughed heartily. 'It seems she is onto me, Katy. After all these years she has finally figured me out.'

Sarah shot Katy a stern look and then her face cracked open into fits of laughter. It was the first time she had heard herself laugh in three months and the release of joy that sprang up inside her made her realise that she had secretly desired to feel happy again. She just hadn't known how.

'Come on, let's get some food in your belly; I'm sure my sister has starved you,' Edward smiled, winking at Katy. 'After lunch we can all start doing our part in preparing for dinner.'

Edward sat Sarah down at the kitchen counter and proceeded to make her a cheese and tomato sandwich, as Katy sauntered off to plant herself firmly on the couch and watch some television.

While Sarah ate, she called out the ingredients she needed for the cake she would bake with Edward, and he meticulously set each one down on the counter as he fished it from the cupboard.

Sarah watched him move. His movements had a sense of control and purpose, reminding her how nothing he did in his life seemed to be without reason. He was ruggedly handsome yet his light hazel eyes still gave away the ten year old boy she had played with.

He was tall – not awkwardly tall, just tall enough to make you feel the strength of his frame and the security he exuded. He spoke in a deep voice etched in softness and had dark brown hair full of untamed curls flopping lazily around his head. His mouth was adorned with full lips, which were a deep shade of red.

He looked at her eagerly, waiting for her to call out the next ingredient on the list. 'Blueberries,' she blushed, realising she must have been staring at him. He was dressed in an emerald green cashmere sweater and blue jeans that fitted perfectly to his muscular frame.

'So, do we have everything we need?' His eyes lifted off her as he scanned the countertop, checking the ingredients.

'Yes, I think that's about it.' She motioned to him to step aside and take a seat as she stood up to start baking.

'Hey, don't brush me off; I don't want to be accused of not contributing! You need to set me to work – it's your one chance to boss me around so you'd better take full advantage.' His eyes were fixed on her and he couldn't help wondering if she was aware of how her beauty mesmerised everyone she met.

'Okay then, mister. You'd better sift the dry ingredients while I cream the butter and sugar.'

'What are we making anyway?' he asked, leaning forward so that his elbows were on the countertop.

'A blueberry crumb cake. I hope I remember how to make it; I haven't baked in over a year.'

'Really?' Edward questioned. 'As I recall, Mom couldn't get you and Katy out the kitchen – you were always baking up a storm. And leaving the kitchen floor covered in flour.'

Sarah laughed at the memory. It's true they'd loved to bake, always trying out new recipes and redoing them until they had created a masterpiece. This past year had been so busy that she hadn't had a chance to bake and had forgotten how soothing the process was.

She handed Edward a sieve and bowl and set him to work while she creamed a stick of butter and caster sugar together until they were light and fluffy.

She looked up to find him staring at her intently and knew he was aware how therapeutic baking was for her. 'So what's next, boss?' he asked.

'How about you grease the cake tins while I finish off the rest and if the cake tastes bad, I will blame it on you.'

'And if it tastes good…?'

'Well, I take all the praise, of course! No one will ever believe you could bake. Unless Jasmine is so blinded by love, she only sees starry skies and rose petals when she's around you?'

Edward looked away quickly and he buttered the tins, wondering suddenly how the night would be with all five of them in the same room.

Chapter Three

John was first to arrive and Sarah greeted him at the door. She was the first to have got dressed, in light blue jeans that sat so low they exposed the upper curve of her hips. She had thrown on a white button down shirt and quickly painted her finger and toenails a dark red before putting on her gold pendant earrings.

John was startled when she opened the door, clearly expecting someone else, or shocked by her appearance. Before she could utter a word, Katy came running up behind her and planted a long kiss on his lips. She turned around to face Sarah. 'John, meet Sarah, my best and oldest friend, and Sarah, this is John, my fiancé.' Sarah let out a shriek and threw her arms around John and Katy, before realising that was probably the incorrect way to be greeting a stranger.

'You didn't tell me you were engaged!' Sarah exclaimed, letting go of them both and pulling them into the living room. 'Katy, I'm shocked that you kept this from me, why didn't you tell me?'

'With everything that has been going on, I didn't know when the right time was,' Katy said defensively, taking a seat beside John on the couch.

'You know now, Sarah, that's all that matters. Katy really wanted to tell you, she just wanted it to be at the best moment.'

Sarah watched as Katy and John exchanged loving glances. Katy unclasped the chain around her neck to reveal a one carat diamond ring. She placed it where it belonged, on her left ring finger. Sarah was overwhelmed with joy but couldn't help feeling guilty that Katy felt the need to hide her engagement because she put Sarah's needs first. She felt a pang of sadness that if she hadn't been so caught up in her own pain, she might have noticed Katy's happiness sooner.

Edward came into the room, carrying glasses of wine, and handed one to each of them. 'Well, now that everyone has caught up to speed with the good news, I think this deserves a toast. To Katy and John, congratulations on your engagement! We wish you all the joy in the world,' he announced, raising his glass.

'Absolutely!' Sarah cheered, clinking her glass against everyone else's, happy that Edward had come in at just the right moment.

The doorbell rang and they all watched as Edward went to open it. He leaned over and kissed Jasmine gently on the lips as he ushered her in. She was breath-taking, with platinum blonde hair hanging pin straight just over her shoulders. She was tall and slender, wearing a mocha coloured trench coat and cream skin-tight pants. Sarah realised she was holding her breath as she watched Edward remove her coat to reveal a gold knit sweater. Sarah suddenly felt underdressed for the occasion, next to this South African goddess and her sun kissed skin.

'Jasmine, you know Katy and John, and this is Katy's best friend, Sarah, who is staying with Katy for a while.' Edward motioned towards Sarah.

Sarah held out her hand and Jasmine shook it warmly, her beautiful dark blue eyes changing shades in the light. 'Sarah, it's lovely to meet you. Edward has told me so much about you.' She leaned in closer and whispered, 'Although you must be just as crazy as the two of them to have survived an entire childhood together.' Her smile was broad and engaging, and Sarah immediately felt herself relax and warm to her. She could see why Edward was in love with her; she had a way of drawing you in.

Edward led her to sit next to him on the couch, where Katy and John cuddled together lovingly. Sarah sat almost hiding in a single wingback chair, feeling strangely like an outsider in this new world. Edward had poured Jasmine a glass of wine and she sat drinking it steadily, nodding earnestly in agreement with the conversation taking place around her.

Sarah became occupied scanning the dynamics of the two new people now included into their "family". From what she could tell, John seemed almost as starched as a well-placed doily, in stark contrast to Katy's laid back manner. He was only a few inches taller than she was, with jet black hair and eyes that told no story, except for when they shone lovingly at Katy. He seemed unable to look remotely relaxed and even as Katy lay with her head nuzzled on his chest, he sat as straight as a pole, his arm bent over her like a branch of a tree. For the life of her Sarah could not imagine the similarities between them. He seemed opposed to any sort of fun, with his smile barely reaching the corners of his eyes, yet they softened when he was smiling at Katy. However, he gave off a sense of dependability and security and seemed like the type of man who would lay down his life for his wife. It was that secure presence he exuded that made Sarah see why Katy loved him. Their polar opposite personalities seemed to somehow work harmoniously, and it was then that Sarah remembered Katy's words about the tea cups: '*Sometimes differences are what make things symmetrical.*' Katy wasn't just talking about the tea cups, she had also been referring to her relationship with John!

Sarah turned her attention to Jasmine. It was clear she was accustomed to being the prom queen, with her well-manicured nails and designer clothes. What Sarah couldn't figure out was what had drawn Edward to her initially. Granted, she was beautiful and lit up a room when she walked in, but she also gave the sense of a woman who expected to be pampered. It was hard to imagine her being willing to cook or play any sort of role as a wife.

'So, when is the wedding day?' Sarah offered, trying to add a contribution to the already brewing conversation. John and Katy exchanged smiles.

'Well, we know its short notice for everyone, being the end of June already, but we would really love to have it this December, on Christmas Eve. Just a small intimate wedding with family and friends.'

Edward shot Katy a confused look, 'I thought you were planning it for next year in August? Why the change? You know I'll have to rearrange my work schedule to make sure I'm in the country from the beginning of December.'

'That's exactly why I'm warning you now.' Katy's response was mischievous and she gave no explanation about the change in dates.

'Okay, well that just means we will have to move along with the wedding plans. There is no time to waste, especially planning a Christmas Eve wedding. Most catering companies close during the festive season,' Sarah said excitedly.

'Well, Sarah, I'm glad to see you are so eager to help, because I'm relying on you to make this wedding perfect.'

Sarah smiled as her friend spoke. This was the moment they had both dreamed of: the day Katy would walk down the aisle. She'd known from the moment she heard of the engagement that she would do everything to make this day as special as she could.

'Katy has some non-conventional ideas for our wedding though, Sarah, I must warn you,' John remarked cautiously. He sounded almost nervous at the thought of doing something different.

'When has Katy ever been anything but unconventional? If she wanted a textbook wedding I would be checking her temperature.'

The room filled with laughter as they were all in agreement that Sarah couldn't have been more accurate. Katy was unconventional and it was what they all clearly loved about her.

The conversation quickly turned back to their everyday lives, with all four settling into comfortable conversation.

Sarah sat quietly, looking from person to person as they chattered with each other.

'I'm going to go and set the table and get the supper ready, if that's okay, Katy?'

'Sure, Sarah, do you need any help?'

'No, you relax. You know, the bride to be needs all the rest she can get,' she said quickly, looking forward to the chance of getting away from them all and having a moment to herself.

Sarah quickly gathered the cutlery and crockery and began setting the table, listening to their excited chatter just a few feet away. She took the roast lamb that Katy had prepared earlier out of the oven and set it on a platter, slicing just enough pieces for them to eat. She left the balance to be sliced later should anyone want a second helping. She placed the roast potatoes and vegetables in a neat pattern around the lamb and breathed out lightly.

'Hey, are you okay?' she heard Edward's voice whisper at the nape of her neck as he covered the small of her back with his hand.

'Yeah, I'm fine, thanks. Just trying to get everything done. Just the gravy to pour and we can eat.'

'Are you sure you're all right? I watched you drift into bouts of silence in there. I know you were never one for crowds.' Edward paused. 'I'm sorry we've all been rather self-absorbed in our own conversations.'

'You know me too well,' she smiled, just enough for him to know she appreciated his kind gesture. 'I'll be fine, I just need to get to know everyone. Soon enough I will be more than comfortable to dominate the conversation.'

'Okay, well you pour the gravy and I will get the salads and we can get this show on the road.' He teased playfully, heading towards the fridge.

She smiled and poured the gravy into a serving jug, grateful that she could be herself around him.

Dinner was delicious; Katy had always been a sensational cook. Sarah knew that even her tiny appetite would not be able to resist her friend's cooking.

'I hope you all have room for dessert; I baked a blueberry crumb cake,' Edward teased, winking at Sarah while putting the cake and clotted cream on the table.

'Now I find that hard to believe,' Jasmine chuckled. 'I have never once seen you anywhere near the kitchen! So, who really baked the cake?'

Laughing cheerfully, Sarah came to Edward's defence. '…I can't say Edward baked the cake, but he was instrumental in motivating me to bake it.'

'Hey, I did more than just motivate you. This cake would have no dry ingredients if it weren't for my technical method of sifting them all together. You can't bake a cake with butter and sugar alone.'

'Okay, okay, you helped, I admit it and next time you will be baking all on your own!' Sarah pointed at him, wagging her index finger as if he were a naughty child.

They laughed as Edward neatly cut the cake and gave each person a slice.

'This is delicious, Sarah; I've never had a blueberry crumb cake before. It's soft and moist,' John offered kindly.

'It's my mom's secret recipe, perfected by me, of course,' she smiled, thinking of her parents and making a mental note to call them and let them know she was safe and sound.

Soon the night was over and Sarah was walking sluggishly to her room, leaving Edward and Katy still chatting in the lounge. She heard the distinctive click of her bedroom door closing behind her as she climbed into bed, not even bothering to change her clothes.

Edward was already fast asleep when he heard the faint cries of someone screaming. He jumped out swiftly and followed the screams to Sarah's room. Opening the door, he saw Katy kneeling beside her, trying to wake her up from her tormenting nightmare.

'Christopher, don't leave me, please don't leave me,' she moaned, tossing and turning in her bed.

'Sarah, it's me, Katy. Shh, you are with me now. It's okay, you were just having a nightmare.' She touched Sarah gently on her shoulder, hoping to wake her, but trying not to startle her. Edward knelt down beside Katy just as Sarah opened her eyes. Tears began to stream out of them as she curled into herself like a foetus in its mother's womb, her body shaking from the pain in her dreams. Katy got onto her bed and laid down next to her, taking her in her arms and rocking her back and forth, trying to lull her back to sleep.

'It's going to be okay. We are here with you; you're not alone,' she comforted. She looked over at Edward out of the corner of her eye, wondering if they could ever fill the hole in Sarah's heart. She was trying to figure out why she would leave family and friends who had held her hand through this tragedy to come back and live in South Africa. Was she trying to start over, or running away from something? Katy couldn't help wondering about this as she wiped the tears from her eyes.

Edward sat down on the wingback chair by the window, watching as Katy finally got her to calm down and go back to sleep. Climbing gently off the bed, Katy came and sat on the chair beside him.

'I think I need to take her away to our cottage in the mountains,' she whispered. 'The scenery and tranquillity out there might be healing for her.'

Edward nodded silently, his heart aching for her. He watched her breathe slowly in and out as she lay curled up on her bed. Her hair was wet from her tears, clinging gently to her face, and he was grateful that, at least for now, she seemed at peace. 'I think that will be good for her right now. I will tie up some loose ends in the office tomorrow and then come and join you. It's good you took leave from work. I don't think we could have left her alone just yet,' he replied, trying not to speak too loudly, afraid to awake Sarah again.

Katy got up and took two blankets out of the cupboard, gave one to Edward and wrapped the other around herself. 'I think we should just sleep here with her tonight, just in case she wakes up again. I want her to know we aren't going to leave her.'

Edward sank into the chair, pulling the blanket over him, wondering if he would ever sleep now and feeling helpless in his efforts to comfort her.

Chapter Four

Sarah held on to the steaming cappuccino Katy had given her. They were on their way to the Drakensberg mountains, a three hour drive from Katy's home. Sarah watched as the landscape changed dramatically as they headed inland, from one of ocean and high rise buildings to that of green grass and rolling hills. She noticed how the temperature dropped the higher they climbed above sea level, and she cuddled into her jersey a little more tightly.

The Drakensberg, Sarah recalled from geography class, was the highest mountain range in southern Africa, rising over three thousand metres in height. The mountains were named by the local Zulu tribe as uKhahlamba which meant the Barrier of Spears, and it was a wonderland of mountainous terrain.

Sarah looked around as they drove: the lush yellowwood forests displayed sheer natural beauty with a wealth of biological diversity. The smoggy city air faded quickly as they wound their way along the highway, and Sarah couldn't help but gasp at the sight of the awe inspiring snowcapped mountains reminding her that it was still winter here. She could already feel the tension begin to drip off her skin like cool water.

'I have a few surprises lined up for us before we get to the cottage,' Katy said smugly.

'What type of surprises? You'd better not leave me alone in the middle of nowhere, trying to fight off jackals and snakes,' she laughed, wondering what her friend had in store.

They had been driving for over an hour now with Katy leaving Sarah mostly to her thoughts while they listened to music playing softly in the background. Sarah watched as Katy drove off the N3 highway following a board that said "Howick, South Underberg", and at the junction they turned left, driving until they approached a large cream coloured plaster brick house with "Peel's Honey Shop" painted in red and black writing across the façade of the building.

As they jumped out of the car, Katy took Sarah by the arm and walked towards the old house. It was a perfect example of a midlands farmhouse in the Natal Verandah Style, with a multiple-ridged complex corrugated-sheeting roof painted in a wine red colour. Inside, the place felt rich with history with oak shelving, uneven white walls and curtains that draped the windows in a floral printed fabric that looked as old as the shop itself. Being established in 1924 the shop carried a sophisticated charm, with jars of honey lining up endlessly on the shelves.

Sarah looked around at all that was on offer from honey fudge to honeycomb and even creamed honey and lip balm. She settled on a jar of orange blossom honey and almond nut brittle. The packaging was simple, with the product on display inside a clear plastic jar, covered with a honey coloured yellow lid. The label was a yellow sticker, stuck around the jar with red writing in a font that had probably been around since the nineteen twenties.

Sarah dipped her finger in the orange blossom honey allowing the sweet liquid to slowly play with her taste buds. She set her jars on the counter next to Katy's selection of honey scotch brittle and *fynbos* honey, and watched as the friendly cashier wrapped them all in a brown paper bag in exchange for their money.

Sarah smiled at this quaint shop. It was unique to the region, and their honey products were sought after all across the country. They made their way back to the car, as Katy re-set her GPS with new coordinates, taking them to their next destination.

Sarah closed her eyes briefly, feeling sleepy but unable to fall asleep. Before she knew it, she felt the car steer off the long stretch of tarred road, onto a dusty dirt road. A short drive along this road brought them to a farm: a small piece of heaven overlooking the misty Balgowan valley. They were greeted by two golden Labradors wagging their tails lazily at the two new visitors.

'Welcome to Indigo Fields,' they heard through their half opened doors.

Standing on the passenger side was a sturdy looking grey-haired man probably in his fifties, with a smile so broad it was disarming. He opened the door for Sarah as she climbed out of the car.

'Hi, you must be Sarah?' he asked smiling down at her. 'Katy has told us to expect you. My name is Grant, and I will be helping you both to de-stress today.'

Katy smiled and came around the car, throwing her arms around this familiar friend.

'Thanks for letting us come up here at such short notice; I know how busy you are this time of year. I'm glad you managed to fit us in.'

'I will do anything for you, Katy. You're my oldest and dearest customer, let alone friend,' he said, motioning to them to follow him through a winding cobblestone paved pathway adorned with bushes of planted lavender on either side.

They entered a large thatched roof cottage, which had a small table covered in a white tablecloth with antique silver cutlery surrounding stark white plates and cream napkins folded neatly on top, with some roses tucked beneath its folds. The smell of freshly baked, rosemary-infused bread wafted gently up their nostrils arousing their hungry bellies.

'This is where we will serve your breakfast before we take you to your first treatment,' Grant said handing them a questionnaire and a pen on a clipboard. 'Catherine will be in shortly to take your orders. Make yourselves comfortable in the meantime. There are gowns and slippers for you to change into, and a fleece poncho for you to put over your gowns. It gets rather cold in the *bomas* you know!' He nodded towards Katy. 'I'm sure you will get Sarah up to speed with the plans?'

'Yes, of course,' Katy said, clearly delighted by what was in store.

Grant left the room just as Sarah shot Katy a questioning look. 'Treatment?… Bomas?… What on earth have you got me into?' she said, gesturing towards the ponchos and gowns.

'It's time for you to relax,' Katy explained, 'Indigo Fields is an African Spa; they will pamper and massage us in the grasslands on the farm.'

'Trust you to bring me into the bush to relax! There'd better not be any snakes here, because a snake falling on my back while they massage me will definitely not be classified as relaxing at all!' Sarah laughed as she hugged her friend, knowing that she was in for a day of exquisite tranquillity.

Only once they had eaten breakfast, filled out their guest cards, and put on their gowns and ponchos, were they escorted by Grant into an uncovered safari vehicle. They were each given a blanket and hot water bottle for the journey to help fight against the biting cold. They drove along a dusty road to their first boma pitched deep within the bush. The scenery on route was soulful, with the road running parallel to fields of scented flowers and horses trotting steadily in the grass.

Grant stopped the vehicle and pointed out to them a wooden plank pathway just off the dirt road that would take them into the bush, and onto a raised platform covered with a tent-like structure that they called a boma.

Sarah and Katy walked in the icy wind up the pathway, a river trickled under the wooden walkway and they could hear the crashing of a waterfall in the distance. As they approached the boma they were greeted by two Zulu therapists, who welcomed them in and motioned for them to take a seat on the hand carved wooden chairs. Inside was a brick and cast iron fireplace on the far end of the wall, with massage tables set up on either side. The room smelt of lavender and rose petals, and Sarah breathed in deeply, allowing the familiar aroma to unwind her mind.

'I am Thembi and this is Ayanda – we will be your therapists today. We will be treating you to a neck and shoulder massage and then Grant will be back to escort you to your next treatment,' they said as they bent down, placing Sarah and Katy's feet on a hot water bottle wrapped in a towel and they then helped them manoeuvre out of the top of their gowns just enough to expose their shoulders. Tying up their hair with an elastic band to expose the skin on their necks, they dipped their hands into warm massage oil and gently began to massage their muscles in rhythmic pulsating motions, from their necks down to their shoulder blades.

The warmth from the fireplace and the scent of the oil became so intoxicating and hypnotising that neither Sarah nor Katy were able to utter a single word; all they could do was allow these African queens to soothe their weary muscles with their healing hands.

Their day continued to ooze with the pleasures that this place had to offer. Every hour they were transported to a new part of the bush, with new sights and sounds, as their backs were massaged, their feet were pampered until finally they lay in a steaming hot jacuzzi looking out over the valley, under the African sky.

It was almost five in the evening when they finally left, with the sky darkening as night fell. They lazily dragged their pampered feet into the car. They endured what now felt like a painstaking drive to Katy's cottage. Their muscles were so relaxed that they fought them with every kilometre enticing them to fall into a deep relaxed sleep. After another hour's drive they veered off the main road and ventured up a long, bumpy and winding dirt road to Katy's family cottage.

'I've arranged for the staff to make us dinner,' Katy said jumping out of the car. 'I'm sure you are starving by now.'

Sarah nodded just as a well-rounded woman headed towards them.

'Good evening, Katy. We have been expecting you. I have set dinner out on the verandah, and I will take your bags inside.'

'Sarah, this is Gladys. She looks after the cottage while we are not here,' Katy said, pointing to the motherly looking woman in front of them.

'Nice to meet you, Sarah. I know you will enjoy your stay here,' Gladys said as her cheeks swelled like lollipops into a smile.

'Thanks, Gladys, I'm sure I will,' Sarah said softly, still feeling the sleep beckoning to her after their massage.

Gladys led them up onto the verandah, her short stumpy legs moving swiftly as she climbed the stairs to where she had set the table for their dinner. 'Your dinner will be served shortly,' she said, motioning for them to sit as she took their luggage inside.

'So this is the infamous cottage,' Sarah smiled, breathing in the cold night air, looking into the darkness. Katy had told her numerous stories of their family time up at the cottage. Sarah had never visited them here, despite numerous invitations; she just had never seemed to get a chance to come.

'Yes, it's our hiding place when we just need to take a break from it all,' Katy shrugged.

Gladys returned with steaming hot plates of spaghetti and meatballs. 'Enjoy your dinner,' she said placing the food in front of them.

'Thanks, Gladys,' Sarah and Katy chimed together in perfect unison, their rumbling stomachs appreciating the food now within arm's reach. Gladys smiled politely, and wandered off back into the cottage leaving them to eat.

'So, tell me your plans for the wedding?' Sarah asked taking her first mouthful of food.

'Well, I want something small and intimate, with just our parents, siblings and closest friends. I've always loved the idea of a pudding party, and thought since I have my baking partner back home, we could turn this wedding into a pudding party?'

'Sounds interesting.'

'We could have it here at the cottage in the garden, and there is more than enough space for everyone to stay over for the night. We can set up the gardens for both the ceremony and reception. Nothing fancy, just us celebrating with everyone we love.' Katy's eyes gleamed as she spoke.

Sarah sat silently, her mind racing as she tried to imagine it all.

'Okay, we can create a makeshift aisle for you to walk through, leading from the door of the cottage all along a pathway into the garden, where we could have everyone sitting on bales of hay covered in fabric overlooking the mountains,' Sarah said watching as Katy's face broke into a huge smile. 'We could then have another part of the garden set up for the reception in the evening, with a dance floor and seating and one long table to the side where all the puddings would be laid out. Do you want a formal place to sit and have speeches, or do you just want everyone to lounge around eating and chatting at their leisure?' Sarah asked.

'I knew you would get it!' Katy exclaimed, 'You've envisioned it better than I could have. I don't like formal speeches. Perhaps we could just do a toast before the reception goes into full swing?'

'That sounds perfect,' Sarah smiled, knowing her friend loved a more relaxed environment than a formal one, and even though this was an occasion that would call for a more formal approach, she knew that wouldn't make Katy happy. 'So what colours do you want everything to be?' Sarah continued.

'How about an antique shade of gold with hints of pale pink and cream, I think?' Katy shrugged unsure of her choice.

'I think that would look perfect out here. I will take care of everything, and we will probably have to bake back at your home, and then transport everything up here the day before. We can hire people to do photography, hair and make-up on the day, and I will arrange everything else. Don't worry, I will make it magical.' Sarah smiled leaning onto the table, excited about this happy occasion.

'I realise that whatever brought you here was not the best of circumstances, but I truly am grateful you came just in time for my wedding. You're like the sister I never had, and I couldn't imagine this day without you.' Katy jumped up and threw her arms around Sarah, kissing her gently on the cheek.

'Hey, that's what sisters are for, right?' Sarah said, feeling the ache in her heart at the mention of the word sister.

'Now come along, let's get you inside; I'm sure you want to get to bed. This drive up here has made me so sleepy, or was it the massage?' Katy shrugged, taking Sarah and leading her into the cottage.

The cottage was charming and whimsical in every way, with the lounge to the right and the dining room to the left, and a clear pathway leading from the door to the rest of the cottage. Sarah rotated as she took in the wooden flooring and exposed stone chimney of the lounge. Every piece of furniture was a different colour, with deep reds, royal blues and emerald greens being the colours of choice, each sofa blanketed with cream cashmere throws. On the floor by the fireplace was a fluffy coffee coloured shabby chic rug, and the walls on either side were covered in endless shelves of books. Sarah loved how the dining table was a rough piece of untreated timber, with cream cushioned wooden benches on either side. There were no ceiling lights in the room, only cream and white lampstands with shades placed at random points around the room, creating a soft glow.

Katy led Sarah further into the cottage, and she was amazed at how much larger it was than she had initially thought. As they entered into the hallway, she saw a large kitchen to her right and turning to her left was an endless passageway of bedrooms on either side.

'How many bedrooms are there in here?' she asked amazed.

Katy chuckled, clearly amused by Sarah's reaction. 'Nine, with the main bedroom at the end of the hallway. All have en-suite bathrooms and toilets, so you have complete privacy.'

Sarah followed Katy down the passage. 'So, choose a room,' Katy offered.

'Wow, how do I even begin to choose?' Sarah shrugged clearly overwhelmed.

'Each room is inspired by a different colour,' Katy said, pointing out how each door had a word written across it in the colour that inspired the room. Sarah immediately noticed the door that had "Sunshine" written in bright yellow writing.

'This will be my room,' she smiled broadly.

'I knew you would like the Sunshine room,' Katy teased.

Sarah opened the door and immediately loved her room. In the centre was a king sized bed. The same pale cream and yellow linen fabric had been used for both the bed covering and curtains. At the end of the bed was a chaise longue covered in cream velvet with gold stitched edges. To the left was a large antique desk, and to the right a doorway leading to the bathroom. The walls were covered in paintings of the ocean, with golden beaches and blue skies. She stepped inside and felt the plush cream carpet beneath her feet, seeing her luggage had already been deposited against the wardrobe.

'I was so confident you would choose this room that I had Gladys prepare it for you before we arrived. There is Lindt chocolate on the bedside table and everything you would need in the bathroom. Make yourself at home and have sweet dreams,' Katy said as she closed the door behind her.

Sarah threw herself on the bed, enjoying the warmth the bright sunny room brought. For a moment, just a moment, it blocked out the world around her.

Chapter Five

Sarah couldn't sleep, and after tossing and turning in bed until four in the morning she decided to wake up, shower and make Katy some breakfast. She found her way into the kitchen with her Lindt chocolate in hand, and rummaged through the cupboards for ingredients to whip up some crumpets for breakfast. After using all the crumpet batter to make a pile of crumpets so high that they threatened to tip over, she left them covered on the kitchen counter with golden syrup and honey positioned on either side, ready for Katy when she awoke. For the life of her she couldn't imagine Katy eating so many crumpets, but the process of mixing and flipping them one by one, was what keep her going; it was her early morning therapy session.

Moving swiftly through the kitchen, she warmed some milk in a pot on the stove and, once hot, poured it into a mug. She broke pieces of chocolate, and let them plop one at a time into the steaming hot milk, allowing them to sink to the bottom of the mug, melting into oozing brown streams as they sank. Leaving the chocolate to melt and mix with the milk, she made her way to a sofa in the lounge and pulled a cream cashmere throw over her legs.

She wrapped her fingers tightly around the warm mug of hot chocolate, and watched through the window as the landscape dawned before the eyes. The beauty of a new day always carried with it a sense of hope. Each day could be so vastly different to the one before. Life could change in an instant, from joy to sorrow and from sorrow back to joy. Nothing in life was guaranteed, no one held the promise of another day. She was determined to try to live each day as best she could. Eventually the darkness had to give way to the light. The rising of the sun each day testified to that.

The door suddenly opened jarring her thoughts as Edward sauntered into the cottage, dragging his suitcase behind him.

'Good morning, Little Miss Princess. I thought I would sneak in while you were both still asleep,' he said, pulling his luggage through the door. 'Why are you awake so early?'

'I struggled to sleep, and decided to stop fighting the inevitable, so got up and made some crumpets. They are still hot in the kitchen if you would like some?'

Edward darted for the kitchen without saying another word and returned with four crumpets stacked high on a plate and the bottle of golden syrup in hand. He fell into the couch beside her and peered into her mug. 'Mmm, hot chocolate made with real chocolate, just the way I taught you to have it,' he said raising one eyebrow.

Sarah thought for a moment before responding, 'I had forgotten you introduced me to "real" hot chocolate,' she laughed. 'It just became so much a part of me, that I had forgotten where I learnt the recipe,' she mused, looking into her mug and seeing the pieces of melting chocolate swirling around.

She laughed suddenly recalling how she first came upon his recipe. He had come up into Katy's and her tree house when they weren't there and stolen the hazelnut chocolate they always kept hidden inside there. He had denied point blank that he had taken it, insisting he would never do such a thing. Later on in the evening he sat merrily in the lounge sipping on some hot chocolate, and as Sarah peered into the mug she saw a hazelnut pop to the surface, just as the chocolate holding it to the bottom had melted setting it free and exposing his sneaky little secret. Edward made Sarah promise not to tell Katy he had taken the chocolate. She had agreed, on condition that he shared his hot chocolate with her. From then onwards, it was the only way she knew to make hot chocolate.

Edward saw her laugh and realised she must have remembered their secret. 'Hey, you still have to keep our secret, you know! Otherwise you can no longer use my recipe! Any other way of making hot chocolate should be banned, and these crumpets are delicious," he sighed, licking his fingers, enjoying every bite. 'I'm glad you're awake and dressed, because today is my turn to take you on an adventure. Katy had her moment of fun yesterday, and today you're all mine.' His eyes lingered on Sarah's face for a moment before he peeled them away.

'You would swear I'm a child in the middle of a custody battle,' she protested, clearly amused by his choice of words.

'Well, today you are in my custody, under my rules, so I suggest you put on a jacket, grab yourself some crumpets and I will meet you back here once I've left my luggage in the room.' He wiggled his finger at her as he gave the instructions. Getting up and grabbing Sarah's mug of hot chocolate, he took a huge gulp.

'Hey, that's not fair. Get your own,' Sarah giggled in protest, punching his arm. He said nothing. Instead he handed her back her mug, and touched the tip of her nose before taking his empty plate and carrying his bags into the passage.

Sarah was still exhausted from her lack of sleep, but decided to follow his instructions anyway, and was back in the lounge just as he grabbed his car keys and opened the front door for her.

'So, where are you taking me?' she quizzed, wondering what Edward had in store.

He smiled mischievously as he led her outside to his car. Opening the car door for her, he waited until she was comfortably seated before responding.

'I would suggest you close your eyes, and try to rest. We have about an hour's drive before you get any further clues from me,' he smiled, his eyes twinkling as he moved to get into the driver's side. He started the engine and put the heater on as Sarah closed her eyes, a smile lingering on the corner of her lips as she wondered where she was headed to next. So far, coming back to South Africa truly had felt like an adventure. She was exhausted, and the steady movement and hum of the car seemed to lull her to sleep.

'We've arrived,' Edward announced proudly, shaking her gently to wake her as he stood holding the car door open for her to get out. Sarah looked out around her to see a small white house overlooking a river. It looked like it had always been there – a serene sweet and simple whitewashed structure just a stone's throw away from the shimmering river.

'Please don't tell me you are going to make me get into that river?' she pleaded, 'It's the middle of winter out here.'

Edward laughed, and took her hand gently as he led her along the paved driveway towards the house. He knocked on the navy blue door and they waited as they heard footsteps slowly approach. The door creaked opened and a short silver-haired man peered out of the doorway.

'Oh, Edward, it's you,' the old man exclaimed, opening the door widely for them to come inside.

Edward took Sarah's hand and led her into a tiny house that smelt strongly of turpentine. They waited as the old man closed the door and then followed him through to the back of the house. It was cluttered and colourful, nothing matching, everything strewn everywhere, with every room painted a different colour and the walls covered in so many paintings that the colours of the walls were almost invisible beneath the many paintings. There was something strangely unpretentious about the place.

Sarah didn't see a book that was lying on the ground, and she lurched forward just as Edward caught her by the arm.

'You will need to look where you're going in here,' the old man called, his feet still shuffling along through the house. 'At my age, one cannot waste time cleaning up,' he smiled, his face shrinking into loose folds of wrinkles. 'Come along. I have set everything up Edward, just the way you requested.'

Sarah followed them to the back of the house which led onto a wooden deck overlooking the river below. On the deck sat two easels positioned back-to-back, and beside each easel were trays of oil paints, cloths, paintbrushes and turpentine. Sarah looked at Edward, confused as to why there were here.

'My name is Joseph,' the old man continued looking towards Sarah, 'Edward has asked me to set up an art class here for you to paint whatever is in your heart. I will leave you both to it, and will be back a little later with lunch.' He smiled at Edward, as he hobbled along back into the house.

'An art class?' Sarah asked confused, looking around at all the art supplies.

'I confess it's a little different, but I know how you love to paint. So I thought we could spend the day painting something that would remind you of this part of life's journey. You do not need to explain to me what you are painting; all I want is for you to allow whatever is in your heart to be displayed on canvas,' Edward explained, hoping he had made the right choice bringing her here.

Sarah examined the white canvas; it had been years since she had painted. She looked over at Edward's sincere face, and smiled at him gently. 'Thanks, Edward,' was all she managed to mutter, as tears began to well up in her eyes.

Painting had always been her way of expressing her emotions, and for so long now her emotions had been bottled up so deep inside, she wasn't sure she knew how to express them on canvas any more. She picked up a piece of chalk and began to sketch the scenery around her, the rolling shapes of the mountains, the parallel boundaries of the river, the blades of grass, and the slats of the wooden deck. Right now her mind could not imagine life beyond this point; all she could draw was what was in front of her.

Edward watched her closely as her brow deepened and her muscles tensed with concentration, as she allowed herself the freedom to express whatever part she so desired. He looked down at his own canvas. He had known before he had arrived here what he wanted to paint. It was a scene he had pictured in his mind the whole drive up here – a scene etched in his imagination for many years, and he knew he would be relieved once he had it etched forever in oil on his canvas.

The comfortable silence merged into swooshing sounds, as they dipped their brushes into the paint and swept them in large strokes across the canvas, each stroke releasing with it the raw emotion that lay beneath the hand that moved it. Sarah felt the rush of the water as she painted the river – like the rushing of pain that engulfed her heart. She watched the pounding and crashing of the water as it hit against the rocks, slowly eroding it bit by bit, giving her shivers down her spine as it mirrored how eroded she felt by the pounding of the hand life had dealt her. The tears slowly began to pierce through her eyes like bursting fountains, as she allowed herself to bleed onto the canvas. Edward watched as she cried, afraid to go over and comfort her, not wanting to stop the release she was feeling. He gave her the space she needed to grieve, to heal, to remember, to feel, knowing that she had this opportunity to lock her emotions beneath each stroke of paint that graced her canvas.

The morning slowly transitioned to noon, and they barely noticed as they both felt lost in the moment.

'I've prepared some lunch for us all, if you are able to peel yourselves away from your paintings for a moment,' Joseph said motioning towards a blanket that had been set up on the grass patch between the river and the deck. It was laden with a picnic basket and cushions upholstered in old French grain sacks positioned neatly on top.

Sarah jolted out of her thoughts as she stepped back and looked at what she had already painted. Although the entire painting was done in dark shades of grey, black and blue, with highlights of white, she still knew it was a painfully beautiful portrait of her inner self. She set down her paint brushes, and wiped her hands on a towel, before walking with Edward towards the picnic blanket as they joined Joseph on the grass.

'Thanks for having us here today, Joseph. It's always breathtaking this time of year.' Edward said earnestly.

'Anything for you,' Joseph smiled so that his eyes shone. Opening the picnic basket he handed them both a chicken and avocado sandwich and some mango juice.

'So, how do you and Edward know each other?' Sarah questioned, wondering how Edward seemed so close and comfortable with someone more than twice his age.

'Edward met my wife and me years ago, when his family would come out here on holidays. My wife offered art classes in the area and Edward would come when he was on holiday from college,' Joseph smiled at Edward, recalling the memory. 'Some years later my wife passed away, and it was a very difficult time for me. When Edward found out, he would make trips to come and see me every few months during his holidays, and would spend the week with me painting in memory of my wife. At first it was difficult to paint again, as the memory of her was too painful. But with Edward's persistent love and support, he helped me to turn my pain into joyful memories of my wife, as we painted scenes of all the places she loved.' His eyes began to water at the fond memories. 'When Edward told me about you I didn't hesitate to have you come over, because I knew that if painting could heal my broken heart it could surely heal yours too. Edward taught me to remember the good times, instead of only focusing on the sad times. He taught me that it's not necessarily time that heals all wounds, but it's what we do with that time that brings healing to our wounds. I hope you can walk away from here today knowing that even though you have lost much and felt great pain, having friends around you who love and care for you as deeply as Edward does overshadows any pain you might have.' He looked sincerely into Sarah's eyes. 'Any friend of Edward's is a friend of mine, and you are welcome in my home any time.'

Sarah threw her arms around this old man, feeling a deep connection to him. She knew now exactly why Edward had chosen to bring her here. He knew she had wounds that desperately needed healing, and hearing Joseph's story gave her hope that her wounds would be healed.

'Thank you so much for sharing your heart with me,' she said to Joseph, and turning to Edward she paused, unable to find the words to say. Her eyes filled with tears, and he came towards her and held her. 'Thanks,' she whispered into his chest as the tears streamed down her face. Edward wiped her tears and looked deep within her soul, 'You are not alone in this,' he said, the sincerity in his voice going straight into her heart. Sarah breathed in deeply and nodded as she soaked up the stillness and the beauty which this day held.

They sat, talked and ate. It was the sort of place where you could easily, and gladly, lose track of the hours, and be lost in the magic of the place. Eventually they returned to finish their paintings. Joseph promised to courier the paintings to them once they had dried.

The sun was beginning to make its descent towards the horizon in a beautiful display of majesty. They jumped back into the car and drove on their way back to the cottage. Sarah felt the nostalgia of the place, a knowing that there are some places that leave an indelible impression on you, occupying your daydreams, nagging at you to return, and she knew this was one such magical place.

'Thanks for today,' she said, looking at Edward as he drove, 'I appreciate what you did for me. That's probably a moment I'll remember forever.'

Edward's gaze met hers and he saw the gratitude in her eyes. 'It's my pleasure, and I meant what I said: you are not alone in this. I am with you every step of the way. I might not always physically be around because I have to travel on business, but if you call me, I will drop everything if you ask me to.'

'I know you will,' Sarah said, as she realised just how much he meant it. 'So, tell me about your latest design project, Mr. Architect,' she teased.

'We are in the middle of a new design for a hotel some investors are erecting in Dubai. I need to go and present my designs to them next week, and if they approve them, then we will start to break ground in the next month, we hope,' he said, ignoring her teasing remarks. 'I was hoping you would consider working with me. I could use a brilliant interior designer like you on my team; I know we would work well together.'

'I don't doubt we would make a formidable team, but I don't think I want to go back into interior design just yet. I just need to do something less demanding for a while. I've been thinking of working on a series of textile and wallpaper designs, getting them manufactured and stocking them in niche retailers. It will be a more accessible product line for the public who feel they want to play their own hand at interior design in their own homes. I will also do specific designs if approached by designers for specific projects they are working on, where they need something unique for the space. Before I came here, I had already sourced a company who can manufacture some designs I already have. I now need to get them printed and then pitch my ideas to the buyers of these niche stores across the country.'

'Seems like you have it all figured out,' Edward said, sounding somewhat disappointed.

'Hey, no need to sulk because I turned down your proposal to be your business partner,' Sarah joked, punching him in the arm.

'When will you ever take me seriously, Sarah?'

'Who said I didn't take you seriously? I would love to work together with you, but maybe at a later stage, once I've found my footing again.'

Sarah watched as Edward's expression softened, and he turned to face her as he pulled the car to a stop up alongside the road.

'I will hold you to that,' he said. 'Now wait here; I will be back in a moment,' and quickly getting out of the car, he walked up a narrow driveway disappearing behind the bushes.

Edward appeared sometime later with a box in hand. 'Here, this is for you. Only open it when you cannot sleep,' he instructed. 'What's this for?' Sarah asked excitedly.

'You will know when you open it; now promise you will not open it for any other reason other than if you are unable to sleep?' He said in earnest.

'I promise, pinky promise,' Sarah giggled, holding out her baby finger to him so he could lock his with hers as a symbol of her promise, as if there were still in school. She looked down at the box. It was a square box, covered with handmade white embossed paper and a red ribbon tied in a bow around the box. Nestled between the knots of the bow was a single stem of lavender tucked neatly through it. Sarah smiled as she held the box, wondering what mystery lay beneath its borders.

Chapter Six

'What are you doing here?' Edward mumbled, as they entered the cottage.

'I came to surprise you,' Jasmine shrieked, running up to him and looping her arms around his neck, kissing him passionately on his lips. 'I knew you would be excited to see me,' she beamed.

Edwards jaw tensed, as he freed himself from her embrace. The sun had just set on their drive back to the cottage and he could feel the evening chill suddenly deep within his core.

'Hi, Jasmine,' Sarah greeted, surprised by her sudden lunge towards Edward as he had entered the doorway, 'It's lovely to see you again.'

'Thanks,' Jasmine said, laughing delightedly in her skin tight red mini dress. 'Edward told me he was coming up to the cottage and I knew I had to surprise him. We are all going to have so much fun together,' she beamed.

Sarah watched as a dark shadow seemed to cross Edward's face, and then suddenly, as if trying to resurrect the sun, his lips broke into a smile.

'Come along then, Jas. I will show you to your room,' he offered, pulling her arm in a desperate attempt to move her along quickly.

'Oh, no need, darling. Katy has already arranged for all my bags to be put into your room. No sense pretending we don't sleep in the same bed just because we are around family,' she drawled, running her fingers up and down Edward's chest before moving to plant herself firmly down on the couch.

'Yes, of course,' he said, glancing towards Katy as she came into the lounge.

'Oh, you are both finally home. I was wondering where you had gone to all day. The note you left didn't give much detail!' Katy smiled, patting him on the arm. 'Now, tell us all about your little adventure,' she said, motioning for everyone to sit down, as she opened a packet of marshmallows and handed one to each of them on a stick for them to roast over the fireplace.

Edward took an exaggerated deep breath before responding. 'I took Sarah down to Joseph's place for the day.'

'Who's Joseph,' Jasmine asked, confused.

'He is a friend of the family,' Katy explained

'Oh, so he is someone Sarah knows as well?' Jasmine looked between all three, waiting for someone to bring clarity to this man's significance.

'I hadn't met him before today,' Sarah interjected, suddenly sensing Edward was not comfortable sharing this with her. 'Edward just wanted to show me that part of the mountains and knew he had a friend who lived there, so he took me to visit him,' she lied, not willing to share with Jasmine the healing mystery the day held.

Edward looked at her with relief in his eyes, as if she had saved him from an inquiry. His shoulders slowly began to ease from the sudden tension, and the softness behind his eyes reappeared through the curtain of anger that had overshadowed them. Sarah could not understand his reaction to seeing Jasmine; she would have imagined he would have been delighted to have her here. Something had changed. Jasmine was showing an almost desperate attempt to plead for Edward's affection, and he seemed too polite to openly reject her.

'I'm going to get into something a little more comfortable for dinner,' Jasmine chimed, getting off the couch with such elegance despite the tightness of her dress.

'I'll join you,' Edward said quickly, following her towards the passage, their rumbling chatter echoing somewhere through the walls.

'Something doesn't seem right with Edward,' Katy questioned, 'What did you do to him?'

'Me?' Sarah gasped, 'He was perfectly fine until he walked through the door and found Jasmine sitting here! You would swear he is irritated that she came up here to surprise him.'

'Well, whatever it is I'm sure they will work it out. They have had an on-again, off-again relationship for years. I just don't know if Edward will ever settle down – it's as if he just can't meet the right person. No matter how long he dates someone the minute she wants to get serious he bolts.'

'Maybe he just isn't the commitment type?'

'I doubt that. All he talks about when we are alone is meeting someone whom he can love and adore, and have a family with. His whole face lights up when he speaks. I doubt that's the reaction of a commitment phobic,' Katy said, her voice in a whisper, not wanting to be overheard.

'Well, let's hope he meets the right woman soon, because your marriage might make him feel more alone, since you will be more occupied with your own life'

'That's what I've been worried about; I don't want to see him alone for the rest of his life. He has so much to offer a woman. If he would just decide to give love a chance.'

'True,' Sarah's voice trailed off as she thought of how kind he had been to her all day today. 'He will make someone the happiest woman in the world. He just needs to allow his heart the freedom to love,' she muttered.

An hour later, Sarah laid the table for supper, and wandered through the passage towards her bedroom to leave the box Edward had given her on her bedside table. She could hear angry chatter as she passed his room, and slowed her pace down to listen a little more closely, feeling slightly guilty for being so nosey but intrigued by what had got Edward so annoyed by Jasmine's presence in the first place.

Edward and Jasmine's door suddenly flew open, just as she had paused in front of their door. Sarah's startled expression went unnoticed, as they stormed out like puffing dragons, nostrils flaring and cheeks burning from anger

'Hi, Sarah,' Jasmine spoke in a high pitched pretentious tone, as she walked into her in the passage looking heavenly in a jade-green cotton jumpsuit, which accentuated her curves beautifully. Edward stomped out of the room saying nothing, and avoided all eye contact with Sarah, his brow knit and his hands and jaw firmly clenched.

'Umm… see you both at the dinner table,' Sarah said quietly as she scurried towards her room.

Leaving the box, she threw on a gold knit jersey over her t-shirt and walked out of her room. She felt slightly untidy in her jersey and jeans, but was not willing to do a wardrobe change for dinner like Jasmine had. She knew that no matter what Jasmine wore she would still look like a beauty queen, and Sarah felt strangely like a peasant girl next to her. She entered the lounge and saw the chilling stares Edward was sending Jasmine, and chose rather to escape into the kitchen to help Katy bring out the food.

'Oh good, you're here. Listen, it seems Edward and Jas are having some sort of fight. I think maybe we should all play "Thirty Seconds" after dinner just to lighten the mood. I can't take this sombreness she has brought with her to our happy cottage.' Katy said, clearly unimpressed that she needed to now tiptoe around them both.

It seems her good intention to bring Sarah up here to relax and feel happy was now a distant memory in light of the feud that seemingly brewed between her brother and his high maintenance girlfriend.

'Yes, sure,' Sarah shrugged, grabbing the dish of lasagna and heading towards the dining table.

'Dinner is served,' Katy called, and everyone filed onto the bench at the table. 'Dig in everyone; I hope you are hungry. Gladys cooked this, so I can't take credit for it. There is dessert as well which we can have later. Sarah and I thought we could all play a game of "Thirty Seconds" after dinner,' she said more as a command than a gesture, her eyes darting between Edward and Jasmine.

Edward locked eyes with Sarah who was seated opposite him. She returned him a pleading look indicating it wasn't fully her idea to force them all to play a game under these circumstances. He put his head down in defeat just as Gladys came in, checking if they had all they needed before she retired for the evening.

'Could you bring me the bottle of chocolate vodka I brought and some shot glasses?' Jasmine asked, her eyes darting mischievously around the room.

'I don't think that's a good idea,' Edward interjected.

'Oh rubbish, Edward. If we are going to have to play a boring board game, I might as well do it drunk and enjoy myself.'

She watched as Gladys returned with the bottle as requested, and she proceeded to pour everyone a shot.

'None for me,' Sarah said, just as Jasmine was handing out the glasses.

'We will *all* be having some. I didn't drive all this way with a big bottle all for myself,' Jasmine insisted, as she set a glass down in front of everyone. 'Go on!' she said bossily, picking up her own glass and throwing it back down her throat.

They all watched as she poured herself another shot, and refilled their glasses as soon as they had drunk their own.

'Jas, I think one is enough – let's eat first, okay?' Edward said, his voice stern and pleading for her to calm down.

'This will be the last one we have before we eat,' she said, 'but it's not the last for the evening. Now, stop being so stiff Edward and just lighten up a little.'

Sarah and Katy exchanged glances; they could tell this was going to be an interesting evening if Jasmine continued along this path. Sarah watched Edward as he ate, his face strained – an undeniable contrast to the relaxed and content image it had reflected towards her all day. What could Jasmine possibly have done to make Edward so frustrated, and why was she suddenly behaving so loudly and obnoxiously. Granted, Sarah knew that she didn't know Jasmine well enough to pass judgment. However the Jasmine she encountered tonight was a bizarre contrast to the Jasmine she had met a few days earlier.

They all filed into the lounge after dinner, and Sarah stood patiently by the fire as Edward rearranged the furniture in the lounge to best suit the game. He pulled two couches closer together and put a wooden coffee table in between them. Katy brought in the peppermint crisp dessert as Jasmine set up the board game on the table, pouring more chocolate vodka into the shot glasses. The flames from the fireplace leapt and licked around the wooden chunks, the sizzle of the burning wood warming Sarah's beating heart as she finally settled on the couch opposite Edward and Jasmine, wrapping herself snuggly in the cream cashmere throw.

'I think we should change things up a bit; how about Sarah and I be on the same team and you two can be on your own team,' Jasmine said enthusiastically picking up her shot glass. Edward kept staring at the floor, clearly lost in thought, barely hearing her request.

'Fine by me,' Katy said, taking her seat next to Sarah, 'Edward and I have had years to practise our skills. Isn't that right, Edward?' she said as she slapped Edward on the knee, trying to jolt him from his daydream.

'Mmm, yeah,' he shrugged. 'We will go first.' He rolled the dice.

'One,' he said, reading out the number on the dice before pulling a card out from the box. Facing Katy, he started.

'It's the day you want to get married,' he said, excitement suddenly in his veins as the sands of the thirty second timer dripped quickly in the timing glass.

'Umm... the twenty-fourth of December!' Katy shouted.

"No, no, what's the day called?"

'Ooh, ooh, Christmas Eve!'

'Yes, next one... He was the first black president in South Africa,' Edward said hurriedly

'Nelson Mandela,' Katy replied.

'Time's up!' Sarah called, just as the last grain of sand ran through the timer. She moved Edward's piece one move ahead.

'Okay, okay, it's our turn,' Jasmine said, her eyes glistening with anticipation. Sarah's heart pounded. She wasn't one for board games where she needed to be under pressure. She gulped down the shooter that was lying on the table in front of her, and watched as Edward flashed her a surprised glance.

'Okay, I'm ready,' Sarah panted watching as Jasmine rolled the dice.

'Zero,' Jasmine called as the dice fell. 'The capital of Ghana?' she spoke speedily.

'Accra'

'Good, good. The female actor in the movie *Maid in Manhattan*.

'Jennifer Lopez,' Sarah said, feeling the adrenalin pumping.

'Name the band that John Lennon was in?'

'The Beatles.'

'The place in South Africa where they keep wild animals?'

'The Kruger National Park,' Sarah said, sitting now on the edge of her seat. They just had one more question to answer and they could move a full five spaces ahead and be in the lead if the timer didn't run out.

'The inventor of the light bulb?'

'Thomas Edison,' Sarah screamed as Jasmine leapt over the table and high fived her.

'It seems we have some serious competition here,' Edward laughed, clearly amused by their competitive edge and forgetting his earlier frustrations with Jasmine. He rolled the dice as Katy pulled out a card.

'Sarah's favourite book?' Katy asked, watching the timer out of the corner of her eye.

'*Wuthering Heights*,' Edward replied without thinking.

'How on earth did you remember that?' Sarah asked, shock resonating through her voice. She stared at Edward. She knew Katy would know about her love for *Wuthering Heights* because she was her best friend. But how on earth did Edward even bother to remember what her favourite book was? Her head suddenly began swimming either from the shooters she had drunk, or the surprise at Edward's memory.

'Shh, you can ask us questions later,' Katy laughed. 'The capital of Italy?' she asked quickly, her attention back on Edward and her mind in the game.

'Rome.'

'The first man to walk on the moon?'

'Neil Armstrong.'

'Time's up,' Jasmine shouted.

'Sarah, we should get an extra point because you slowed us down with your questions,' Katy protested.

'No charity points here,' Jasmine sneered, 'If you were foolish enough to let her interrupt you, then that's your own problem.'

'Sorry, Katy, I was just surprised that's all. I guess I didn't realise you both remembered so much about me.'

'Of course we do,' Edward said, looking down sheepishly. 'We remember everything.'

'Listen, if you guys are going to look for excuses and sympathy points then I'm out of here,' Jasmine said, wobbling as she tried to get off the sofa. She threw herself on Edward's lap and kissed him drunkenly. He stood, lifting her in his arms, and headed for the doorway.

'I'd better get her to bed,' he muttered wearily as he left.

Katy and Sarah sat and giggled at Jasmine's behaviour. 'She is a piece of work, I must say, and my brother tries so hard to be patient with her,' Katy laughed.

'Lucky girl,' Sarah replied, thinking how she had never been that lucky in love after all in her own life.

Sarah walked over to the window and peered out into the darkness. The only lights out here were those of the stars and the moon. Tonight the moon stood proudly in its full splendour, glowing out through the night sky. She was reminded of something her mother had once quoted her: darkness cannot drive away darkness, only light can do that.

She looked at the moon and how it pierced through the darkness. Where there was light, darkness was no more. She knew she needed her life to be filled with light, and the only way was for her to surround herself with people who loved her and people who brought her joy. Only with their support would make the darkness in her heart disappear.

'Penny for your thoughts?' Katy asked, standing beside her.

'I'm just admiring the moon. If we had no moon we would have no hope of the sun shining tomorrow. The moon reminds us that the sun is just around the corner.' Sarah smiled reflectively, speaking more of her own life than of the moon.

'I know,' Katy smiled. She admired Sarah for her strength and positive attitude. She could have curled up and died if she so chose, but instead she wanted to look for hope even in her valley.

'Do you ladies want to sit on the verandah?' Edward asked, coming up behind them.

'Hey, I thought you had gone to bed?' Katy questioned.

'Not a chance! I just put Jasmine to bed! She was getting out of hand.'

Sarah and Katy shot each other amused glances as they recalled Jasmine's star performance.

'I will meet you both on the verandah. Let me make us some coffee,' Katy said, turning and heading for the kitchen.

'Come along, Little Miss Princess,' Edward said, pulling from the sofa one of the cashmere throws before ushering Sarah outside to sit on the porch swing.

He sat down alongside her, silently tucking the throw over them both as he pushed the swing with his legs, making it rock back and forth in a gentle lulling motion. Sarah smiled at him silently as he rocked her. Today had been a bizarre day.

For as long as she could remember she and Edward were always playful with each other, poking fun at each other, never serious for one minute. Yet since she had returned to South Africa she had connected with him in such a comforting way. She knew from all he had said and done that he knew her better than she knew herself right now.

He had remembered her love for baking and art, and her love for reading. She still couldn't fathom how after so many years he seemed to know exactly what she needed to heal. Seeing Joseph today testified to that. Over the years she had lost herself, yet he seemed to remind her of who she really was. He reminded her of the parts of herself that she loved, and the parts of herself she could reach into as tools for her healing.

She turned to him, and saw his eyes were already fixated on her. 'Thanks for today, Edward. You have exceeded your brotherly duties.' She added the last bit in an attempt to lighten her gratitude.

Edward looked away, and Sarah noticed a strange pained expression on his face.

'I didn't do it because I view you as my little sister,' he muttered.

Sarah look at him confused. He seemed irritated by her gratitude; his sudden annoyance made no sense. Katy came in carrying a tray with their coffee and some rusks. She saw Edward's face and Sarah's puzzled look, and stopped in front of them holding the tray.

'Did I interrupt something?' she asked confused.

'No. I need to get to bed,' Edward muttered, getting up and taking his cup of coffee before walking back into the house.

'What is up with him?' Katy exclaimed, irritated once more by his strange mood.

'Wish I knew. I sat here thanking him for taking me to see Joseph today, and he seemed annoyed at me for doing so.'

'I don't know if I will ever dissect that brother of mine. He just makes no sense sometimes.'

Sarah nodded at Katy, feeling slightly annoyed by Edward's reaction. If he and Jasmine had their problems he shouldn't take it out on her, she thought. She turned back to the view of the moon as Katy began to chatter excitedly about her wedding plans. Sarah was grateful for the distraction.

Chapter Seven

'Where should I put these?' Katy called, heaving over a large box.

'I think it should go in Kevin's office; we can sort it all out later,' Sarah replied, looking outside at the pile of boxes the courier had just delivered from London. 'When I requested my work files be sent over, I didn't imagine there were so many.'

Kevin smiled knowingly as he helped to carry in the remainder of the boxes; he knew sorting through these files would be a mammoth task that he was willing to take on.

Sarah looked around. It had been two weeks since they had come back from the cottage, and the estate agent Katy had hired to find her office premises had called informing them of a property in Umhlanga that was available. She had spent the last four days moving into the offices and hiring Kevin, who would be her personal assistant. Sarah had tasked Kevin with the research, logistics and administration of the business, so that she could keep her focus on the design aspect. She was excited that she had found offices so soon, and had already given Kevin his first assignment to source more manufacturers, get quotes and arrange meetings, so that she could get the fabrics and wallpapers printed and present them to buyers of the niche décor stores.

'I will need a few more filing cabinets,' Kevin mused, as he looked around at the piles of boxes in his office. 'I think I will stay in late tonight; I can't work in such a mess. I will need to arrange everything today so that I can get cracking on work tomorrow.'

'Don't worry, Kevin. Katy and I will be here as well. We need this office in perfect working order so we can settle in properly.' Sarah frowned. 'And the first order of business is to get a coffee and hot chocolate machine in here pronto!' she laughed.

Kevin chuckled. He already loved working for Sarah, even though it had only been a few days. He knew they would get along perfectly. She was beautiful and driven, with a fighting spirit behind her eyes, and a passion for design. He had read about her work previously in *Elle Décor* magazine, where she was commended for her work in restoring an old castle that had been declared a heritage site. Her reputation preceded her, and he wondered what she was doing here in South Africa. Surely there were greater prospects in England for an interior designer? He didn't ask however – he was just grateful for the opportunity. Having done an internship at Cecile & Boyd's in Cape Town for a year, he had moved back to Durban and this would be his first official job since his return. He was excited to learn all he could from her.

'I'm going to run out and get us something to eat,' Katy offered. 'I'm starving and definitely need a break.'

'Thanks, Katy,' Sarah and Kevin echoed, as she beelined for the door.

'So what do you think, Kev?' Sarah asked, wheeling herself around as she took in the office.

'It's taking shape, sweets. Once we've unpacked the boxes and the rest of the furniture is delivered it will be complete,' he sighed.

'I still want to get a TV and projector in the boardroom for presentations, and we need to stock that fridge with some goodies or we will starve to death in here.'

'Good idea,' he smiled, watching as she moved quickly unpacking the stationery, and filled their drawers with its quota of pens.

'So, what brought you back to Durban?' Sarah quizzed, wondering why he would leave Cape Town.

'My girlfriend lives here, and I had no intention of moving to Cape Town permanently. I'm a Durban boy through and through so it wasn't much of a decision to make.' He paused, 'If I didn't return I would have missed this great opportunity to work for you,' he smiled.

'Mmm, well I'm not sure I'm a great opportunity,' Sarah laughed.

'Let me be the judge of that,' he said seriously.

Sarah looked up at Kevin – he seemed genuinely excited to work for her. He had a degree in interior design, yet he was willing to be her personal assistant in her new wallpaper and textile business. His portfolio of work was amazing, and she knew he could contribute valuable design input to her business. She knew when she saw his designs that she couldn't keep him as her assistant for long. With talent like that she would need to promote him to a designer soon. She hadn't mentioned that to him though. He had an aura about him that was bright and cheerful – just the type of person she needed to surround herself with. He had darkly golden skin, with hair more caramel than brown, his hazel eyes popped against his glowing skin, and his smile was broad and engaging. He had a face that could only be described as beautiful, with flawlessly clean shaven skin.

'Where must these go?' Kevin asked, pointing to some boxes marked "lamps".

'Oh, those need to go in the reception area outside your office. Once the chairs are delivered we can set up that area properly.'

'I'm back,' Katy called, with bags of Chinese food in hand. 'I didn't know what you guys wanted, so I got some beef chow mein, sweet and sour pork, chicken chop suey and some honey prawns with rice.'

'Geez, are you planning on feeding an entire country?' Sarah laughed, helping her with the bags and placing them on the table in the kitchen.

'I thought we could have a mini buffet, kind of taste a little of each thing,' Katy shrugged.

'Hey, I have a man-size stomach, so no amount of food is ever too much,' Kevin said, joining them at the table.

'Oh Kevin, you fit in perfectly with us,' Katy giggled.

Sarah shook her head and laughed, pouring them some Fanta. She sat back and relaxed, watching as Katy and Kevin chatted about their love for Chinese food and feeling for the first time the pain throbbing in her feet. She was happy with the offices they had found. They were a perfect mix of ocean villa and countryside heaven, with the entrance to the office having a winding stone driveway, flanked on either side by box-shaped hedges and rose bushes with benches placed neatly at the entrance. The reception area had exposed brickwork with wooden flooring, which she planned on decorating with a Chesterfield sofa in a blue and white striped fabric and brown woven chairs, with oversized paintings gracing the walls. Kevin's office led off from the reception area with the kitchen and meeting rooms to the right, and her office at the back of the building with an awe inspiring view of the ocean.

'The telephones will be connected today, and I have already ordered your business cards based on the logo design you gave me,' Kevin said, interjecting Sarah's thought.

Sarah lifted her head lazily, 'Thanks, Kev. I think I ate too much, because now I just feel sleepy.'

'Come, come, no time for resting here!' Katy pulled Sarah to her feet, 'The sooner we get back to work the sooner we finish, because I have a steaming hot date lined up with John tonight. Oh, and while I remember, don't wait up for me!' She said, her eyes twinkling with mischief.

'You're going to leave me home alone?' Sarah protested.

'Hey, you're a big girl; you will manage on your own.'

Katy suddenly felt guilty, as she realised what she had just said; she hadn't left Sarah alone since she arrived. 'Unless you would prefer I stay home with you, if you need me. I can cancel with John – I won't mind at all?' she added quickly.

'No, you go and enjoy yourself. I need to get used to being alone since I will be moving into my own place soon.'

'I hope not too soon, I've just got used to having you around.'

Sarah hugged her friend. She had got used to being with her as well, but didn't want to get too dependent on her. It was her time to heal and move forward, and she knew she had to draw on her own strength to do it. It was time to live her own life.

'The furniture truck has just arrived,' Kevin called from the front door, as a large trucked pulled to a halt at the end of the driveway.

'No rest for the wicked, hey?' Sarah laughed as Kevin went ahead to the truck to coordinate the delivery.

'At last,' Sarah signed more to herself than to Katy. At last everything was delivered, and now this new aspect of her career was about to begin.

By the time Sarah and Kevin had finished in the office it was well past midnight. She had sent Katy off much earlier to kick-start her romantic evening with John. They had brought in all the furniture and set it up in each room. They hung the curtains and blinds and finished off the reception area with all the soft furnishings. In her office they hung her 3D renderings of previous projects she had worked on, from hotels, to villas in Spain, castles in England and even an eco estate in Kenya. Her framed drawings would stand as a reminder of her achievements in her career, a reminder of how she fought to be the best designer she could be then, and she would fight to be the best designer she could be now. At some point she would carry on with her illustrious career as an interior designer, but she knew she would then need to travel again, and right now she didn't want to travel. Right now she felt she needed her feet to be firmly set in one place, so that the trembling in her belly could stop, and she could once again feel like she was on solid ground.

Sarah finally arrived home, exhausted from the day's work as she stumbled into the house. She took off her shoes and let the pain subside in her feet while she set some milk on the stove to boil. There was nothing a warm mug of hot chocolate couldn't fix she thought. Her mind spun with ideas and urgencies. She knew money was not an issue – even if she hadn't opened her business straight away she could have managed financially for a few years – but her career was not about money. It was a reminder to herself that life had to go on, that she couldn't curl up and die, that she had to keep hoping for the sun to shine again in her life.

Sarah sat on the couch with her mug in hand. She knew there was no way she could sleep. She hadn't spent a night alone in ten years but she couldn't let Katy know that as she had done more than enough for her already, so she just had to manage this night alone on her own. She remembered the box Edward had given her in the Drakensburg, the box he made her promise never to open unless she couldn't sleep. There had been many nights before now she hadn't slept, but had never felt them bad enough to peek into the box. Tonight, however, she knew was that night.

She went to her room and opened her cupboard, and took out the neatly wrapped box. The piece of lavender had started to dry out, and she removed it as she pulled on the strings of the silk red ribbon surrounding the box. She unwrapped it slowly, ensuring not to tear the wrapping paper. She found inside a red and gold box and she opened the lid and saw ten rows of chocolates arranged neatly in gold casings. On top lay a note. She opened it and read:

Taste the first chocolate in the box:
It represents your life now.
Taste the last chocolate in the box:
It's a promise of your future.
Edward xxx

Sarah lifted the first chocolate to her lips; it was bitter and hard. She shivered, as the bitterness lingered on her tongue.

She took a bite of the last chocolate and it was soft and smooth with a sweet liquid caramel centre that clung to her lips gently. She smiled, knowing Edward was right; the best was yet to come, and her best days were before her.

She lay on top of her bed and hugged her pillow. It was hard to imagine that just a few months ago she was blissfully happy with no cares in the world; her life seemed perfect, and in a blink of an eye it all evaporated. She had left everything behind in hope to start afresh, but she knew she was also running away from her past, and at some point she would have to face it.

For now she needed to regroup, she needed to find her strength, so that when she did face it, she would have healed somewhat. She would be bold enough to deal with the grief, the hatred, the betrayal. She would rise above this; no one would destroy her. She remembered something her grandmother would always say when she came home crying from school: 'This too shall pass,' she would whisper, as she stroked her hair and soothed her tears. And right now, in this place of hiding, she was waiting for the pain and darkness to pass, so that she could rise above it all and live once again. She longed for the day when real joy would engulf her, when real happiness would pursue her, and for when she would hold onto the part of the past that meant something and be able to let go of the painful memories.

She turned over and looked at the giraffe she had placed on her bed, and now next to it lay the box of chocolates. For now, this was all she would hold onto; this was a piece of her past that meant something, and this was a hope for her future. She held tightly onto the giraffe as her thoughts slowed down and her breathing got heavy, until finally her fears and sadness gave way to the weight in her eyelids, as she drifted off to sleep.

Chapter Eight

Sarah couldn't take her eyes off the light dancing over the ocean: the crashing, swirling waves as they played blissfully with the shoreline, dissolving into ripples of dazzling topaz waters. It was one of those days when the view was more hindrance than help, wrapping around her like a hypnotising trance disabling her from focusing on work. She wanted to melt in the heat spots in her office, chasing after their whimsical light as they moved around with the dawning of the sun.

'Sarah?' he asked, his eyes fixated on her, 'Sarah are you ok?'

Startled she moved, unaware that anyone had come in, 'Umm, Kevin. Sorry, I didn't see you there. What time is it?'

'It's eight o'clock. How long have you been sitting in here?'

'Since dawn, I guess,' she shook her head, clearly still lost in the crevices of her mind. How had time gone by so quickly – she felt as if she had just arrived.

Kevin walked around her office, his eyes constantly on her. She sat still on the leather couch as he took some files off her desk. 'I will start to set up appointments for today. Are you up for it?' he said finally.

'Yeah, I will be fine,' she nodded. 'There is a lot to do, so we'd better get started,' she said, stirring from the glue that had bound her until now. 'I will make us some coffee.'

She stood up and walked dazed into the kitchen. She needed to snap out of whatever had got a hold of her; this was go time, and right now she needed all the strength she could muster. Slowly and meticulously she moved through the kitchen; switching the kettle on; pulling the cups out; measuring sugar and coffee and dividing it between them. She felt divided. She longed for what she had, longed for what she missed, longed for birthdays and Christmases and milestone moments that she would never have, never see, never touch. He was gone, there was no bringing him back, and time could never be reclaimed, redeemed.

'Need some help there?' Kevin remarked, feeling unsure of what to do.

'Nope, all done,' she said, handing him his coffee and forcing a smile that barely left her lips.

'Your estate agent, Julie, left a message on the answering machine. She has found a few places for you to look at, if you're up for it today?'

'Sure, perhaps set it up for this morning, and arrange appointments with suppliers and manufactures for this afternoon. Would you mind coming with me to view the apartments?'

He stared at her, she was clearly fragile, and even though he knew he needed to help her in every way with her business, he could see today she needed him for this too. 'Of course, let me just set up the appointments for later today, and we can jet off and see those apartments.'

'Thanks, Kev,' she said politely as she made her way back to her office. 'I've got some croissants in here, if you're hungry?'

'Thanks, but no thanks! In order to keep this six pack I'd better watch what I eat,' he laughed, cracking through the stillness. She smiled. She was glad Kevin was here with her.

Sarah returned to her office and laid her designs out patiently on her desk. Her aim was to have three main ranges of complementary textiles and wallpapers. She wanted a range for children's rooms, orphanages and schools; a range for offices, homes and hotels; and a custom made range that was specific images designed to custom fit a space.

From her research she knew that the manufacture of wallpaper was divided into those used in residences and those hung in businesses and public buildings. The two categories of paper differed in weight, serviceability and quality standards. Residential-use wallpapers were made from various materials and could be purchased pre-pasted or unpasted. This would be the range she would offer to buyers to stock in niche retail décor stores. The commercial-grade wallpapers, however, went through a different process, and were divided into categories based on weight, backing composition, and laminate or coating thickness. All commercial-use wallpapers must have a vinyl surface and pass rigorous physical and visual tests. She planned to offer these to interior designers and architects to use in their designs in commercial spaces.

Her textiles she wanted printed with soft furnishings in mind, such as scatter cushions and curtains, with an extended range for upholstery of occasional chairs and couches.

Her eyes grazed over her designs, as she began casting a critical eye over her work – her two main designs were a design of the South African flower, the protea, which was indigenous to the region, and the mother and child design of the giraffe. Both designs were done in various styles, from abstract versions to life-like portraits to child-like renditions; all were easily able to fit into all three product ranges and could be woven into fabric or printed onto paper.

'You ready?' Kevin interrupted. 'The estate agent is waiting for us at the first property.'

'Okay, great,' Sarah said, grabbing her coat as they made their way out of the office.

Shuffling through the glass paned doors, they meandered up a winding staircase with white wrought-iron balustrades. At the top of staircase was apartment twenty-two. Julie opened the door to the apartment and moved aside to allow them in.

Sarah walked inside and looked around. The apartment was empty, hollow and dark, with a musty smell. The pine wood flooring extended into every room, with evidence it had been chewed by borer. She stepped towards the large sash windows and heard the creak of the floorboard beneath her. Despite its sombreness, this place had a subtle charm with high volume ceilings and wood-panelled windows, each room interleading with French doors.

She heard a sudden thump, and ran to the window. Someone had just rammed their car into another. This apartment was built right on the roadside, the sound of traffic a constant hum that never seemed to ease up.

After a few more minutes of bewildered browsing, she knew this wasn't the place for her. 'I just can't see myself living here, Julie. It's too dark and it's built right on the edge of the main road. The sound of traffic is deafening; I need something more spacious and light, a place I can relax.'

Julie smiled knowingly, 'There are two more places I have to show you, but the second is similar to this, so I think we should make our way straight to the third. I have a feeling you might like it.'

Kevin put his arm around Sarah as they made their exit. 'Don't worry, we will make sure we find you the perfect place,' he said comfortingly.

Sarah was taken aback as they entered. The space was bright and inviting, with stark white ceilings and butterscotch walls and carpets. The apartment was fully furnished, and Julie explained that this was the owner's holiday home, and they had now decided to rent it out, as it was.

'I love it,' Sarah exclaimed, searching every inch of the place.

It was perfect – she could move in tomorrow without the hassle of looking for furniture. She let her eyes wander around the bright and airy apartment. The living room was open plan, with the kitchen, lounge and dining areas all seamlessly interlocking. The lounge had a glass and stainless steel coffee table with an Ascotcouch in an ivory wheat fabric and two boudoir chairs in fuchsia pink. The scatter cushions were upholstered in white and gold striped linen and the walls adorned with black and white photography with a large bookcase on the far wall.

'They took all their books away,' Julie interjected, as she noticed Sarah's eyes fell on its empty shelves.

'Oh, that's fine. I will soon fill it with my own collection,' she smiled, surprised by her sudden love of this place. 'It's beautiful; the view of the ocean and city skyline is breathtaking. It just feels like home. The proportions of the rooms are perfect, with a perfect mix of crisp feminine and masculine details throughout. So when can I move in?' she beamed excitedly.

Julie and Kevin laughed, delighted at her response. 'I will speak to the owners. They will require some documentation from you, as they will need to do the necessary credit checks, but I'm sure I can arrange for you to move in here by Thursday. All you will need is linen for the king size beds in the main and guest rooms and your clothes. Everything else is already here,' she said cheerfully.

'Perfect! That gives me three days to get Katy and myself used to the idea of me living on my own.' Sarah nodded; it was like some kind of mission statement. She knew she would have to wrap her head around it more than Katy would. She hoped she was ready.

Chapter Nine

'Sorry I'm late,' Katy grinned, peeling off her turquoise trench coat and falling into the seat beside Sarah, as the waiter set down two cappuccinos and yoghurt parfait.

'I ordered for you already,' Sarah said, motioning to the coffee.

She had arrived an hour earlier, parking her car on the main road and taking a slow walk to what now had become their regular Saturday morning spot since she had moved out. It was positioned behind several old Victorian styled homes, tucked quietly away, as a secret haven only the locals knew existed. The restaurant was actually two bright red mirrored shipping containers that had been set up perpendicularly to each other and converted into seating areas. Sarah and Katy always opted to sit outside at the back of the containers underneath the mango trees which came alive at night, sparkling with fairy lights twinkling around their branches.

'Thanks! So what news do you have for me? Is everything in production?'

'Yes, thank God, finally. I was starting to lose hope with the back and forth, but we seem to be making headway.' Sarah breathed dramatically, playing idly with the black and white ceramic salt and pepper shakers in the shape of sausage dogs.

It had been a tough month, running around liaising with the manufactures to get samples made, ensuring each design was in the correct palette that would be marketable, and guaranteeing there were sufficient designs to form a collection, as the buyers wanted to stock only a wide-ranging collection, as opposed to one or two line items. Three stores agreed to stock her products, and she planned to launch them all sometime during the following month, once production of the textiles and wallpapers was complete. She had sent samples to each buyer as well as leading magazines, as she needed them all at her product launch. The difficult part had come in sourcing the correct manufactures and suppliers; she needed sustainability as well as large volumes produced. As much as she wanted to support smaller businesses, she needed to be confident that they could handle the high order volumes as the business expanded, to avoid any teething problems.

'Good, so that means we can move forward with my wedding.'

Sarah laughed, opening the leather bound folder she had on the table. 'I have made you this schedule with all you need to know for the wedding. I have booked 'Make-Up-Your-Mind' to come through on the day to do your make-up, as well as Will Taylor for your hair.'

Katy shrieked; they were both considered the best, and Katy knew Sarah would have had to have bribed someone to get an appointment at this late stage, and to get them to agree to drive all the way to the Drakensberg on the day.

'I've also arranged for us to do wedding dress shopping tomorrow, and I've ordered that extravagantly glamorous Louis Vuitton sandal you were eyeing in Glamour magazine, as my wedding gift to you. They will be delivered the week before the wedding.'

'You did what?' Katy screamed almost knocking over her cappuccino. 'Sarah those shoes cost a fortune and I was just dreaming of having them as my wedding shoe. Never in a million years would I have expected to actually be walking down the aisle in them,' she beamed, reaching over and covering Sarah's hand with hers. 'How could I ever repay you for such a gift?'

'You have done more than enough for me. I am actually the one indebted to you, and I couldn't resist seeing you pull off those heels. You are the only person I know brave enough to wear gold, navy and black five inch heels with her white wedding dress instead of the conventional white and silver shoe.' Sarah laughed delighted to see her friend's reaction. The shoe was made from suede baby goat leather featuring spectacular ostrich feather trim with an Art Deco-inspired gold metal and black lacquered heel – it was as unusual as she was.

'You love me for being different,' she chuckled, 'and I have one more favour to ask you and then your debt is paid in full.'

'Name it'

'John and I want you to be our maid of honour. That's if you're up for it? Edward will be the best man, as John has no brothers. So what do you say? Would you do us the honour?'

Katy knew before the last words left her mouth what Sarah's answer would be, as she saw the tears gleam in her eyes, and her smile stretched across her face like a Cheshire cat.

'I would be honoured, Katy. I thought you didn't want a conventional retinue at your wedding?'

'With you and Edward a part of it, nothing could ever be conventional,' she giggled, recalling the time all three of them had played "the wedding game" with Sarah and Edward being the bride and groom, and Katy the minister. Sarah knew immediately what she was thinking, and they both burst into fits of laughter.

'Do you remember how Edward so valiantly repeated his vows after me, and was more eager to kiss the bride than anything else,' Katy giggled.

'Yes, he was hoping I would be his first kiss. Shame,' Sarah laughed, thinking of how she almost punched him in the face as he had lunged in, raspberry lips puckered, waiting for his kiss.

They both laughed hysterically, getting glared at by the other patrons seated beside them clearly annoyed that they had disturbed the peace. Sarah stifled her laugh quickly, noticing the old lady opposite her giving her a penetrating glare, as if scolding a school girl when she had misbehaved.

'I wanted to host a housewarming party at my apartment this Saturday, if you aren't all busy?' Sarah offered, after they had finally managed to calm down.

'Yes, sure. John and I were planning an evening in, so we will come to you instead.'

'Great, will you check with Edward and Jasmine if they're available, and I will see if Kevin and his girlfriend would also like to come?'

'Sounds perfect. Could we perhaps bring anything?'

'I will do the cooking, you can bring the dessert?'

'It's a deal!'

'Hey, did I tell you my parents sent over these beautiful black and white Ralph Lauren framed photographs of the Chaumont La Guiche Stables and the Versailles La Grande Stables. They said they are to remind me of our time horse riding in France. I've hung them up in my bedroom; they are beautiful.'

'How are your parents?' Katy frowned, realising this was the first time Sarah had made reference to her former life since she arrived.

'They are well. I miss them dearly, but they understand that for now its best I am here. Would you mind them coming to your wedding? I wanted them here for Christmas, and I know they would be delighted to see you walk down the aisle and to see your parents again.'

'Of course!' Katy exclaimed, 'I would be honoured to have them there.'

'Great, it's settled then, I will add them to the guest list,' Sarah said in her most cheerful voice. Despite her excitement to see her parents, she felt a sudden chill. It would be the first time she would have seen them in months. She knew she hadn't given them the goodbye they deserved, with her leaving them a hurried voicemail of her intentions to leave the country, before getting on the plane. It had been a shock to them, and they were deeply hurt she didn't talk it through with them before making such a major decision. She loved her parents, but she knew she couldn't bring them into the horror of her life. She couldn't allow them in the middle of it all; it was not their fault and they didn't deserve to be torn at the seams by it. It was easier for her to leave, to get away. That way they didn't have to choose. That way they didn't have to stare at her with sympathy in their eyes. She refused to be a victim, the one everyone spoke about in hushed tones at family dinners, and she would not be the problem child.

'I've got to go,' Katy said standing up, 'I'm meeting John and Edward for lunch. We are going to ask him to be the best man, with strict instructions that's it's John who gets to kiss the bride, and not he who gets to kiss the maid of honour,' she giggled delightedly. 'Although judging from our last encounter with Jasmine, she will kill him if he tries!'

Sarah laughed as Katy kissed her on the cheek, 'See you Saturday at seven o'clock, and don't forget to ask Edward as well.'

'Consider it done,' Katy beamed, turning on her heels and leaving the restaurant with such drama and pizzazz, as only she could.

Sarah wandered up the road, deciding to walk through the makeshift market stalls before heading home. Being a Saturday, all the stallholders were frantically busy, running back and forth trying to get small change, and rummaging through bags and boxes for more stock. The patrons seemed laid back and relaxed however, walking as if all time were on their side. The day was brightly cheerful despite the winter chill, and Sarah twisted her fingers through the fringes of the knitted scarf she wore. She recalled when she had received it – it was a happy day – and he who she would rather forget had given it to her as a birthday gift. He was so grand in her eyes then, so strong and sturdy, valiant and unchanging. He was her everything. She pulled her leather jacket tightly around her remembering his eyes; his smile; the way he laughed with such a thickness that if you didn't know him well enough you would mistakenly think he was coughing.

She walked silently, passing the stalls one by one, crowded with people trying to find the bargain of the day. A tired woman pushing her baby in a pram peered over the eager shoulders into one of the stalls, and two children ran merrily blowing bubbles into the air, chasing them as if they held within their soapy moulds sprinkles of fairy dust to help them fly away.

She smiled, recalling the days when she, Edward and Katy would run through the forest next to their house imagining they were the characters from Enid Blyton's *Enchanted Forest* series of books, looking for the "Far Away Tree" and "Moon-face" hidden within. They longed to escape into the fantasy worlds the book recounted – it seemed so magical, so blissfully enchanting.

The hairs on her neck suddenly stood up; a feeling as if she were being followed. She swung around scanning the throngs of people. She saw a man in a black woollen coat who seemed to slow his pace down the minute she turned around. His face looked familiar, as if she had seen him the week before whilst she had walked on the beach. No, it can't be, she thought. She must be imagining it. Who would follow her? *Sky News* always reported on the crime rate in South Africa, but she had never heard of stalking being one of the crimes. She must be mistaken. She looked around again – he was gone, nowhere to be seen. She shook off the creepy sensation that had engulfed her. Finding a bench, she sat down to catch her breath.

'Hi, can I sit with you?'

She turned to see a little boy, probably five or six years old, standing beside her in cargo shorts and a baby blue golfer, holding two balloons tightly in his hands.

'Sure,' she said, watching as he quickly ran around her and wriggled his tiny self onto the bench.

'What's your name,' he asked, beaming up at her, his big brown eyes and thick lashes fluttering dramatically as he spoke.

'It's Sarah, and yours?'

'Jamie. Why do you look so sad?' He gave her a look and frowned deeply as if imitating the look on her face.

'I'm not sad, sweetheart; I was just thinking that's all. Where are your parents?'

'My dad is around somewhere, shopping.'

'Don't you think you should get back to him? He will be worried not knowing where you are!'

'Umm, he won't. He knows I always come and sit on this bench. We come here all the time.'

Sarah smiled; he was delightful, his chocolate brown hair flopping around freely as he spoke. He was so tiny, yet spoke like a little gentleman. She wanted to hold him tightly, but she restrained herself.

'I want you to have one of my balloons,' he said cheerfully, handing her his yellow balloon and holding on to the blue one for himself.

'Oh, thank you, that's very kind of you. But I can't take your balloon. It just wouldn't be right.'

'Yes, you can,' voices echoed.

She turned around to see sea-blue eyes staring down at her. He was leaning against the back of the bench, watching her notably, his gaze not moving from her as she registered his pale blue golfer and cream cargo shorts very much like the little boy's, with dark blond hair and an angular jawline, strong and ridged.

'Hi, I'm Jake, Jamie's dad,' he said, stretching out his hand for her to shake it. She put her hand in his, noting how soft his skin was and how piercing his gaze was on her, as if he had already undressed her with his eyes.

'You're beautiful,' he stated, releasing her hand, his eyes not leaving hers for a second.

'Umm, thank you,' she stuttered, shifting in her seat. She turned to face Jamie whose hand was still outstretched with the balloon. 'Thanks for the balloon, Jamie. That's very sweet of you.' She took the balloon from his hand, and suddenly out of the corner of her eye, noticed the man in the woollen coat taking her picture. 'What the heck!' she screamed, jumping up and running across the road, trying to find him. Before she could even get across he had disappeared behind the trees.

'What happened?' Jake asked, having followed her across the road.

'Some guy has been following me, and now I caught him taking pictures of me.'

'You're shaking,' he said, putting his arm around her as if they were old friends. He held onto her as he led her back to the bench and sat her down. 'Now tell me more about this man.'

'He… he… I can't describe him, I just know he wore a woollen black coat. Every time I see him I never get a chance to see his face clearly. He ducks or disappears.'

'Do you know why someone would be following you? Is there anyone you can think of that would want pictures of you?'

'No, I can't think of anyone.'

He knelt down beside her, and cupped her face in his hands. 'It's going to be okay. I will give you my phone number. I want you to try and look at him properly next time to get a good description, or use your cellphone to take a picture of him. Then I want you to call me and I will find out who he is, okay?' He handed her his card with his name and number on it. 'Now, why don't the three of us go and get some frozen yogurt, and then I will walk you back to your car?'

'Thanks, you don't have to do that though.'

'I want to, and Jamie would be disappointed if you don't join us for frozen yogurt, won't you, Jamie?'

Jamie nodded, obviously still startled by Sarah's reaction.

They walked over to one of the stalls, and chose their yogurt. Sarah chose the "strawberry delight", Jamie the "caramel swirl" and Jake had "praline chocolate". Jake led them further up the road to a park, and they all sat down on the grass licking at their cones delightedly.

'I didn't get your name?' Jake asked, watching as Sarah twisted a piece of her hair idly.

'It's Sarah,' Jamie chimed in. 'She's real pretty, isn't she Dad?' his eyes beamed up at Sarah.

'Pretty is an understatement, Jamie. She is breathtaking!' he said, the last statement directed more at Sarah than at Jamie.

His eyes clocked her body: the curves of her hips; the nape of her neck; the way her lips parted as if waiting and ready for him to kiss them. He watched as she looked away shyly, almost embarrassed by his attention. If it were any other time, any other place, he would have kissed her so hard, so hungrily, taking off her clothes to explore what treasures he could plunder that lay beneath, but he knew now wasn't the time.

'I'm going to play on the swings, okay, Dad?'

'Sure, Jamie,' Jake smiled, watching as he ran off to play with the other children.

'So where is Mrs. Jake?' Sarah asked, trying to throw him off her scent.

'There isn't one,' he mused, aware of what she was trying to do. 'She left some years ago, abandoned us and never returned.'

'I'm so sorry.'

'No, it's okay. We are better off anyway.'

'Have you tried to find her?'

'Yes, I have. I finally found her living in Johannesburg, high on cocaine. I begged her to come home for Jamie's sake, but she wasn't interested. She said she had never had a motherly instinct, and couldn't be bothered what happened to us.'

'Oh Jake, I'm sorry. I don't understand how a woman could abandon her child – that's heartbreaking.'

'It's been hard to try to explain it to Jamie. He asks for her often and I don't know what to tell him.'

Sarah turned and watched Jamie play with the other kids. Her heart ached for this little boy. He was so loving and kind hearted. He didn't deserve to be rejected that way. She longed to just wrap him in her arms and keep him safe.

'At least he has you to love him,' she said finally.

They sat together chatting about Jake's work. He was an investigator for a large corporate company, looking after the interests of the business, spying on the competitor to ensure they always had the competitive edge. Sarah found it all a bit sinister and underhand, but she knew that was the nature of the business. Jake noticed how Sarah offered no personal information; she seemed guarded, not willing to tear down the walls that imprisoned her. She thought they kept her safe, but all they did was trap her within the fortress of her past.

Eventually the roads became quieter and the people disappeared. The stallholders counted their money and folded up their remaining merchandise, and Jake and Jamie walked Sarah to her car.

'Call me if you see the stalker again. I know many people in high powered positions. It won't take me long to find out who he is,' Jake said, leaning in and kissing Sarah gently on the cheek, his stubble grazing her as he pulled away.

'Thanks,' Sarah muttered, pink cheeked from the close contact. She bent to hug Jamie. 'Thank you for my balloon, sweetheart. I will keep it safe, and think of you always.'

'It's a pleasure, Sarah,' he said, wrapping his tiny arms around her neck.

Her heart leapt. His embrace was so genuine, so loving; she didn't want to let him go.

Chapter Ten

The breeze swirled around her, toying with her loose ponytail as she pushed harder on the pedals along the narrow paved pathway. But she pressed on, cycling harder. She needed to cleanse her mind from the horror that provoked her sleepless nights. This had become her only way of dealing with the lack of sleep – it was her escape.

She knew the day was fast approaching when she would have to face her nightmares, her fears, but today was not that day. Today she could allow her mind to meander as she moved along the beach feeling the burn in her thighs. She had found this place soon after she found her offices, and by now knew every bend in the path, every familiar face cycling or walking past her each morning.

Pedalling harder as the incline grew steeper, she felt the force of the wind slow her down as her speed diminished. It was dawn, and the glare of the sunrise suddenly blinded her eyes, as the sky's portrait changed from a dusky dark blue to a bright blue and orange glow. She stopped at the top of the incline, and looked out over the horizon; she couldn't help but look around frantically for the man in the woollen coat. Ever since her encounter with him last week she felt paranoid each time she stepped outside, looking in every crevice where he might be hiding, stalking, watching.

She checked her watch; it was six thirty. Katy had cancelled their regular Saturday morning breakfast, as they were coming over later for supper. She ran through the list of groceries she needed to buy: chicken, fresh cream, spices, filo pastry and prawns. It would be refreshing to have some company at home for a change. The loneliness was getting to her, despite her days being filled with meetings and Kevin's chatter. Somehow the contrast between her busy work life and her silent home life was stark, and the walls of her apartment now served as a silent reminder of all that she had lost.

Work had been productive, however. Her reputation had preceded her, and she had already been commissioned to design wallpaper for the reception area of a new eco-friendly hotel, and textiles for its guest rooms. The project had given her greater purpose, and even though she had been asked to interpret their interior designer's vision for the hotel, she was still able to add her own signature touch to the designs. Her very own range of wallpapers and textiles was finally complete and out of production, ready to roll out into the stores which had agreed to stock them. Delivery would commence next week, and the following week would be the launch party at her offices. *Elle Décor* magazine had agreed to do a feature article on her designs and lists of stockists; she had also set up an online store for delivery to areas where her products weren't in retail as yet. She was excited about her achievements and eager to finally see profits from her labour.

It had been a highly productive few weeks, and she was grateful to Kevin for his unfailing assistance. He was organised and on top of things, having a plan B whenever plan A had failed, and she planned on giving him a raise as soon as she made a profit. She knew she couldn't have done it without him, and he never failed to remind her of such.

She looked around once more for the stalking stranger, then pushed forward as she continued cycling, watching as the sun ascended higher and higher over the horizon's edge. She passed the cafés as she pedalled, that were starting to set up their tables and chairs on the side of the pathway, ready for business. Here people flocked to the beach for breakfast as early as seven in the morning with their families. Parents would sit in the cafés having breakfast as they watched their children build castles in the sand. They had a clear view of the ocean from where they sat, and it allowed for perfect leisure time for parents and children alike.

Passing the Dinky Doughnut stand she inhaled the smell of freshly frying doughnuts, with their liquid chocolate dips tantalising her taste buds. She realised she was hungry as she felt the familiar growl in her stomach, which now served as a noble sign that her appetite had finally returned. The ice cream lady sauntered lazily along the path, ringing her bell, pushing her ice cream box. In spite of it being winter, it was never cold enough out here to deter people from consuming ice cream even in the winter chill, and with September just weeks away, the signs of spring were fast approaching.

She made her way to the end of the path, approaching the red and white lighthouse that identified this area. She braced herself for the final incline as she pumped her legs harder on the pedals, half standing off the bike, pressing on upwards, feeling her heart come alive as her blood worked harder to supply her body with its dosage of oxygen.

At the top, on the main road, she slowed down as she cycled towards her car. She had had her car fitted with bike racks, and she rapidly manoeuvered off the bike and strapped it onto the roof of her car. She felt sweaty, and pushed back the few wet curls that clung to her face. Checking her watch again, she realised it was eight o'clock; the shops would be open now. She could go and get her groceries, and prepare dinner for her guests.

The setting of the evening sun streamed into her apartment, as it made its final curtain call for the day, soaking her sitting room with a sleepy musky glow, amplified by the aroma of lavender seeping through the wooden scented sticks she had purchased on her way home from the Charlotte Rhys store. She heard the rumbling knock on her door of someone eager to come in, as if time were not on their side. Wiping her damp hands on her apron she looked through the peephole to see whose hand had half ruptured her door, her heart racing as thoughts swirled of the stalking stranger. Recognising the familiar bright eyed face on the other end of the peephole, she opened the door.

'Edward, thanks for coming early,' she said, kissing him on the cheek. She noted how his skin was baby soft, and and the scent of his aftershave exuded his masculinity and the giddying effect he seemed to have on woman.

'Hi, Little Miss Princess. I think you just wanted me here to help you cook,' he teased, eyeing her already messed green and white apron as if witnessing a scene from an old fifties movie of a curly haired beautiful woman cooking hearty food for her family to eat. He noticed how, regardless of her apron's desperate attempt to hide the slender curves of her figure, her tight black spandex dress beneath was far less modest in revealing each landslide mountain and valley, rise and fall from her hips to her waist to her breasts. Each angle was in perfect proportion to the next, creating with it the perfect silhouette that existed in artists' dreams.

'Well, now that you mention it, I could put you to work, if you don't mind?' she asked, raising one eyebrow waiting for him to protest, as she closed the door.

'As long as I get to wear one of those sexy aprons you have on,' he chuckled, following her through to the kitchen and setting down the bottle of red wine he had brought with him.

She handed him a pale pink apron with frills, and giggled as she watched him put it on and model around the kitchen as if imitating her movements as she cooked.

'First things first,' she said, her face suddenly serious. 'We need to sort out the wedding plans. I have made you a folder documenting all your best man duties.'

'Wow, you are well prepared,' he smiled, opening the folder she handed to him.

He watched her closely as she articulated his duties: make sure the groom gets to the wedding on time; take him shopping for his suit and shoes; keep the wedding ring safe; keep him calm; book appointments for your haircut; don't overdo the alcohol at the bachelor's party; and absolutely no strippers, she had written in big red writing.

He smiled, noting the gleam in her crystal-blue eyes that he hadn't seen since she arrived; a sense of purpose and excitement seemed to envelope her as she spoke.

'Are you listening to anything I'm saying?' she pouted, observing how he hadn't once viewed the folder, his eyes constantly fixated on her.

'Yes,' he grinned, quickly recounting for her all she had said, watching as her adorable pouting pink lips slowly began to curl upwards into an amused grin. She realised he was paying more attention to her than she had thought.

She shook her head pugnaciously, 'Why do I have a feeling I will have to keep a close eye on you for this wedding?'

'Hey, you can trust me. Have I ever let you down?'

She pondered for a moment, and shook her head earnestly, unable to recall a single moment where he had not honoured a promise he had made. 'No, you haven't. Now let's get cooking before everyone arrives.'

'What are we making?'

'For starters, prawns in filo pastry baskets, and for mains, butter chicken.'

'Sounds scrumptious,'

'Well, we can only hope.' She smiled wearily.

She set him to work cutting the chicken into small bite-sized cubes and marinating it in the yogurt and spices she had previously set out on the kitchen counter, whilst she got busy, moving rapidly with the filo pastry to prevent it from drying out. She meticulously peeled each layer off and brushed melted butter between them. Then putting the pre-cooked prawn mixture in the centre, she pulled up the pastry edges and twisted them around, as if making a closed basket gently nestling with prawns.

'How's it going there?' Edward asked, watching her brow furrow with deep-set concentration. She worked with speed and diligence as if her life depended on it.

'Mmm, so far so good,' she sighed. 'Where is Jasmine? I thought you would have brought her with you.'

'Umm, she couldn't make it.'

Sarah looked up at him, watching as he made sure not to make eye contact with her as he spoke, his long silky eyelashes easily covering the hazel eyes she knew all too well.

'You're lying,' she protested. 'What really happened?'

'I told you, she couldn't make it,' his voice croaked.

'Whatever! I know when you're lying! You can never make eye contact with me, and you've done it since you were a child. Remember that time you stuck a frog in my lunch bag? And when I asked if it was you, you denied it flat out! I know you are lying now because you did the same thing! You hid your eyes from me! You know, I can always see the truth in your eyes!'

He looked up at her suddenly, serious, his eyes staring unswervingly into hers, displaying flickers of fire beneath their hazel mask. 'And what are my eyes telling you now?' he asked huskily.

Sarah looked quickly away; the look in his eyes was so intense, so penetrating, that she felt he could see into the depths of her soul with a desire that transcended space and time. His eyes didn't flicker, didn't falter, they remained transfixed on her face, challenging her to respond.

'How about we get back to cooking,' she said hurriedly, putting on the stove and reaching up trying to retrieve a pot from the back of the cupboard.

Edward came up behind her. 'Here, let me get that for you,' he said, pressing himself against her body, preventing her from moving past him. He reached effortlessly above her head to get the pot.

His touch was like a lightning bolt running through her, crowning her head and moving with intended purpose rapidly down her spine. She felt the heat of his body, and the brush of his flesh against hers. Every part of her was tempted to lean back into him and rest her head against his chest, wishing he would wrap his strong muscular arms around her. She felt him pause as he slowly brought the pot down, and without moving his body from hers he reached around her and set it down on the stove. His breath tickled her neck as he leant in closer, causing her tiny hairs to respond and stand to attention in honour of his proximity. Her heart stopped. He moved his hand up to the nape of her neck and gently moved a stray curl to one side, as if teasing her with his closeness, enticing her to respond. She was certain he could feel her heart flutter in the veins of her neck, as his fingers lingered fractionally against her skin. She held her breath.

'Is that one okay, princess?' he whispered softly in her ear. She noted how he had dropped the "little miss" from the nickname he had always called her, all childish innuendos gone, his voice raspy, his breathing shallow, as he allowed the words to take on their intended purpose, exposing within them the desire and passion they bore.

Slowly she felt him peel away from her, inch by inch, as if somehow their bodies had been entangled together by some unknown magnetic force, taking painstaking effort to tear them apart. Her face burned, her body tingled in places she had forgotten existed. She closed her eyes, knowing that she needed to brush off whatever it was she had just experienced; there was no way anything good could come of it. No way. She wasn't prepared to allow herself such pleasure ever again. She wasn't willing to be vulnerable in that way ever again. Straightening herself abruptly, she moved slowly towards the fridge ensuring her face was hidden from his at all times.

'Thanks,' she mumbled, opening the fridge door and allowing the cold air to caress her face, cooling it down from its rosy pink hue.

He watched her, aware of her every move, inhaling her scent that now lingered on his shirt. He knew she felt it too. He so desperately wanted to go up to her and pull her into his arms, but he knew this wasn't the time; he was willing to wait for as long as it would take. He moved silently towards the stove, putting the chicken into the pot, allowing her to fluster around aimlessly in the fridge. There was an abrupt knock on the door, jarring them both from the spell that had immobilised them. Sarah rushed to the door, grateful for the sudden distraction.

Chapter Eleven

Katy sauntered in, seven o'clock on the dot, followed by John, watching closely as Edward and Sarah moved sheepishly around the kitchen, one cooking dinner, the other pouring them a glass of wine. Katy went to the stereo and put on some music, delighted as Mafikizolo blasted through the speakers.

'I see you've wasted no time getting reacquainted with local South African music,' Katy quipped, as Edward handed them each a glass of wine.

'That's thanks to you for always keeping me abreast of local music,' Sarah laughed, kicking off her shoes and joining Katy in the sitting room as they sang along to the song. Their wine glasses serving as their imaginary microphones.

John and Edward stood on the sidelines watching them dance to each song as if oblivious they were still in the room.

'Have they always been this way?' John asked, turning to Edward as he spoke.

Edward threw his head back laughing, 'Ever since I can remember! Although the only thing that's changed is that back then, their microphones were hairbrushes.'

John watched, clearly amused at the sisterly bond the two girls shared. Katy had often spoken of her friendship with Sarah, but seeing them together had opened his eyes to a childish innocence Sarah seemed to awaken in Katy. He had initially wondered if their friendship was just a fantasy they both held onto from childhood, one that would not be able to transcend the years they had spent apart. But ever since he had witnessed them together, he could see that what they shared was something thicker than blood; it was a strange cord that looped between them both, tying them together in a way no outsider could comprehend. It was as if they were predetermined to be sisters whilst playing in heaven as angels before they were born, and God allowed them to keep their promise to each other even after they were born into different families.

The doorbell rang and Katy opened the door ushering Kevin and his girlfriend in. Kevin kissed her merrily on each cheek and then made his way around the room introducing his girlfriend to everyone. Sarah noticed how she was the complete opposite to him. Her chestnut wavy hair was shabby, as if she had never met a brush in her life. It looked as if she had used her fingers instead as a rake to mop it up into a loose bun. Her skin was pale, almost milk white and she wore a crimson red lipstick that stuck out like a clown's red nose on her white face. She plodded along rather than walked, but her round face was warm and inviting as if you had known her your entire life.

'Sarah, this is Annie,' Kevin said proudly, standing up with his chest thrust forward as if announcing the queen.

'Pleased to meet you, Annie,' Sarah smiled sweetly. 'Kevin has told me wonderful things about you. You must be doing something right, as he is clearly smitten by you.'

Annie threw her arms around Sarah, hugging her tightly. Her short stature only allowing for her head to reach as far as Sarah's chest.

'Thanks, Sarah.' She giggled, 'Kevin loves working for you. He talks of you so often I feel as though we have already met.'

The rupture of her giggles were as if bubbles were erupting from her throat.

Sarah squeezed her gently, and announced to everyone to take a seat at the table in the dining room. Dinner was ready to be served.

Edward insisted that Sarah join the others at the table to relax and socialise with her guests. He took the liberty of running back and forth serving each person their starters and mains, and topping up their glasses like the perfect host should.

'I think this should have been Edward's housewarming party,' John laughed heartily, tucking into his second helping of butter chicken and rice. 'You would swear this is his home. I've never seen him so domesticated and comfortable in the kitchen before.'

'Me neither,' Katy smiled, watching as Edward looked away clearly embarrassed by the sudden attention. She was struck by the way he treated Sarah: so gentle and caring, almost doting on her and only following through with their childish banter if she provoked him to.

'Yes, Edward has been great,' Sarah offered, sitting back in her chair, feeling the weight of the food she had eaten settle in her like lead. 'I've got all confidence he will be an outstanding best man after his dedication to the cause today. I had my doubts earlier, but he has proven himself worthy,' she winked.

Edward's eyes met hers and he smiled, grateful that she noticed his efforts to help her. He wanted nothing more than to see her happy and content, and if today that meant allowing her time to socialise with everyone while he took care of the logistics of the party, then he would do it with pleasure.

'How about we all move into the sitting room. I will make us all cappuccinos and bring out the dessert that Katy made,' Sarah said, pushing her chair backwards as she arose from the table and made her way into the kitchen.

Each guest moved effortlessly to the sitting room, and made themselves comfortable on one of the couches, maintaining the constant chatter that had graced the evening. Sarah set out the coffee cups in a neat row on the kitchen counter, as Edward took a knife from the drawer and cut the cheesecake into slices.

'Why don't you go and relax,' Sarah said, motioning to Edward to join the others in the lounge.

'If we work together, we can both relax,' he smiled, reaching for some saucers and placing a piece of cake neatly on each plate, then garnishing each plate with slices of strawberries and sprigs of mint.

Sarah observed him amused. He clearly considered his handywork an achievement to be proud of. She popped a Nespresso pod one at a time into the coffee machine, and inspected as the black liquid oozed out, swirling lazily into each cup. The robustly opulent aroma wafted up her nostrils instantaneously liberating all tension tangled up within her, as if audacious enough to challenge her muscles in a showdown for her peace. Edward made his way to the sitting room carrying the cheesecake and handing it to each guest. Sarah refilled her sugar bowl with extra sticky brown sugar and her milk jug with fresh full cream milk. She set them down neatly beside the coffee cups on a silver tray and walked cautiously towards the lounge, taking each step in her stride, ensuring not to spill anything.

'We've all brought you housewarming gifts,' Katy said, impressed by the pile of gifts on the carpet in the centre of the room. Sarah steadily handed out the coffee, smiling as she too eyed the pile of gifts.

'You guys didn't have to do that; I didn't invite you here for gifts.' Sarah laughed, plunging on to the floor beside the gifts once the coffee was safely in each person's hand, and shaking each box, trying to guess its contents.

They all tittered at her excitement, as if Santa Claus had arrived with a sack full of toys and had publically proclaimed she was on the "nice list" this year.

Sarah prudently unwrapped the first gift, to reveal a series of cooking books inside. Two books were by Nigella, one by Ina Garten and another by Jamie Oliver.

'I know who this is from,' she grinned up at Katy. 'Thanks, my friend. I guess you will be expecting to taste one of these recipes soon.'

'You bet ya!' Katy smiled down at her. 'I didn't buy them to collect dust on your bookshelf.'

She laughed, watching as Sarah got up and placed her books on the empty shelf.

Sarah sat back down alongside the next gift which was placed inside a green and blue polka dot gift bag. She opened the bag to find a dazzling set of crystal glasses. She looked up wide eyed, trying to see who had bought these for her.

'They are from Annie and me.' Kevin beamed. 'I hope you like them. I know this place came fully furnished but there is nothing like your own glasses.'

'Aah, thank you both so much. I will treasure these, I promise.' She proceed to reach for the next gift. It was in a large orange box. She unfastened the ribbon and lifted the lid. Inside was a digital camera, a photo album, and a diary.

'I thought you could start a new set of memories, and record them along the way,' John smiled as Katy reached over and held his hand.

'That's a really thoughtful gift, John. Thank you. I will make full use of it starting with today.' She grinned, running her hand over the box's contents.

'Umm, I left your gift in the car,' Edward spluttered, 'I will go and get it later.'

'Thanks, Edward, although there was no need for any of you to indulge me like this.'

Sarah smiled fondly at her magnificent group of friends. 'Having you all here is a gift all on its own.'

She got up off the floor and flung herself into her fuchsia pink boudoir chair, taking her feet and tucking them neatly under her thighs. Reaching for her cake, she sank her fork into the soft mousse texture of the cheesecake, savouring its rich tangy flavour as it made melodies on her tongue.

They sat together listening to the soulful sounds of Kenny G crooning softly in the background, their faces highlighted in the soft glow of the lampstands beside them. Katy and John spoke excitedly about their upcoming wedding just over three months away. Sarah couldn't help but feel a shudder in her heart as Katy detailed their lifelong plan to love each other forever and exclusively, forsaking all others, caring for each other in sickness and in health, in good times and in bad times.

Sarah allowed her mind to ramble back to her life in London; she pondered how things must be now that she was gone. Had anything changed? Did anyone miss her or even notice she was gone? She had left no forwarding contact details, just arranging for her business to be closed down and its contents to be shipped over to her. She swore her secretary to an oath, never to reveal her whereabouts to anyone but her parents. It seemed to have worked as no one from her past had tried to contact her, and she felt relief and rejection encircle her all at once.

'Sweetie, we're going to go now,' Katy peered at her, holding her arm. It had been an hour since they had enjoyed their coffee and Sarah seemed to have drifted into an alternative space, leaving them all to chat amongst themselves. Kevin shot Katy a worried look, and she just shrugged, not knowing what had caused Sarah to seem so distant suddenly.

'Oh okay, no problem,' Sarah said standing up, jolted back to this new life. 'Thank you all for coming. It was delightful having you all here with me. This house feels like a home now that you came here.' She smiled tearfully looking from one person to another.

Edward ran outside to get her the housewarming gift he had promised, whilst everyone else hugged and kissed her goodbye, filing one by one out of the apartment.

'This is for you,' Edward panted, standing at the door, having run up the five flights of stairs to get back to her. 'Please don't open it in front of me,' he said, handing her the neatly wrapped gift. 'I would feel too embarrassed.'

'Why should you feel embarrassed?' Sarah enquired, wondering what could possibly be inside the gift that would embarrass him.

'Someday I will explain,' he said, leaning into her and kissing her tenderly on the cheek. The edges of his mouth grazing the boundaries of her lips. 'Goodnight Sarah. Thanks for an enchanting evening,' he said, all sincerity lacing every word.

'Thank you. I don't think I would have coped without your help.' She smiled, grateful for the strength she seemed to always draw from his presence.

He touched the tip of her nose fondly, and turned and walked away, his cologne lingering as she closed and locked the door, making her way to her bed, her present in hand.

She sat down wearily on her bed, putting on the bedside lamp beside her. She looked at the gift concealed in the familiar white embossed wrapping paper, skillfully held together with a red satin ribbon knotted in a looping bow. She noted how this gift had no lavender in the bow, like the previous one had. She pulled at the ribbon, allowing it to flop onto her lap as she peeled away the white wrapping. She gasped, as she saw what lay beneath: a leather bound vintage copy of *Wuthering Heights*. She picked it up carefully, inhaling the weathered smell of the fraying leather and yellowing pages, imagining how many hands had held this book before her, how many had got lost in its pages, cried in its torment, longed with its sorrows – a harrowing heart wrenching tale of love, bound through time, resonating with all who delved into its pages, pulling them into the world the author had brought to life. She ran her hand over the leather cover and wondered how Edward had managed to find such an old copy of the book. She knew he must have gone to great lengths to find something so rare. Opening the book she saw scrawled in the cover a note to her:

'This is my gift to you:

A constant reminder that death and life can never conquer love.'

She turned over the page and saw written on the next page another note, clearly still written in Edward's handwriting, but neater than the page before:

'May the book's words grace the shelves of your bookcase,

Adding to it a sense of nostalgia that nothing is forgotten.

Edward xx'

Sarah ran her hands over the handwriting, recalling when he had told her that he remembered *Wuthering Heights* was her favourite book the night they played "Thirty Seconds" at the cottage in the Drakensburg. She skimmed through the pages of the book, and was about to close it when she saw stuck between some pages a dried piece of lavender that seemed to have been there for ages. She lifted the book to her nostrils and inhaled the lavender scent that still lingered, entrenched in the pages it clung to. Closing the book she switched off her bedside lamp and put her head on her pillow, clinging to the book and the giraffe lying next to her. She breathed in deeply as she drifted off to sleep.

Chapter Twelve

Sarah leaned closer into the mirror, dipping her brush into her neutral shade of eyeshadow.

'The secret to a good smoky eye is blending,' her mother had once told her while teaching her the specialised technique. Sarah's lips curled fractionally at the memory. Sweeping the brush over her eyelid she swiftly applied her neutral base, her muscles recalling the movements she once knew so well. Over that she brushed on a shimmery bone shadow to add light to her crystal blue eyes. She followed through with a lavender hue adding it most intensely at the lash line, blending it towards her perfectly arched brow bone. Picking up her tiny liner brush with a steady and unwavering hand, she lined her eyes with a plum shadow and to create the much needed drama her eyes so desired she swept black eyeliner closely against her silky eyelashes. Finally for the last act of magical illusion and without missing a beat, she coated her eyelashes with two coats of mascara with perfect perfection.

She looked at herself prudently in the mirror. This was the first time she had worn make-up since returning to South Africa – a stark contrast to her life in London. There her face was constantly hidden behind its colourful mask, concealing the hollow she knew existed all along, but trying to deny it was there.

Kevin came in wearing an Italian-made charcoal two-button suit, perfectly tailored to his trim silhouette, crafted from lux virgin wool. Sarah caught her breath.

'You clean up pretty good, hey,' she teased, trying to conceal how impressively handsome he looked.

'Well, tonight's a special occasion! I see you're looking ravishing yourself,' he smiled, his eyes panning over her sexy ensemble.

She had chosen an elegant floor length gala purple evening gown. Crafted in soft matte jersey, it clung to her figure as if its life depended on it, revealing in its wake the supple flesh of her left shoulder in its one-shoulder design. She had finished it off with a glistening embellished rhinestone brooch at the top of her right shoulder. Her hair had been pulled to one side in an array of curls with a fringe spanning across her forehead towards her right eye. Her make-up was flawless and Kevin noted how she looked breathtaking with or without make-up.

'The guests will be arriving shortly. Do you want me to give you a walk through before they arrive?' he asked, extending his arm to escort her through.

She linked her arm through his. 'Kevin,' she paused, looking up at him, her face suddenly filled with sincerity, 'I just want to thank you for everything you've done. Our hard work has paid off and I know that this product launch wouldn't have been possible if it weren't for all your assistance, sleepless nights and planning every last detail.'

'You're the brains and I'm the brawn,' he smiled squeezing her hand. 'It's an honour to work with you; I wouldn't trade it for anything.'

She reached up and gently kissed him on the cheek as he escorted her out of her office and into the garden.

'It's stunning,' she breathed, seeing it all lit up in the night's sky for the first time.

Kevin led her to the beginning of the garden, through which the guests would enter.

'As you can see, I have a table here with goodie bags for each journalist and designer,' he said, pointing to the turquoise bags lined up embossed with her initials "SL" and filled with a catalogue of the collection and a gift for each guest. She had decided her company name would simply be her name: *Sarah Lewis Designs.*

'Each guest will receive a cocktail on arrival, courtesy of Liquid Chefs,' he continued. Sarah appreciated how the company, Liquid Chefs, had set up a bar at the entrance that lit up in a soft pale blue glow. She watched, mesmerised, as their bartender theatrically began mixing different drinks.

'Everything is set up "exhibition style" with each of your collections showcased on a raised platform.'

Sarah followed Kevin's eyes as he spoke, seeing how there were four exhibitions set up in the garden on either side of the pathway. The first was of her "Opaque Collection" which consisted of wide-width lightweight sheer fabrics with a subtle sheen and slight moiré effect. There were twenty-two shades in the collection, mostly neutral and natural. The stand was set up with the sheer fabric suspended as curtains, with a glittering view of the garden visible through its sheer finish, fluttering gently in the evening breeze. White leather couches stood in front of it with a wall to the left covered in stark white wallpaper that had a subtle gleam embedding inside to complete the collection.

The next collection was called "World Traveller" and it was showcased with hammocks hung from the branches of trees in the garden. Old antique leather suitcases sat stacked up beside the hammocks, to create an old school lazy traveller effect, with a wall behind it showing the fabrics and wallpapers. The collection encompassed a whimsical journey referencing popular cities and places from around the world. The fabrics and wallpapers alike were well proportioned with graphically novel and classic designs suitable for offices, bedrooms and hotels. Sarah had based this collection on all the places she had visited in her lifetime.

The third collection was simply called "Safari", inspired by Sarah's initial giraffe design. It was a charming range of printed cotton fabrics and wallpapers providing endless opportunities for all sorts of interiors. The six novelty patterns would be a worthy addition to children's rooms and schools alike, whilst the more classic deconstructed patterns and spots would sit well in hotels and game reserves, as well as home interiors. The colour palette was gentle and sophisticated with shades of "Baked Coconut", "Golden Harvest" and "Mystic Copper". This collection was exhibited on a stand depicting a child's room designed as if on a safari.

The final collection called "Fynbos and Protea" was a collection of wallpapers and fabrics based on the South African fauna and flora that graced its shores. All fabrics were polyester, giving it a chic shiny look, and all wallpapers were embossed, creating a three-dimensional effect. Whilst the design and technique were traditional the yarns and colours were not, "Citrus Splash" nods to high fashion being a bright lime green, whilst other colours stayed fashion-focused in shades of "Beige Rose" and "Green Shrub". The display set up depicted a fashion conscious lounge, in bright cheerful shades of green and fuchsia pink.

Sarah smiled broadly at Kevin. 'You have brought my vision to life!' she exclaimed.

He beamed excitedly, leading her further up the path. He felt in his element here, basking proudly in his achievements in a job he grew to love more and more each day.

Kevin pointed out the seating areas for all guests with couches to the left and tables with bar stools to the right, that lit up with feature lighting positioned strategically to set a sophisticated yet relaxed mood. Just outside the entrance to her offices was a small podium for Sarah to do her speech. A photographer she had hired stood waiting patiently to capture each moment and a DJ ready to get the party started.

'Thanks, Kevin. It all looks perfect,' she breathed.

'I'm glad you're so pleased. Now go back inside and read through your speech once more and I will come and fetch you as soon as all the guests have arrived.'

She nodded in agreement and headed off back inside, anxious at how her guests would respond to the collection; she had a lot riding on it all.

Sarah walked with grace and poise from person to person, answering each question with professional elegance and sitting down for each interview with journalists with perfected boldness and confidence. This was the stage to which she performed, a comfortable place being lost in conversation regarding her designs and ability. This was her forte and she dazzled the crowd with ease.

Everyone was overwhelmed by the collection, and the response was outstanding. Buyers who had previously rejected her request to stock her range, suddenly begged her to represent her brand. She loved the excitement and craze her designs seemed to evoke in all who viewed them. She observed each guest networking and socialising seamlessly, as they all chatted while snacking on canapés and winding down on cocktails.

She had given her speech earlier to overwhelming applause, her previous nerves uncalled for, now leaving room for her to finally relax with her guests and form formidable alliances.

Suddenly her eyes met his strong dark stare – the stalking stranger. He was here. She froze, unable to think of her next move, paralysed by his proximity, her thoughts racing as to why he was here and how he knew they were having this function. Her heart beat faster. She began to move slowly as she noticed he tried to conceal himself within the crowd, hoping he could be masked as one of the guests, uncertain whether she knew who he was.

Eventually fear lost its grip on her and she remembered Jake's words to try and get a picture of him. She moved slowly trying not to let him know that she was keeping a watchful eye on his whereabouts and signalled to her photographer to take a picture of him, urging him to get a clear shot and not to alert him to their intentions. As soon as the stalker spotted the bright flash of the camera pointed straight at him, blinding his eyes, he darted from the party at high speed.

'Kevin!' Sarah started, pulling Kevin's arm to get his attention. 'Is there someone at the entrance checking the guest list to ensure there are no uninvited guests here?'

'I was the one doing that earlier, but once everyone arrived and all names were ticked off the list, I came and joined the party,' he replied, noticing how shaken up she was. 'What's wrong? Is there someone here who shouldn't be?'

'There was, he is gone now.'

'You're shaking, Sarah. What's the matter?'

'Someone has been stalking me for some time now. In the past week I hadn't seen him but he was here tonight; I saw him. I know it was him.'

She turned to the photographer and took his digital camera out of his hands. Scrolling through the pictures she found the image of his face, glaring straight into the lens. She shuddered, fear gripping her every thought.

Chapter Thirteen

Jake knocked urgently on the door, waiting for Sarah to open it. She had called him the night before, frantically explaining she had seen the stalker and had managed to get a clear picture of him. Since their meeting in the park she hadn't called him once, and despite his hopes to see her again on happier terms, he hadn't been granted such an opportunity.

He waited for her to open the door, holding tightly onto the man beside him. Sarah had sent him the picture straight away, and with his contacts in law enforcement, he had managed not only to identify the man but track him down as well. He had spent the morning casing the man's home, waiting for him to leave, and once he set foot onto the pavement, Jake moved swiftly to grab him. After rummaging through his home, he dragged him to the car and brought him to Sarah's apartment, having confiscated every picture he had taken of her, and waited to interview him once Sarah was in the same room.

Sarah opened the door. She had been waiting for Jake; he had called to warn her he was on his way, and he would be bringing the stalker with him. She watched as Jake dragged him in by his collar, handcuffed, and set him down on the couch. He handed Sarah an envelope filled with all the pictures the man had taken of her.

'His name is Angelo Bramley,' Jake began, not taking his eyes off him. 'From what I've seen in the photos he had of you, he has been tracking you ever since you arrived in South Africa.'

Sarah suddenly went pale and Jake rushed to her side as her body became limp at the thought of it all. He sat her down on the other side of the sitting room and took his place beside her.

'I'm here with you,' he whispered. 'You're safe now.'

She nodded silently, looking into the stranger's dark eyes, unable to get a sound out of her throat. Jake turned to Angelo and began the questioning on her behalf.

'Do you stalk women for fun?' he began harshly.

'No,' the man replied, clearly unwilling to speak.

'So, you just decided to stalk Sarah?' Jake continued aggressively, not willing to back down, eager to get answers.

'I told you earlier, I was not stalking her.'

Sarah suddenly found her voice. 'So watching my every move and photographing me wherever I go isn't considered stalking?' she asked, strengthened by her fury.

'No!' he protested.

'Now, listen here! I warned you before, if you don't tell us exactly why you are stalking Sarah, I will have you arrested and thrown in jail without a court hearing. Don't test me,' Jake warned sternly.

The man sighed, as if defeated. 'I am a private investigator. I was hired to find Sarah, trail her and report on her whereabouts by one of my clients.'

'And who's your client?' Sarah demanded.

'Adam,' he stated, not offering even a surname, aware that the name alone would reveal to Sarah his intended purpose.

'Who is Adam?' Jake asked, turning from Angelo and seeing the recognition in Sarah's eyes.

'Someone from my past,' she mumbled, not willing to offer any more information than that. Turning to Angelo she said firmly, 'You go back and report to your client that he will no longer have me followed. He has no right, and I will lay a charge against him if he continues to try. Tell him I want to be left alone. Do you understand me?'

'Yes, I will pass the message on.'

'If I see you anywhere around her again, I will personally make you regret it,' Jake threatened him, his eyes sending a clear message how serious he really was.

Jake uncuffed the man and walked him to the door. He went back to Sarah and watched as her lip began to quiver and the tears began to fall. Putting his arms around her he held her tight until eventually she calmed down.

'Thanks, Jake, for your help. You have been kind to me. Considering I'm practically a stranger, your kindness is even more valuable.'

'You are no longer a stranger. You stopped being a stranger from the moment you took hold of Jamie's balloon,' he smiled, stroking her arm.

Sarah arose and made her way to the kitchen, silently pouring him a glass of pomegranate juice.

'Would you like to tell me why the name Adam seemed to shake you more than the stalker did?' he asked tenderly, wishing she could tear down the walls she used to protect herself.

'I'm not ready to talk about him, or think about him. I just can't,' she said, taking her seat once again beside him on the couch and handing him his drink. He set the glass down on the coffee table and began to trace her face with his hand, wiping the tears that had left stains on her flawless skin. She looked at him, grateful for his protectiveness and help. Slowly he leaned in, his lips searching for hers through the air that separated them. He felt her hot breath against his skin as he got closer still. Parting his lips he kissed her full on her mouth, only to realise her body had suddenly tensed, and her lips were screwed tightly shut in protest to his advances.

He pulled away abruptly. 'I'm sorry, Sarah, I shouldn't have done that. I wasn't taking advantage of your vulnerability, I swear. I just thought we had a real connection that's all,' he stammered, watching her face closely as her jaw remained clenched tightly shut.

'Sarah? Please don't let this ruin our friendship,' he begged.

Her expression softened, and she looked up at him. 'I'm sorry if I gave you the wrong impression, Jake. I'm grateful for all you've done for me, but if you're hoping our friendship will end in some whirlwind romance, then I had better shatter your fantasy right now. I don't plan to ever love again or get involved with anyone again. I just can't,' she said firmly.

'I understand,' he said, clearly defeated, realising that whatever happened in her past, must have closed her off to relationships. He rose and kissed her softly on her forehead. 'I think I should go now. Perhaps we can meet for frozen yogurt again sometime? I know Jamie would love to see you again.'

'I would like that very much,' she said, watching as he let himself out of her apartment.

She pulled a cushion close to her and hugged it tightly, allowing the tears to fall violently from her eyes.

For the life of her she couldn't understand why Adam would have her followed; why did he care where she was or what she was doing? Her heart fluctuated from anger to hatred, to sadness and loneliness. Once again the silence the walls bore stood as a grave reminder of all she had lost. Just yesterday she was revelling in the success of her launch, with the initial orders the buyers had made now being tripled as they fell in love with her collection. Today it all felt meaningless in light of her discovery.

She made her way to her bedroom and drew the curtains; despite it being early afternoon she couldn't bear to live through this day. Crawling beneath her heavy duvet cover, she pulled it over her head. Right now she wondered if she could ever outrun her past, and if the pain it held would ever seize. She forced herself to sleep, dreaming of the joy she once held just a few months before. Now it was all gone, and she lost hope of ever feeling that kind of joy again.

Chapter Fourteen

Music blared from every angle. The room was so crowded that there wasn't enough space to swing a cat. Everyone was dancing as the bass resounded from the speakers to the floor, vibrating to the beat, travelling up everyone's excited bodies. Sarah had planned to have just a few of Katy's friends and colleagues over for her bachelorette party, but by the time Katy had handed over the list of names of who she needed to invite, it seemed she had included every female in the city of Durban.

Despite all these people not being invited to the wedding – as Katy had definitively expressed her desire for family only – it did not deter anyone from ensuring she had a proper send off from her current bachelorette status to her soon-to-be married position.

'Great party,' someone screamed in Sarah's ear. Sarah squinted in the dim lighting trying to decipher who the stranger was; eventually defeated, she nodded politely and smiled.

The party was being held in Katy's apartment, and Edward was hosting John's bachelor party in his home. Initially they planned to have them the night before the wedding. Sarah, however, was paranoid that Edward would deliver a hungover groom on the wedding day, so she had opted to host them the week before the wedding. Looking around she wondered whether Katy might be the more hungover of the two as she witnessed her dancing on the couch downing tequila shots and screaming wildly at the top of her lungs.

Sarah let her gaze drift around the room. She knew none of the faces there except for Laura, whom Katy had introduced to her a few weeks prior. Laura and Katy worked for the same law firm, and had been friends ever since they studied together in law school. She watched as Laura stood leaning against the sofa, bottle of tequila in hand, pouring Katy another shot with an ever ready grin plastered over her plain face. Sarah already didn't like Laura, and she knew why; she was mature enough to admit it. She was jealous. She knew she had been gone for all these years, and Katy possessed a life apart from her, but now that she was back she almost expected Katy to once again belong solely to her in friendship. The knowledge of someone else being her "bestie" was one thing, but seeing it thrust in her face was another. She watched as Katy threw her head back, downing yet another shot, and stumbled off the couch, beelining straight for Sarah.

'Why aren't you dancing?' she sputtered drunkenly, her finger wiggling unsteadily in Sarah's face.

Sarah shot Laura a furious look. She had not wanted Katy sloshed before the party properly began. How dare she ruin her plans.

'I'm making sure all your guests are comfortable and have enough to eat and drink,' Sarah said, holding Katy steady to prevent her from falling over.

'Mmm, I think I've had a little too much to drink,' she said, hiccupping between naughty giggles. 'I'm not sure how much more I can take; I think Laura got me drunk.'

Sarah fumed. She wanted Katy to enjoy her bachelorette party, not have her passed out drunkenly on the carpet. She sat Katy down and asked one of the ladies walking past to please go and get her something to eat and pour her a strong black cup of coffee. Storming over to Laura she pulled her by the elbow into the bedroom, away from the thumping music.

'What are you trying to do? Have Katy so drunk she cannot remember her hen party?' Sarah hissed at her.

'Shut up. You're just pissed off because you aren't the one giving her a good time. If it were up to you, we would all be sitting sipping on English tea and eating scones. Katy loves me because I'm as exciting and enthralling as she is, and it kills you to think I'm the one she has had all her fun experiences with.'

Laura spat her words into Sarah's face, each word loaded with venom and anger, and Sarah noticed that she too disliked her for her role in Katy's life.

'That might be true, but I'm the one she chose to stand beside her on her wedding day, not you! I'm the one planning this wedding, and I'm the one she entrusted with it! She knew I might not be as spontaneous or adventurous but I'm responsible and sensible enough to put her best needs first.' Sarah thrust her fingers into her chest as she spoke, pointing to herself, animatedly announcing Katy's appointment of her and not Laura to the prestigious role of maid of honour.

'Are you implying I'm a useless, irresponsible friend?' Laura screamed, thrusting her face and fingers aggressively at Sarah's face.

'No, I'm just telling you that you aren't her friend, period! Because a true friend would put her friend's needs first! A true friend would make sure her friend is safe, not get her so drunk she passes out before the fun begins.'

'Hmmft, what fun?' Laura scoffed. 'I don't need to hang around and witness your lame excuse for a bachelorette party. I'm out of here; there are more interesting places to be,' and with that she turned on her heels and marched exaggeratedly out of the apartment.

Sarah stood still for a moment, watching her go, her heart still racing wildly from the confrontation. The audacity she posed: first she got Katy drunk, then she left the first chance she got. Baffled, Sarah made her way back into the living room, scanning the crowd for Katy.

Katy was lying on one of the sofas, her hand covering her eyes from the blinding light. Sarah saw a half-eaten sandwich lying beside her.

'Katy, here, take this,' Sarah offered, her hand outstretched with two pain tablets. 'Make sure you drink this entire glass of water; it will help with your hangover in the morning.'

'The room is still spinning,' Katy slurred, reaching for the water and swallowing the tablets.

'I know. I will get you a blanket, some steak and salad. Sit here and eat it. When you feel better you can carry on enjoying the party.'

Sarah went through to the kitchen and dished up a huge serving of steak and salad for Katy, still burning with anger from her conversation with Laura, a pulse of disbelief churning at the nerve she had sabotaging Katy during her own party.

By the time the belly dancers arrived, Katy had somewhat recuperated. Everyone gathered in the centre of the living room as Sarah moved all the furniture against the walls and started the rhythmic tribal music, giving over her reigns to the belly dancing instructors.

They handed each woman a belly dancing belt, which was richly ornamented with beads, sequins, crystals, coins and a beaded fringe.

'Tonight we will teach you all how to lure your men in through the art of belly dancing,' the instructor purred, grinding her torso and hips to the rhythm of the music.

The women shrieked with delight as they became hypnotised by her hips punctuating the music and accenting the beat.

'Today we will be learning the "percussive movement". I will show you hip drops, vertical hip rocks, outward hip hits, hip lifts, and hip twists,' she said slowing, demonstrating each action as she spoke. 'Trust me, your man will thank you for it,' she whistled.

The women gyrated and shimmied their hips from side to side, articulating their torsos in multiple directions, giggling from adrenalin fuelled excitement and sheer self-consciousness, as they moved together discovering the sensuality in their own hips. Eventually they all felt like experts, swinging their belly dancing belts from side to side as they thrust their hips, feeling a freedom of expression and lowered inhibitions as they moved in circles clapping and dancing to the music.

Sarah watched as everyone laughed, imagining how they would apply the technique in their bedrooms later that night.

'Thanks for this,' Katy giggled, thrusting her hips, 'I'm sure John will thank you too,' she laughed, delighted by her new found bedroom acrobatics. 'I'm glad I was feeling well enough to participate. I would have been disappointed to miss out on this!' she exclaimed.

Sarah smiled brightly; she too was glad. She knew her friend well enough to know what she would like best, and no one could convince her otherwise. The bachelorette party was turning out to be a resounding success and she was proud of it.

Chapter Fifteen

The countdown to the event of their lives had begun. With just three days until Katy walked down the aisle, Sarah was frantically arranging all the finer details, ticking her list and checking it twice.

Logistically it was a nightmare; she needed to drive back and forth between Durban and the cottage in the Drakensburg taking florists, caterers and ministers up there for them to plan the fluidity of the day. Besides running around for Katy's wedding, she and Kevin were full swing into the bursting demand on her business. The demand had officially exceeded the supply. And despite her best efforts to avoid such a disaster, especially during the festive season, it had been inevitable, with manufactures unable to meet the bountiful production demands that had sprung forth virtually overnight. Sarah's mind swirled constantly like a tornado sucking up information on its path to its final destination, ensuring nothing was left to chance, every detail of utmost importance to make the wedding and her business a resounding success.

The warm summer sun streamed scorching into Sarah's apartment, as she made a step by step schedule for Katy's big day. She had hoped her business could close for two weeks during the festive season, but with production schedules so far behind, they had to keep a watchful eye on their manufactures. She thanked God once more for Kevin, having come to fully rely on him to manage the business. He knew her gratitude, however, as she summed it up in the hefty increase and bonus she gave him, motivating him to push harder during crunch time.

Everything was virtually completed for the wedding. John and Edward had bought their beige three piece suits the week before, and her dress was being hand delivered tomorrow by the dressmaker. Katy's Louis Vuitton shoes had arrived earlier that week, and her wedding dress had already been transported to the cottage on Sarah's last trip there. All décor, chairs and lighting had been delivered to the cottage, waiting for her to go up and begin to set up the day before the wedding. She had entrusted Kevin to assist in getting everything pristine on the day, ensuring it ran without a glitch, and from his stellar performance at her product launch she knew he was fully capable.

The only major thing left to do was for them to make all the desserts and puddings the day before the wedding. Sarah had tried talking Katy out of it, offering rather to hire a pastry chef to do it for them. But Katy had refused insisting it would be more personal and special if they did it together. Sarah knew their common love for baking was what helped them through every stressful situation they had both faced, and she knew this would be Katy's way of de-stressing before her big day.

The first time they had used baking to de-stress, was when they had perfected their triple-chocolate mousse cake after Sarah had broken up with her first boyfriend in Grade Eight. At the time, Sarah thought he was "the one". She giggled to herself recalling how she had cried for months, staining the letters he had written her with soggy tears, dreaming of their first kiss. He had sucked her entire face looking for her lips, half drooling down her chin. At the time, she thought it was the best thing ever. The thought now, however, gave her shivers. If only she had known then how much better kissing could be, she never would have wasted her time longing for his sloppy drooling kiss.

Katy had helped her overcome the pain of the breakup, by spending every day mixing, beating and baking cake after cake, until the pain was gone and the layers of dark chocolate, milk chocolate and white chocolate oozed together with dustings of hazelnuts, tantalising their taste buds. The therapy of baking created amnesia of boyfriends and heartbreak alike.

The chiming tunes on her iPhone warned merrily of an incoming call as it thumped out the rhythm of Mariah Carey's song "Beautiful", jolting Sarah out of her meditating thoughts. She reached for her phone, tapping the answer key before checking who was calling.

'Hello?' she asked questioningly.

'Hi, Sarah it's Dad,' she heard her father's strained voice on the other end of the receiver.

'Dad, hi. Where are you? Weren't you supposed to be on your flight already? I'm supposed to pick you up from the airport in three hours, aren't I?'

'That's why I'm calling, Sarah,' her father's voice grew faint on the other end of the line. 'It's your mother; she isn't well and we couldn't make the flight.'

'What happened?' Sarah panicked. Her mother had never been ill; it had always amazed her how her mother was as strong as an ox. When everyone else would come down with the flu or bronchitis, her mother would be unaffected, taking on her age-old role as caregiver, fluttering between them like a mother hen smothering her chicks with love.

'It seems she had an undiagnosed heart condition and will need to go in for bypass surgery. They have scheduled it for the twenty-ninth of December. I know it's Katy's wedding on the twenty-fourth, but I was wondering if you could fly over after that? We need you here, Sarah – your mother and I cannot go through this without you.'

'Of course I will be there,' Sarah said without hesitation, before realising that to be by her mother's side would mean she needed to face her nightmares.

Her father heard her throat gasp for air. 'I know this is hard for you, my angel. I will be here with you, but I also need you here with me,' he said reassuringly.

'I will book the earliest flight I can get, Dad. Please give Mom my love, and tell her to hang in there.'

'Call me with your landing details; I will come and fetch you to stay in the house with us.'

Sarah paused, 'It's fine, Dad. For now I will stay in a hotel, but I will be there, I promise.'

'Okay, Sarah. Just know your mother and I love you very much.'

'Thanks, Dad. I will call you with the details of my arrival.' Sarah hung up the phone, collapsing on the carpet, feeling the swell of sobs rupture from within her, bursting forth like an overflowing dam, waiting to be set free from its retaining walls.

Edward knocked at the door, softly at first, then more urgently. He knew Sarah was home; her car was parked in her parking bay. She had asked him to come over today to go over wedding plans. He was half an hour early.

Worriedly, he turned the door handle, checking if the door was unlocked. It was. He stepped inside, dropping the package he held in his hand as he spotted her crumpled body lying on the carpet, her sobbing so violent, so loud, that she was unaware he had even entered the room. She writhed with anguish, pulsating as each burst of sadness rummaged through her body, causing her to roll with pain, unable to stop the floodgates that had opened.

He knelt down slowly beside her, trying not to startle her. 'Sarah, it's me Edward. It's okay, I'm here,' he whispered, gently stroking her hair. Her eyes creaked open marginally as she acknowledged his proximity, unable to contain her lament. His heart ached as he watched her, helplessness washing over him and covering him like fog. He felt powerless to help her. What comforting words could he offer to heal her pain? Nothing he could muster up felt appropriate, and a part of him suspected there were parts of her past that she still kept hidden from Katy and him.

He gently scooped her up into his arms, and carried her into her bedroom. Laying her gently on her bed, he covered her with a cashmere throw and lay beside her, moving her head onto his chest, wrapping his arms safely around her. He held her. For now that was all he knew to do. He needed her to know she wasn't alone; he needed her to feel the love he had for her. Minutes turned to hours as he held her, watching as the sun slowly made its routine descent in the west, leaving in its glide a husky golden afterglow.

Her tremors ceased, her tears dried, and soon the anguished trance that had so strangled her gave way to the tenderness of his embrace. He ran his fingers lovingly through her matted hair, letting her know he was with her. She would be okay. He stroked her face, running his fingers from her forehead to her lips, wishing he could kiss her tears away.

After what seemed like a lifetime she stirred, lifting her head so that her swollen eyes met his. 'My mother is sick, Edward, really sick. She is having an operation and I need to go back there to be with her. I don't know if I can do it. I don't know if I can go back there. I can't bear to lose my mother and I can't bear to go back to my home. How will I cope?' she questioned, her voice barely a whisper, thickened by the strain her tears had asserted on her vocal cords.

'I will come with you, princess; I won't let you face this alone,' he whispered, gently caressing her face, watching as a glimmer of hope seemed to dawn in her eyes.

She closed her eyes, basking in the sincerity in his voice, the promise his words carried and the comfort he brought. She knew she couldn't take him up on his offer though; this was something she needed to do on her own. But the knowledge that she had him to turn to, gave her the ounce of strength she needed. She wasn't alone. She had him and Katy, and they had never hurt her. She felt guilty knowing she still hadn't given him or Katy any explanation as to why she had moved back here. She owed it to them to know the truth. She knew they knew a part of it but they deserved to know it all..

'Thanks, Edward,' she breathed, unable to muster up enough strength to offer him an explanation just yet. Knowing his loyalty towards her had never required any effort or explanation on her part. He displayed unconditional affection towards her, and his embrace healed her aching heart .

Once the storm in her eyes cleared, and the rattling of her body subsided, Edward went into the kitchen to make her some hot chocolate. He rummaged through her cupboards until he found a slab of milk chocolate; breaking it into pieces in steaming milk he brought it to her. She laid there as stiff as a corpse, her body rigid and brittle. Her mind was unable to think; darkness had washed over it in blackened fury trying to devour her hopes and dreams. She knew she needed to snap out of it, she had to pull herself together at least long enough to celebrate Katy's wedding, but right now she felt numb and cold.

Edward watched as she sipped on the hot chocolate, holding the mug in one hand and her toy giraffe in another. She wouldn't let the giraffe go, holding it and stroking it as if it were alive. At one point he could have sworn he saw her lips moving as she looked at the giraffe, as if speaking to it as a person. His heart dropped, plummeting at the sight of her torment. She seemed to have been flourishing in recent months, but now she would have to return to the place she was daily running from. His hope was that somehow, someway, her return would bring a sense of closure instead of another gaping wound.

He remembered the package he had brought with him. Moving swiftly he brought it to her. The sight of the large gift, covered in what had now become his signature wrapping, brought a tiny twinkle in Sarah's eye. That twinkle gave Edward hope as he handed it over to her.

'I brought this for you. I've had it for some time, I just never got the opportunity to give it to you,' he said softly, watching as she set down her mug and moved the giraffe aside to open the gift.

Cautiously she removed the stem of lavender and untied the red bow, taking a deep breath as she opened the white embossed wrapping paper, her lips curling at their corners in what almost seemed to be a smile as she saw her painting.

'Wow, it looks beautiful,' she smiled, as if she hadn't painted it herself. 'It's so full of hope and promise, just like our day was out there.'

'I was hoping that when you saw the painting it would remind you how Joseph had managed to experience joy again, even after the pain of losing his wife. I was hoping that looking at the painting would remind you just how far you've come in your own healing process.'

She leaned her head back against the cold wall, recalling how at that moment when she painted this she couldn't see a future, she painted only what was in front of her because she couldn't imagine life beyond that day.

'My life has purpose again,' she muttered.

'Purpose and promise,' he smiled, 'and watching you these past six months has shown me just how strong you really are. Despite your pain you have triumphed, starting a brand new life, building a company up from the ground and surviving on your own. Whatever it is you're running from in London, I know you now have the strength to face it! Strength you didn't have six months ago when you left. Trust me, you will overcome.'

His words were the reassurance she needed, the glue that seemed to cement her fragmented life back together again.

'Thanks, Edward. I will hang the painting in the lounge as a constant reminder of my journey,' her brow suddenly furrowing. 'Hey, where is your painting? To come to think of it, I was so absorbed in my own painting that day, I didn't even notice what you were painting!'

His eyes sparkled as if lighting up the sky on Guy Fawkes' Day. 'It's a surprise, one I'm hoping to give you sooner rather than later,' his face revealing his inward excitement.

'You have me intrigued,' she said, studying his expression in anticipation. 'You know how eager I get for surprises; you can't keep me in suspense like this!'

'I will make a promise to you, then. On your safe return back to South Africa, I promise that I will give it to you.'

'I'm onto you Edward, making the painting my focus instead of my trip to London.'.'

' You have me all figured out,' he chuckled. 'Am I that obvious?'

'Yes, I'm afraid you are to me,' she replied amusingly. 'Will you stay with me until I fall asleep?' her voice suddenly soft and fragile.

'I already planned to,' he smiled, lying on the bed beside her and taking her into his arms. 'I'm here, and you're safe,' he reassured.

He stayed with her, holding her, watching her, caressing her face, her hair, wiping the tear stained tracks from her face. Eventually her muscles released their tension, succumbing to the sleep she so desperately needed. His eyes never left her face, watching her intensely as she slept, waiting for the moment peace overcame the torment in her dreams – the moment her crimson red lips fought off the scowl and her deep furrowed eyebrows glided to their natural position.

Moving from beneath her, he manoeuvered her head until it rested gently on her pillow. Covering her with a blanket, he tucked the giraffe in with her and stood silently over her. Analysing her face one last time, he kissed her gently on her nose and let himself out of her apartment, his heart and thoughts with her still.

Chapter Sixteen

Sarah knocked hard on the door. She was exhausted. The first part of her day had been spent at the cottage preparing for the wedding tomorrow. She knocked again. Exasperated and tired she opened the door and let herself in.

'Katy?' she shouted. 'Katy, where are you?'

'I'm in here,' she heard between sniffles.

Rushing into Katy's room, Sarah saw her friend's sullen face peeking under the covers.

'What's the matter? Why are you crying?' Sarah questioned softly as she sat on the bed.

'What if this whole thing is a big mistake? What if John breaks my heart?'

Sarah sat silently for a moment. She didn't know how to respond; she was the last person qualified enough to answer such a question.

'Love is about taking chances, sweetie; there are no guarantees. I guess we put ourselves out there hoping for the best, hoping that the person you say your vows to will be an even better person when you are both old and grey. We hope that they will still be there, sitting in a rocking chair with you on the porch, sipping on coffee with your toothless gums,' Sarah joked, hoping to make her smile.

Katy smiled somewhat, as she imagined what Sarah had said. Her mind drifted to an image of John and her sitting in rocking chairs, reading their newspapers, mindful of their gummy mouths, as coffee drooled down their chins.

'If you don't take the chance you could be missing out on something beautiful,' Sarah continued, 'and if your heart gets broken, well then, at least you know that you knew what it felt like to love someone so much that you entrusted your heart in their hands.'

Katy sighed, 'I just don't know. I love John so much it hurts, and we're so different you know. We are polar opposites: he is like a tall strong tree, and I'm like a dandelion blowing in the wind, wild and free, not always rooted like he is.'

'No one said you had to be twins to fall in love. It's your differences that make you perfect. Remember how you told me about your tea set?'

'You got the analogy!' Katy laughed.

'I sure did, and as I've watched you both over time, I've seen just how perfectly suited you are. John's ability to be firmly rooted is your stability – it's your centre of gravity. He is able to keep you grounded. Your free loving spirit is what reminds him that life isn't always serious; sometimes it's okay to take off your clothes and dance naked in the rain. You need that fun and freedom sometimes and you give that to him.'

'You're right; I think John only learnt to smile when he met me.'

They both burst into bouts of laughter. John's sense of humour was as dry as a dry red wine, and Katy's joy was like adding bubbles to turn it into champagne.

'Now come on, young lady, we need to get baking!' Sarah scolded sternly, feeling the exhaustion wash over her again.

Katy grabbed her arm. 'I'm truly grateful for all you've done for me for this wedding. With me being in the courtroom all day, it's difficult to focus on a wedding. You've stepped in and just allowed me to relax, taking care of everything. I couldn't have done it without you. I know you've had your own work challenges, so when all this is over, I will be at your beck and call.'

'I know, I'm amazing,' Sarah joked. 'It's my pleasure. That's what sisters are for, right? And you've been there constantly for me, so it's the least I can do for you.'

Katy kissed Sarah on her cheek, 'Come on now, enough of the soppy stuff. Let's get baking!'

Sarah tapped the sieve rhythmically as white clouds of flour fluttered up as they hit the bowl. The motion was therapeutic, the smells in the kitchen heavenly, as they baked and mixed and made mouthwatering creations to tempt every taste bud.

Katy was rolling the shortcrust pastry she had made, toying with the dough, as she allowed her rolling pin to stretch and pull it wider and thinner in all directions, as if tearing down the muscles that had kept it tightly bound.

'Have you made the chocolate and pistachio filling yet to go into the tarts?' Sarah asked, still engulfed in the flour clouds around her.

'Not yet. You know, I should have listened to you and got a pastry chef. This baking is hard work.' Katy giggled, her fight with the pastry finally over, the pressing pain in her arms a reminder that the rolling pin would be her workout for today.

'I warned you!' Sarah replied, setting down the sieve.

'Well, when we first discussed this you did not mention we would be baking everything in our recipe book,' Katy chuckled, looking around at the state of her kitchen.

'You wanted a pudding party!' Sarah exclaimed. 'We can't do that with one dessert,' she screamed, seeing the horror on Katy's face as she took in the sight of the kitchen.

The kitchen was a right mess. There were cake tins on the floor, cocoa fingerprints on the cupboards and drippings of cake batter on the walls from their disaster with the Kitchen Aid mixer. But the smells wafting from the oven and stove top were glorious. Sarah was busy mixing together ingredients for a rainbow cake. There would be seven colours of the rainbow represented in seven thin layers of cake, sandwiched together with a vanilla meringue frosting.

On the stove was a mixture of Granny Smith apples with cinnamon, nutmeg and sugar, combining together to form the filling for their apple crumble, and in the oven the puff pastry was popping up like pillows, to be filled with a custard filling for the custard tarts.

'We still have to make the *malva* pudding, Nutella cheesecake, cocktail doughnuts and I can't even remember the rest,' Sarah smiled, her hair looking white from scatterings of flour.

Katy grabbed her camera, and snapped a shot of Sarah with her wooden spoon and sieve in hand.

'Hey, not fair. You'd better not blackmail me with that picture when I'm famous,' Sarah laughed hysterically.

'A girl always needs one blackmail picture in case of a rainy day,' Katy giggled, admiring her perfect timing for the picture.

There was a knock at the door. Katy looked at Sarah bewildered – it was seven thirty and she wasn't expecting anyone. She opened the door to find two ladies standing in a Mangwanani Spa uniform, carrying two bags.

'Surprise!' Sarah screamed as she came up behind her. 'It's time for the bride to have her very own pamper party!' Sarah announced.

'You didn't!' Katy exclaimed, her voice growing deep at her surprise. 'But we have so much baking to do?'

They showed the ladies into the lounge.

'Now listen, it's the maid of honour's duty to take care of the bride, and that's what I'm doing! You go and relax, enjoy the pampering, and I will take care of the baking.'

'And you? Are you not being pampered as well?' Katy pouted.

'A little later, once everything is safely in the oven,' Sarah said, giving Katy a quick hug and waving her off to relax in the living room.

Sarah continued to bake, watching Katy in the living room snoring like a lion with her mouth wide open as the ladies massage her back in perfect unison. Sarah giggled – it was good to see her friend relax. Right now she couldn't imagine when she would get time to relax; there was still so much to do. Her bags were already packed and waiting for her trip to London. Her flight would leave at eight o'clock on Christmas evening, which gave her enough time to see to the guests who were sleeping over at the cottage tomorrow after the wedding.

Tomorrow was Christmas Eve, and with Katy's wedding being on the same day, no one had even taken time out to decorate their homes with Christmas trees. Sarah's mind wandered to how life had been so different last year at this time. She was sitting in her living room in London, on their rug by the fireplace, Christopher roasting marshmallows as "I'm dreaming of a white Christmas" crooned softly in the background. She couldn't imagine a happier time; life had seemed so perfect then. She didn't dream it would all be snatched away only three months later.

She checked the clock on the wall. It was ten o'clock: time to take the tipsy tart out of the oven and pour over more brandy so it could suck it all up while it was still hot. She set the tart down on the countertop and inhaled the drunken scent of brandy as it slipped between the cracks of the tart. She was finally done. All six cakes were iced: her rainbow cake, the delectable Red Velvet cake, her vanilla cream sponge, the rich dense coffee cake and her two favourite show stopper cakes – a milk stout and chocolate cake with butterscotch sauce, caramel chocolate shards, and dark chocolate icing (she knew Katy loved this cake), and their other favourite she had made was a spicy pineapple cake with vanilla cream cheese icing, white chocolate drizzle and caramel praline dust. It was pure decadence. No one could resist.

Kevin would come in the morning to collect all the cakes, desserts, puddings and cupcakes and transport them to the cottage. She had caterers who would be serving canapés at the reception for guests who were looking for more substantial food. Katy's wedding cake was being specially made by a wedding cake designer, and would also be delivered first thing in the morning as another dessert option.

Katy stirred sleepily on the sofa as a therapist washed her feet in rose water.

'You've finally come to join me just in time for the foot massage. It's heavenly after all that standing and baking.'

'I've been in the kitchen for six hours. The time flew by but now I'm exhausted,' Sarah exclaimed, soaking her feet in the warm water as the therapist sat down at her feet to massage them. 'It was worth it though.'

Katy smiled and reached over and squeezed her hand, 'You are one in a million Sarah Lewis. They don't make friends like you anymore.'

'I can say the same about you, the soon to be Mrs. John Gates. I was almost losing hope that you would find Mr. Right. You just never seemed to settle down. You and Edward both.'

'Aah, now Edward is a different story altogether. It seems he is waiting for his one true love to appear. Me, on the other hand, I was just out there enjoying the good life. I didn't imagine myself getting serious until John came along.'

'Well, my heart fills with joy knowing you are so happy.' Sarah smiled, 'Ooh, ooh, and I have something for you,' she said motioning to the therapist to pass her bag on the sofa.

'I have something for you as well,' Katy said, picking up a box from the coffee table.

They both looked at each other and giggled like two school girls. 'Our boxes are wrapped in the exact same wrapping paper. How much do you want to bet we bought it from the exact same store?' Katy chuckled.

'Only one way to tell,' Sarah said, ripping open the silver wrapping.

They both gasped simultaneously as they each held a navy blue box in their hands with the silver embossed Swarovski logo. Slowly they opened their boxes, peaking at each other as they lifted the lids in eager expectation.

'Sister, sister,' they both screamed delightedly, as they lifted their identical gifts: a white gold chain with a Swarovski encrusted angel wing pendant.

'I bought it for you because you've been my angel of shelter and protection through each step I've taken this year,' Sarah whispered, tears filling her eyes.

'And I bought it for you because you've been my guardian angel all my life, giving me sound advice to keep me out of trouble.' Katy smiled, reaching over and hugging Sarah, nearly kicking the therapist in the face who was trying to massage her feet.

'Sister, sister,' they chimed, as they clasped the chains around their necks, reminiscing about the days they would watch the TV comedy *Sister Sister* and would dream of being twins. Time and distance had not stolen their bond despite all the odds. In spite of no bloodline to join them they were, and would always be, sisters, and Sarah realised once more how Katy was the only real sister she ever had. She knew it didn't take only blood to make sisters; it took loyalty, friendship, compassion, and unselfish acts of love and kindness.

'How's your mom?' Katy interrupted her thoughts, after she had let the therapists out of the house.

'She is okay. I spoke to her this morning when I called to give them my flight details. She is holding strong, determined to live a full life no matter what.'

'Well, that's the spirit. Please give them my love when you see them. Edward told me you turned down his offer to come with you? You should reconsider; it would be good to have someone with you.'

Sarah sighed. 'I need to do this on my own and Edward is too sweet for his own good. I cannot ask him to drop his life to babysit me half way across the world.'

'He would do it in a heartbeat. He would do anything for you.'

'Yeah, he'd better; I'm like his little sister.'

Katy scanned Sarah's face, wondering if she realised Edward saw her as more than just a little sister. It wasn't her place to tell her though; right now Sarah had enough on her plate. Katy hadn't known how Edward felt until he recently confessed it to her, and she suddenly understood why he always treated Sarah so differently.

'Yeah, you're the favourite little sister,' Katy replied. 'Just want you to know that he wouldn't get on a plane with just anyone to travel half way across the world to babysit them. Its only you he affords such a privilege. Now go and put your pyjamas on. I will bring the mattresses into the living room and we can have a tea and chocolate infested pyjama party. It's my last night of being single and there is nothing more I would rather do than have a pyjama party with you.' She winked as Sarah jumped up merrily and headed for the bedroom to change into her pyjamas.

Sarah knew they needed to sleep soon; somehow she needed to get Katy sleepy enough to fall asleep. She had thought the massage would have done the trick but after her short nap she was wide awake again. She knew the adrenalin for the wedding day was pumping wildly through her veins.

'Okay, I'm all done,' Sarah bounced lightly into the living room in her not-so-sexy flannel pyjamas. She giggled as she saw Katy jumping on the mattresses in her "Winnie The Pooh" printed pyjama's.

'It's the last night I get to wear these,' she giggled, jumping higher and higher. 'From tomorrow night I will have to sleep in a lace negligée!'

'You'd better believe it,' Sarah chuckled, as they switched on the TV and settled onto the mattress, tea and chocolate in hand.

They sat talking, reminiscing about their childhood dreams, and their "wedding games" where they would imagine their Prince Charming riding to their rescue. Sarah prayed silently that John would be Katy's prince – that at least one of them would live the fairytale life.

Eventually Katy fell asleep, and Sarah lay silently listening to her gargled snores as she watched the cooking channel. A chef was on describing artichokes – a vegetable she had never tasted or desired to taste, yet he made it look so delicious.

'Globe artichokes are part of the sunflower family,' he continued, his voice melodically rugged, as if trying to hypnotise her into wanting to eat it. 'Dip in lemony melted butter, and pull out the juicy bottom parts with your teeth. Keep peeling off the leaves until you reach the prized heart.'

Sarah's eyes grew heavy as his words and images skipped through her brain. Instead of artichokes she saw her calloused heart being dipped in love and each hard layer slowly being peeled away until finally her soft, loving heart finally resurfaced – her heart that she had tried so hard to bury away.

Chapter Seventeen

Katy slammed the car door shut, nerves finally getting a grip on her. Today was the day she had been waiting for, and with Sarah waking her up at five that morning she was exhausted, but had managed to get some sleep on their drive up to the cottage. She looked over at Sarah. Her heart sank as she saw the exhaustion on her face. She had done so much for her for the wedding and somehow Katy had failed to realise that perhaps this was too much for her to bear.

'Come along,' Sarah shouted perkily, using every fibre of her being to muster up the last ounces of strength needed for today. 'We've got to get you looking like a queen, waiting to meet her king.'

Katy followed Sarah into the cottage. Sarah had given her strict instructions: 'I will take you to see the ceremony area once set-up is complete, but you are under no circumstances to go to the back of the cottage – the reception area is a surprise.' So Katy had agreed obediently, anticipating the surprise Sarah had in store for her.

Kevin was standing on the verandah as Gladys ran out to greet them and take their bags. Gladys hugged Katy excitedly;

having watched Katy grow up over the years, it brought her sheer joy to see her finally getting married.

'Welcome, ladies,' Kevin greeted warmly, kissing them both on each cheek. 'Katy, I need you to indulge me for a little. Sarah has been working so hard, so I have a tiny surprise for her inside. I know it's your big day, so I hope you don't mind me stealing your limelight for a moment?'

'Of course not!' Katy clapped her hands, delighted that Kevin had thought to do something for Sarah.

'Now, sweetie,' Kevin drawled in his most sophisticated voice, holding the door to the cottage tightly shut. 'I remembered how you mentioned Christmas was your favourite time of year, and since you weren't able to decorate your apartment for Christmas... I took the liberty of...' He held his breath as he swung the door open.

Sarah gasped. 'Kevin, it's beautiful,' she screamed, jumping to hug him and almost bowling him over. 'When did you find the time to do all this?' she shrieked, looking around at the most beautifully Christmas-decorated living room.

'Mmm, let's just say I didn't sleep at all last night, and seeing that expression on your face has made it all worthwhile.'

Sarah's eyes glistened with tears of joy. She walked around the room holding Kevin's arm, taking in all he had done for her. 'This is all for me? You did this just because I told you I love Christmas? Kevin you are amazing! I truly appreciate this; it means so much to me.'

'It's my pleasure, darling. I've got to score brownie points with the boss you know,' he winked at Katy. 'Especially if I want another pay rise next year.'

'You were getting one anyway,' Sarah chuckled, punching him in the arm, 'and no need to score brownie points with the boss. Your friendship won my heart over the first few weeks we worked together. I should be the one doing something special for you! Here you are spending your Christmas Eve with us when you could be with your family.'

'You are my family,' Kevin smiled, bending down to hug her, 'and as long as I have Annie and you with me, it's Christmas already. You've been a great boss and an even greater friend to me, Sarah; this is my way of saying thank you.'

Annie came bouncing into the living room, her pink rosy cheeks puffed up as if they had been stuffed with helium and blown up, ready to soar into the sky.

'You like it?' She giggled, jumping from foot to foot, clapping her hands in front of her face.

'I love it,' Sarah laughed, bending down and squeezing her tight. 'I gather you didn't sleep either?'

'Nope,' she said, her red lips screwing up into a strange rounded shape as she spoke, 'We stayed up all night making sure you would like it.'

'Thanks to both of you. Your attention to detail is astounding. God only knows how you managed to get that huge Christmas tree through the door! And I love the snow on the floor and the reindeer; it's like a scene out of a movie.'

'Ooh, and I love the crocheted Santa Claus cushions on the couches. Can I keep them?' Katy grinned, walking around her cottage that had suddenly transported them into a mystically glorious Christmas.

'Only if Sarah wants to share them with you,' Kevin laughed.

They were all so engrossed in taking in each detail that Kevin had put together that they completely forgot it was Katy's wedding day. Kevin had left nothing out: he changed the lamps to Christmas themed lamps; he had the dining room table set with red, cream and gold settings. The only thing that reminded them it was a wedding day was the cream carpet that ran from the back of the living room to the front door and down into the garden, as that was the aisle Katy would walk down.

'Katy, you will be transported from Christmas in the living room, to your wedding day outside.' Kevin smiled.

'I couldn't ask for better!' Katy gleamed.

'Okay, it's time to get cracking! Kevin do you have everything I need?' Sarah suddenly snapped into business mode.

'Yes, it's all here: your check list, arrival times of vendors, guest lists, and phone numbers. Its eight thirty, which leaves us with five and a half hours to show time. I've set up Katy's room just like you asked, and I've put your dress in your room.'

'Perfect! Now come on Katy, let's get you all settled in your room; it's transformation time. By the time John lays eyes on you he will fall over at the sight of you, and he will be rushing you out of here to get you naked sooner than we would like!' Sarah teased.

They all laughed at the thought. For the life of Kevin and Sarah they just couldn't imagine John as the passionate "sweep you up into my arms" kind of guy. He looked more like the type who would stand in front of her naked and ask rigidly if she would like to have sex now.

Sarah giggled at the thought; she hoped for her friend's sake he would be a more romantic lover than that!

Sarah got Katy settled into the room then went outside to ensure everything and everyone had arrived. She knew Kevin would take care of everything, but that didn't stop her from worrying frantically. She wanted Katy's wedding day to be perfect.

She thought about her own wedding day and how it hadn't been anything she wanted. Her in-laws had pre-determined how everything should be – she had no choice in the matter. She would have loved to have had an intimate wedding like Katy's but instead she had hundreds of people. It was a huge flashy wedding, grand enough to let every guest know that she was marrying into wealth. Even though she had grown up in a wealthy home, her parents had never bragged about their wealth, but her in-laws made sure to let the world know exactly how much money they dripped in.

Her dress was from a designer they chose, the décor by people they chose. They only thing she chose that day was to marry their son. She wondered how they were now – if they ever thought of her. After the wedding they seemed to adore her and were delighted to welcome her into the family, perhaps because she was the perfect doting wife and daughter-in-law, always eager to please them and obey their every wish. She wondered if they ever bothered to know why she had left, or whether they knew the truth. They would probably know soon enough, as they all socialised in the same circles and it wouldn't take long before someone said something.

Right now she had to ensure she gave Katy the wedding she dreamt of. She couldn't stress about her in-laws just yet. Katy had flown up to London the night before Sarah's wedding. She had so wished Katy was there before then because Katy would never have allowed her in-laws to push her around. She would have ensured Sarah had the wedding of her dreams.

Sarah sighed. It didn't matter now. She had married the man of her dreams, only to have it all snatched away. Today Katy was marrying the man of her dreams, and she hoped it would last forever.

Chapter Eighteen

Sarah ran around like a headless chicken, moving back and forth, sorting out last minute details. No matter how perfectly planned everything was, there always had to be some sort of last minute crisis. Today it was the wedding cake. The cake designer arrived, only to discover she had forgotten the top tier of the wedding cake. She was on her way back to Durban to collect it. Sarah crossed her fingers, silently hoping she would be back in time for the reception.

'Are you all right in here?' Sarah asked, popping her head into Katy's room.

She had left her in there a few hours ago with the beautician, who was giving her a manicure and pedicure. Katy had opted for an antique gold nail polish to match her wedding décor.

'I couldn't be better,' Katy lied, trying to conceal the nerves that were pounding like hammers on her heart. In just a few hours she would be Mrs. Gates – the thought both delighted and frightened her. She would belong to someone, she would take on his name and they would be one. She knew realistically that life would never be like the fairytales in the books they had grown up reading. She knew it had its ups and downs, and she also knew that its ups were better than any fairytale could describe and its downs were more terrifying than the villain in each story. But she was committed to John, and he to her, and they would weather every mountain and valley together. They would overcome the storms and wait together for the rainbow.

' Will Taylor has just arrived to style your hair; Kevin will bring him in shortly and Edward called to say they are on their way up here now. They have arranged to get dressed at Joseph's place, and I have given Joseph strict instructions to make sure that he kicks them out of the house at exactly one o'clock so they arrive here on time for the wedding.'

'Please tell me Edward has everything they need?' Katy asked, fearing her brother would by now have misplaced the wedding rings.

'I made sure to call him a million times to check he had everything. Trust me, if he forgets something, I will make him walk back to Durban to get it,' she laughed nervously, hoping Edward kept his promise to follow her instructions.

Sarah made her way outside, greeting Will Taylor as Kevin showed him into Katy's room. She was amazed how everything had come together, and even more grateful that all these people agreed to work on Christmas Eve.

'Hi, Sarah,' a fat woman with blond hair, smiled up at her.

'Oh hi, Molly. Katy is in her room; I think you should start taking photographs of her in there. Terry is currently styling her hair, so those will be charming pics to get. Is your husband on his way to Joseph's place to take pictures of Edward and John getting dressed?'

'Yes, he is. Once Katy is dressed, I will need to take pictures of you and her. So get dressed. I also need to do a detailed shoot of her perfumes, flowers etc, so there is no time to waste.' Molly spoke with the speed of lightening, clearly aware of the time frame and its limitations.

'Yes, of course. If you need me just shout, or look for Kevin – he will help you.' Sarah smiled, patting Molly on the shoulder as she walked outside into the garden. Molly had come highly recommended, and at a rather steep price, which Katy was more than happy to pay for as long as Sarah had managed to book her. Molly and her husband were both photographers, working as a tag team, ensuring they captured every moment from every angle. It was clear Molly wore the pants in that relationship, as her husband moved around her like a sheep waiting to be slaughtered, following her every instruction.

Sarah looked up at the sky. It was a beautiful day, sunny and clear, with a slight breeze to cool off the summer heat. The workers Sarah had hired to help with the set-up were busy arranging the bales of hay the guests would sit on during the ceremony. They set them down neatly in rows in the garden on either side of the cream carpet aisle they had laid down. Sarah had made gold and cream cushions to be placed on top of each bale of hay for extra comfort. She knew they were running a tight schedule with little time in between, but such was the drama in the production of garden weddings.

The ceremony was scheduled to start at two o'clock and the reception at six thirty. The guests would be able to relax in the garden after the ceremony with light snacks to nibble on and a photo booth and props for them to take pictures of themselves. One copy of the picture would be stuck into a memory book for Katy and John where guests could write messages or words or advice, and the guests would be given one copy of the picture as a memento of the special day.

'Sarah, Terry Scott is ready to do your hair now, and the make-up artists have arrived, ready to do both of your make-up.' Kevin interrupted.

'Oh Kev, I don't know if I have time to go and sit and do my hair. The videographer hasn't arrived yet, and neither has the florist.'

'Listen, there is nothing you can do until they arrive. You also need to look beautiful for the wedding, so go and do your hair and make-up. I will take care of the rest. If there is a crisis I cannot handle, I will be sure to call you. It's not like you're miles away, and you cannot be the ugly duckling in Katy's wedding pics.'

'Fine, then,' Sarah said crossly, folding her arms and stomping her feet like a little toddler, walking off but turning around after a few steps and blowing kisses as Kevin. 'You rock,' she giggled, trotting off to Katy's room, her legs feeling like jelly and her feet like lead.

'Aah, darling, you finally graced us with your presence,' Will crooned, as he pushed her down into a chair. 'Look at this hair! When last did you have a trim? These ends look like a rag doll.'

'I'm sure you can work some magic,' Sarah grinned, feeling the weight come off her feet. She couldn't imagine how she would fit her feet into high heels for the wedding; they looked like balloons from the swelling. She had been standing far too long.

'I will have to cut these stray cats off here first,' he said, showing her the tattered ends of her hair. 'We can't have you walking out of here with hair like this; you will be bad for my image.'

'Have your way with me,' Sarah giggled. 'Where is Katy?'

'She just popped into the pee parlour, darling; she needed to squeeze a pee.'

Sarah burst into fits of laughter; the image of Katy 'squeezing a pee' was beyond her. How on earth had he ever come up with such an expression?

Sarah sat and watched as Will went into his zone, pulling her hair in various angles, snipping away at her straggly strands of hair. He snipped and snapped his silver scissors, moving her hair between his hands as if juggling balls. Her hair covered the floor beneath her and she began to wonder what, if anything, was left of her luscious locks. Eventually he threw her hair forward in a dramatic explosion, fluffing and tossing it around her face.

'There you go, darling; you look like a catwalk model already,' he said, manoeuvering her hair around her face. 'I've layered it to frame your face and accentuate those million dollar cheekbones of yours. Pure perfection, I tell you, pure perfection.' He admired his own handywork as he examined her reflection in the mirror.

Sarah studied her haircut. She hadn't had a trim in months. It seemed the upkeep of her hair was the last thing on her mind, with her growing business and preparations for Katy's wedding. Hair that once lay below her supple breasts clung beautifully just above them, with wisps of hair in staggered layers accentuating her features.

'Taking into consideration the dress you will wear, I think the best style for your hair would be a chignon: it's a beautiful, ultra-feminine side bun. It will take the hair up, exposing the silhouette of your shoulders and neckline, and framing your face exquisitely.'

Sarah nodded silently, watching as he combed her hair to the side, then twisted a thick section of hair in a spiral and secured it with bobby pins. Finally he wrapped any remaining outer sections around the chignon, pinning each strand in place in flawless cohesiveness.

'All done! You like?' He asked, tilting her head from side to side for her to view all angles in the mirror.

'I love!' Sarah exclaimed. He had so effortlessly, in one swoop, accentuated her most prized features.

'Ooh, you look breathtaking!' Katy exclaimed, coming into the room. 'I'd better be careful, John might rather marry you when he sees you all cleaned up.'

Sarah laughed, 'Not a chance. You look ravishing!'

Terry had pulled Katy's hair up into a shabby chic bun, allowing for strands of hair to fall softly around her face, and a lace and diamante band served as her tiara.

'I am definitely a sight to behold,' Katy giggled, sizing herself up and down in the mirror. 'Time for our make-up,' she grinned, as two make-up artists walked in the room from Make-Up-Your-Mind.

'Goodbye, darlings. Enjoy your wedding, Katy. Sorry I can't stay, but my family would kill me if I didn't at least show my face on Christmas Eve!' Terry said, kissing them both on each cheek.

'I completely understand. I'm honoured you agreed to come out on Christmas Eve. Merry Christmas and all the best for the new year,' Katy replied gratefully.

They settled into their chairs, as the make-up artists proceeded to do their make-up. Katy and Sarah had both insisted on more muted nude looks – nothing over theatrical. They wanted to feel like themselves instead of Cleopatra plastered in make-up.

'How are you feeling?' Sarah asked, looking at Katy out of the corner of her eyes, feeling the tickle of the brush on her face as the foundation was applied.

'Much better now; the nerves are finally being replaced with excitement. I wonder what John will think when he sees me. I hope he likes my dress. I've kept it so secret from him. I think he is expecting me to rock up in a black wedding dress.' Katy's face split into a delighted giggle. 'He thinks I'm such a nut! I think my eccentricity frightens him a tad.'

'Ooh, he has seen nothing yet! Has he seen the pictures of you in your high school phase, with one side of your hair shaved off?'

'Hell, no. I knew that would scare him off!'

'Remember your mother's face when she came home and she realised we had used your father's hair clippers to do our very own hair creation.'

'She would have grounded me for life, if it wasn't for my dad's pleas for her to let me be. That was the benefit of being daddy's little girl.' Katy beamed.

'Much to Edward's disgust. He was hoping you getting into trouble for your hair would let him off the hook for failing English. Who on earth fails English when it's your home language?' Sarah threw her head back laughing, causing the make-up artist to put eye-shadow all over her cheek.

The look of Sarah's purple cheeks sent Katy into fits of giggles, tears falling down her face uncontrollably.

'Oh my, I'm so sorry,' Sarah apologised to the make-up artists, who were beginning to look unamused, 'We will behave now, we promise.'

They both tried to stifle their laughter and look painfully serious. Sarah decided to start a new conversation that hopefully wouldn't result in fits of laughter.

'So, tell me how you and John began dating? For some reason you never got around to that story,' Sarah asked.

'Hmmm, it's not the most romantic of stories, I guess.'

'I will be the judge of that!' Sarah replied emphatically.

'Okay. I was defending a client for murder. He had stabbed a man to death in his home when trying to rob the place,' Katy paused. 'The man who was stabbed was John's brother. His name was Leon.'

'Oh no, Katy, that's awful. What happened?'

'The case carried on for months. I tried to defend my client but it was pointless; all evidence pointed directly to him. Every day I would notice John sitting quietly in the courtroom watching the proceedings. When the judge was about to announce the sentencing, John asked if he could say something to the man who murdered his brother.' Katy pouted her lips waiting for the lipstick to be applied. 'He stood there, and told my client how he forgave him. How forgiving him was the only way he could live free from the bondage of what had happened. He said he knew in order to live a life of joy, he needed to forgive the man who caused him pain.'

'That's profound!' Sarah gasped, thinking of her own life and wondering if she could ever come to such a place.

'It was profound. I stared at him as he spoke. In all my years of defending criminals all I saw was the hatred, unforgiveness and heartbreaking pain the families suffered from the hands of those murderers. Seeing such love and forgiveness melted my heart.'

'It takes someone with unwavering strength and character to make that choice.'

'Exactly! And every day with John has proven to me he is just that: a good man with integrity, a mighty fortress.'

Sarah sat silent for a moment, thinking of John's bravery in making such a choice. It couldn't have been easy for him, but he had found true love in the process.

'Hey, wait a minute,' Sarah protested. 'You told me how you met him; where is the part of how you began dating?'

Katy snickered, 'I saw him later that day sitting alone in the coffee shop across the street from the courtroom. I asked if I could sit with him. I didn't really think he would say yes, considering I was defending his brother's killer. But he did, and we sat chatting until the coffee shop closed. After that he would come and have lunch with me every day in the same coffee shop, and finally he plucked up enough courage to tell me he had feelings for me and, as they say... the rest is history.'

Sarah sighed. 'Mmm, I think God has a sense of humour, because the Katy that no one could pin down into a serious relationship finally succumbs to a man in the courtroom with a heart of gold. Who would have thought love could blossom in a criminal court?'

Katy laughed. 'John still cannot understand why I choose to defend murderers, but he tries not to pass judgment. I've tried explaining that not all people on trial for murder are guilty, and getting the innocent people off for being wrongly accused makes it worthwhile.'

'You have found a keeper, sweetie!'

'I know,' Katy said smugly. 'My Prince Charming.'

Chapter Nineteen

Sarah stood at the door, nervously jiggling her leg. The seats were already full, and Edward and John were still nowhere in sight. Edward had promised they wouldn't be late, and now it was quarter past two and still no sign of them, and to top it all off, he wasn't answering his phone.

Kevin, of course, was running around trying to remain upbeat, determined not to allow Sarah to think the worst. They were late, only by fifteen minutes. Surely they must have got stuck in traffic, perhaps?

'Why don't you go and be with Katy?' Kevin told Sarah, trying his best to get her not to panic. 'I will go and get her father, so that as soon as they arrive we can get this show on the road. Okay?'

'Okay, Kev, thanks!' Sarah said, scanning the driveway one last time hoping for a sight of Edward and John, before turning around and heading for Katy.

'There you are.' Katy exclaimed, 'Where did you disappear to?'

'I just went to check on some last minute details,' Sarah smiled determined not to alert Katy to her missing groom.

'So can we start?'

'Umm, not just yet; Kevin is just rounding some things up. As soon as he says the word we are ready to go.'

They both heard a knock at the door, and Sarah hoped with all her heart that it was Kevin with some good news.

'Aah, my beautiful baby girl. You look stunning,' Katy's Dad said, coming into the room.

'Thanks, Dad,' she giggled.

'Kevin said to tell you, all is good to go, Sarah.'

'Thanks, Rodney!' Sarah turned to Katy, 'So that means we are ready to walk you down that aisle,' Sarah said excitedly, relief washing over her like a waterfall. Finally the boys had arrived. She was beginning to worry that John could have changed his mind, although thinking back now, she should not have panicked so prematurely – they were only fifteen minutes late for goodness' sake. She sighed, glad this day had finally come; now it would be time to focus on her.

Katy took her father's arm as he walked her to the front door that would lead to the ceremony.

'Are you ready, pumpkin?' he asked, squeezing her arm.

'As ready as I'll ever be,' Katy smiled, her face lighting up like a glow worm.

'I will walk out first,' Sarah instructed, 'and Kevin will signal to you both when it's time for you to make your grand appearance. Okay?'

'Got it!' Katy beamed.

She caught Sarah's arm, 'Thanks again for everything.'

'Anything for you, sweetie,' Sarah smiled, turning towards the door, waiting for Kevin to cue the music.

Edward held his breath as he watched Sarah walking down the aisle towards him. She looked stunning in her blush pink strapless chiffon floor length dress. He watched her skin light up like sparkles as it glowed against the sun's rays. He stepped forward, almost wanting to run towards her and scoop her up into his arms. He caught a glimpse of her thigh, as her side slit teased him with each step, showing just enough of her leg to make him want more. He steadied himself as she came closer, her Chanel perfume already wafting before her announcing her presence.

'You look beautiful,' he breathed into her ear as she took her final step into his outstretched arm.

'Thanks,' she blushed, aware that his eyes hadn't left her once; she had felt them like burning flames licking every inch of her body, caressing every curve, every movement. 'You look pretty good yourself,' she complimented back, feeling his sturdy hand against her bare back, as he led her to the left of the altar.

The violinist played Katy and John's song, "All of Me" by John Legend, as the minister motioned for everyone to stand. A ballet dancer danced up the aisle for the first verse and chorus of the song, laying a pathway of pale pink roses as she moved, ready for Katy to arrive. When the words of the chorus sang out the words, "even when I lose I'm winning", Katy appeared on her father's arm looking radiant. When Katy had explained that she had lost the court case, but had found John, Sarah knew exactly why she had insisted on walking out just as those words sang forth.

Katy had chosen a gorgeous ivory mermaid shaped gown with a fitted bodice and sweetheart neckline that hugged every curve of her body. Sarah turned to look at John. His smile was so radiant and wide that she could see all of his teeth. His eyes glistened with tears, glued to Katy's every move. Katy's dress shimmered with Swarovski crystals and the entire dress was adorned with delicate gold lace appliqué on English net. Everyone gasped at the sight of her, each crystal reflecting the sunlight, and Sarah felt tears begin to fall down her cheeks, grateful to be able to witness her friend marrying the man she loved.

She knew John must have been relieved she wasn't in the black wedding dress he had feared; however, Katy's unusual Louis Vuitton shoes gave away her eccentricity and inner wildness. Sarah noticed how Edward stood with such pride as his sister made her way down the aisle, his hands clasped in front of him and his chest thrust forward like a peacock.

Rodney kissed Katy for the last time as her provider and protector, and handed her over to John, as he now took over the role of caring for his little girl. John beamed as he took hold of Katy, almost leaning in to kiss her before the minister had even begun.

The ceremony was extraordinary, with Katy and John having written their own wedding vows. Sarah was amazed at how much gentler John seemed, his love for Katy being displayed openly on his sleeve; he was powerless to hide how deeply he loved her.

Sarah felt Edward's eyes piercing her during each moment, her cheeks blushed pink each time she looked up at him and caught him beaming back at her. She could feel her heart fluttering at his proximity to her, but she sternly reminded herself that she could not allow her heart to betray her to love. It had been shattered too many times, and she had vowed never to allow it to open up to anyone again.

The minister announced that John could kiss his bride, and John leapt forward planting his lips so firmly on Katy's that Sarah wondered if they would ever be able to be prised apart.

'I present to you, Mr. and Mrs. John Gates,' the minister bellowed enthusiastically as John finally peeled his lips from Katy's and turned to face the crowd.

They both smiled sheepishly as they began to make their way down the aisle, posing at each turn for the photographers to snap the perfect shot.

Edward took Sarah's hand and linked it into his arm. He looked down at her silently as he walked her down the aisle. He didn't need to say anything because his eyes spoke for him, burning with passionate hunger.

Kevin led them off to the side of the cottage that overlooked the waterfall, where they would take pictures. Sarah checked with him quickly if her surprise for Katy had arrived yet, before she allowed Edward to lead the way.

Edward shook his head, 'At some point you need to relax and enjoy the day, princess. Kevin has everything running according to your *very* detailed plan,' he chuckled. 'Trust me, no one could miss a detail, you covered it all.'

Sarah sighed, she knew he was right, but that didn't stop her from worrying.

'Now, let me stand next to you in the photos and make you look good,' Edward teased with a slight smile.

'Fat chance, buster! We all know it's my beauty that accentuates your one handsome feature.'

'Oh, yeah?' Edward said, raising one eyebrow, 'And which handsome feature might that be?'

Sarah blushed, not expecting him to ask her what she found handsome about him. She didn't know what to say, in fear that she would give away that she found every single inch of him ruggedly handsome and irresistibly sexy.

'Wouldn't you like to know,' she teased back, hoping that would throw him off.

'Mmm, I see,' he smiled, sensing her sudden shyness and deciding not to press her for any further information.

'Everyone, could you all stand here,' Molly pointed to a spot on the grass. 'John, I want you to dip Katy, as if you were dancing, and Edward I need you to stand behind Sarah and wrap your arms around her waist.'

Sarah jumped as Edward slipped his hands around her waist.

'What's wrong?' he asked.

'You just tickled me, that's all,' she lied, feeling her heart flutter as she rested her head against his chest.

'That's good, Sarah,' Molly said, motioning to how Sarah rested into Edward, 'Now look lovingly up into his eyes.'

For a moment Sarah was lost when her eyes met Edward's – Molly's words became muffled as if being drowned under water. She heard her giving some sort of instruction to John, but Edward's strong arms around her as he held her tight, caused her tummy to do flips. She held her breath as Edward looked down towards her, his lips so close to hers that she could feel the heat they contained.

'Perfect.' Molly shouted, having taken the shot and motioning to them to move over to another location for a different shot.

Sarah breathed deeply as Edward released her, his hand seamlessly moving from the front of her waist to her back, as he led her on. She felt giddy, confused by the effect he had on her, wondering if he felt it too. She hoped she could get through this day without succumbing to her desire for him, as her body tingled and came alive in rampant heat, betraying her will to resist.

Chapter Twenty

The day wound down magnificently, staining the inland sky with musky shades of golden orange, pink and blue. The smell of hydrangeas wafted gently in the air, and the trees clung to their leaves in a green array of splendor.

Sarah led John and Katy towards the back door of the cottage, their faces alive in eager anticipation of what lay before them.

'My wedding has been an enormous adventure,' Katy said, planting a kiss on Sarah's cheek. 'I doubt there is any other bride who would entrust the details of her day to her friend, and be utterly surprised by the outcome.'

Sarah giggled as they walked. It was true; she had only let Katy in on very few details, and the rest she hoped would be a pleasant surprise. Sarah opened the door to the back yard, and the guests erupted in loud applause as John and Katy appeared.

'I present to you, Mr. and Mrs. Gates,' Edward bellowed through the microphone, grinning from ear to ear in proud adoration.

Katy gasped as she saw what was before her. 'Sarah, it's better than I could ever have dreamt. You took simple and made it elegant,' she breathed, her surprise and joy evident in her eyes.

She looked out at her family and close friends, standing to welcome them in under a canopy of lights strung through the trees, lighting up the night sky, twinkling like stars in every direction.

To her left was a basket with a note that read: "Help yourself to a quilt, and make yourself comfortable on the grass. Welcome home." Katy beamed at Sarah as she lifted the quilt.

'You like?' Sarah asked, almost holding her breath as Katy noticed each detail.

'I love,' Katy shrieked back, amazed at Sarah's ability to capture more than her imagination.

'I thought each guest could choose to sit to the left on the grass on quilts or they could choose to lounge to the right on couches.'

Katy looked to her right as she saw large oversized couches arranged in groups all over the lawn, with golden side tables that lit up from inside. She clapped her hands excitedly as she saw their garden come to life.

'It's awful,' John teased, his eyes glistening with tears, 'Just awful.'

Katy punched him playfully in the arm.

'Is that what I think it is? 'Katy asked pointing to her right.

'Yup, it's a food truck,' Sarah giggled, 'serving only cocktails, and only gold, pink and cream coloured cocktails to match your colour scheme.'

Katy chuckled, 'Trust you to keep the colour scheme going in everything.'

To her left she saw tables adorned with all their puddings and cakes, and in the centre of the garden was a wooden dance floor that had been erected.

Sarah turned to look at her friend, feeling both excitement and sorrow. It was the end of her adventure of having Katy all to herself – she now belonged to John – and Sarah knew that no matter how she tried, their relationship was bound to change to some degree. She knew their bond would never be broken, but no longer would Katy be available every day like before; no longer would she be able to burst in through her doors. Now she would have to call first; now she would have to fit into her schedule with John.

Katy sensed her nostalgia and squeezed her hand tightly. 'You are my best friend, Sarah, nothing will change that.'

Sarah smiled up at her, feeling the tears weigh heavily on her eyelids. 'Let's get this party started,' she replied cheerfully, trying to lighten the moment.

Sarah moved towards the microphone, and took the reins to begin the evening.

'Welcome, everyone, to this momentous occasion, where we celebrate the union of John and Katy. As you can all see, the plan is to relax, party, and enjoy each moment with them. Waiters will come around with canapés, drinks are in the food truck, and dessert is overflowing behind me, as we sweeten you up to our pudding themed reception.'

Sarah motioned to John to come and take over for his speech. He grabbed Katy's hand and they ran up together.

'Thank you all for coming,' John beamed. 'Today is the happiest day of my life! Katy, you are crazy and adorable, and I look forward to this new journey of our lives. You complete me, you excite and delight me. I love you.' He kissed Katy full on the lips, as everyone whistled merrily.

Katy took a hold of the microphone, 'Mom and Dad, I think you both can see how I'm safe in John's care, and Edward has threatened him enough times for him to keep in check,' she giggled as Edward nodded his head so hard Sarah thought it would fall off. 'Sarah and Kevin, you have both been phenomenal – this place is all I wanted and more – and to my darling husband,' Katy giggled as everyone screamed at the mention of the word husband, 'you are my sunshine on a cloudy day, and I love you more today than I did yesterday.'

Sarah's heart melted as she saw their love and affection towards one another. Edward ran towards them, his glass in hand, as the waiters handed everyone glasses of champagne.

'To the bride and groom,' he shouted, lifting his glass, watching as everyone cheered and clinked their glasses. 'Sarah has an announcement to make,' he said, motioning to Sarah to take over.

'Katy, I've got one more surprise for you,' Sarah jumped excitedly behind the mic, looking for Kevin to see whether the surprise was ready; he nodded eagerly with his thumbs up.

'Ladies and gentleman,' Sarah continued, 'I present to you Katy's favourite band... Mi Casa!'

Everyone turned to see a black curtain that had been hung in one corner between the trees, suddenly drop, and Mi Casa appeared on stage as the music started, and they sang 'Heavenly sent'.

Katy ran for Sarah, almost tripping over her dress, as she grabbed her and ran towards the stage screaming, 'How on earth did you arrange this!'

Sarah laughed as J'Something, the lead singer in the band, came off the stage and sang to Katy. John chuckled as he watched Katy's excitement, as she and Sarah bounced happily to the song, their hands raised into makeshift microphones as they sang along to every word.

When the song ended they bounced back towards John, and Sarah once again took the microphone, 'Kevin will hand out Chinese lanterns to everyone. Each person is to light their Chinese lantern, then say a few words of advice to John and Katy before letting the lantern float into the evening sky.'

Each person took hold of a lantern and a lighter, as Sarah led John and Katy towards a couch she had set up for them to sit on and watch as each lantern took flight. One by one each person came towards them and gave them advice on marriage before letting go of their lit lantern. The sky filled with burning lanterns going higher and higher into the night, before their orange glow burnt out.

Edward came towards them with his lantern, 'May you both always remember to run your own race in life, never comparing your love to others, never comparing your possessions to others, and living your best life together in love.' He lit his lantern and everyone watched in silence as it floated up into the sky, the light getting smaller and smaller as it moved on the wings of the wind.

'May you always remember to be faithful to each other, always communicating your hearts to each other. May laughter and joy be the foundation your children are supported in,' Sarah said, as she too lit her lantern and set it free into the wind, her words resonating in the air as they fluttered up with it.

The music began to play and John and Katy made their way to the dance floor. Sarah saw Annie holding onto Kevin, her cheeks popping like caramel popcorn with excitement, and her crimson lips colouring her face with joy.

Sarah whirled around as she felt his hand on her back, 'Would you do me the honour of dancing with the best man?' Edward asked, taking her hand in his. She nodded silently as he led her onto the dance floor, Katy winking at them, as they joined them in their dance.

'You look breathtaking,' Edward breathed on Sarah neck, causing her spine to tingle. His voice was quiet and low, as he swung her out and pulled her back into him, pressing her body firmly against his, his feet moving in perfect rhythm to the music. Sarah's mouth opened, as air escaped with adrenalin, overwhelmed by his sudden intimate nearness. His breath was warm against her skin as he moved her slightly so that her eyes were forced to look into his.

'You are breathtaking,' he whispered again, this time tracing her face lightly with his fingers, inhaling the familiar scent of her hair.

'Thanks,' she muttered, feeling her lips betray her as he gently touched them, lifting her chin even closer to his.

He pulled her closer, so close that she closed her eyes waiting for his lips to meet hers. His breath was warm against her skin, tickling her senses, mixed with the masculine scent of his cologne. Sarah's eyes flashed open, realisation firing through them. What was she thinking! He had a girlfriend and she could never kiss him, never! She saw him staring at her, a frown forming on his brow seeing the change in her eyes, his hand still roaming along her back, as the music moved their feet in perfect harmony.

'What about Jessica?' Sarah spat at him, her voice thick with frustration at herself.

'I broke it off with Jessica after the first night you met her.' His voice was low and urgent.

'But she came up and stayed at the cottage,' Sarah growled, feeling her heart beating faster, pumping through her veins in beats of confusion and a desire to have him.

'She came to try and get me back. She knew I hadn't told anyone of our breakup and she hoped her presence there would force me to take her back.'

Sarah breathed deeply, allowing his words to sink in, wondering if the piercing look in his eyes were correct: he had broken it off with Jessica because of her. She shook her head, looking away; she had to be wrong… had to be. There was no chance he cared for her in that way – her loneliness must be playing mind games with her. Her eyes locked again with his, and she realised how fragile she was against his charms. She had always been, but had never imagined he thought of her as anything other than a little sister until recently – or was it her imagination? Was the electricity between them just something she alone felt? Were his looks towards her just pity and not passion or love.

'Princess?' he asked gently, the change on her face firmly obvious. 'Are you ok?'

She looked away, realising that he could see into the very heart of her: he could see her every apprehension, every wall. He knew her like no other man ever had. She was determined to keep her heart safely guarded by the walls she had built, and she knew that, if she let him, he would tear them down in one instant swoop, breaking through and taking a hold of her, not just in heart, but in mind and body too. Her body stiffed, as her mind began to override her emotions.

'I need to sit down,' she muttered, pulling away from his arms: the arms she wanted to run into, the arms that had kept her safe and warm these past few months. She now knew it was these arms she had to run as far away from as possible before her heart let go and melted at his feet.

'Okay,' he said, sensing her urgency for space. 'You must be tired; it's been a long day.'

He released her and watched her walk away from him, watching her sit on a patch of grass, her legs pulled up into her chest. His heart broke as he wondered if he had shown her too soon how he felt – if he had lost her forever.

He walked towards her and sat beside her. 'I'm sorry if I said something to frighten you.'

Her eyes filled with hot tears of confusion, 'You could never frighten me. I... I'm just tired, that's all.'

He said nothing, instead he stretched his arm around her, pulling her into his chest, deciding not to push her for a truthful answer but sensing somehow he had scared her off.

Chapter Twenty-One

The sun rose steadily; it seemed to be the only certainty Sarah felt today. She knew that in just a few hours she would be getting onto a plane headed for London.

She stretched her legs further out on the couch pulling the blanket around her, feeling cold despite the summer heat. Resting her head on her arms, she watched as a butterfly flew past the window without a care in the world, moving from flower to flower. She was exhausted, having been up until late with Kevin and Edward, packing up everything from the wedding, and sending Katy and John off on their honeymoon to Mauritius. The guests lay fast asleep in the bedrooms, and Sarah knew she should get up and start making breakfast before they all awoke.

Dragging her feet she moved towards the kitchen, her eyes burning from a lack of sleep. Despite her best efforts and sheer exhaustion, the dooming fate that awaited her seemed to prevent her from sleeping, poking and prodding at her like needles in her heart.

She took out the eggs and began to crack them into a bowl large enough to feed all the guests. Fortunately most of them had decided to face the long trip home, wanting to spend Christmas morning with their families, but John and Katy's immediate families had decided to spend the night, and Sarah knew she needed to see to them before they left.

'What are you doing awake already?' she heard a voice croak behind her 'I was coming to make breakfast; you should be resting.'

She felt Edward come up behind her and take the fork out of her hand. He turned her around and kissed her cheek. 'Merry Christmas, Sarah,' he said sweetly, leading her to a stool and sitting her down. 'Today you relax. I will take care of everything,' he said, feeling as if he were talking to himself. Her silence cut deep into the atmosphere, as he saw her mind adrift in a faraway place.

Kevin sauntered in already dressed, holding an envelope in his hand. He stood beside Sarah. 'Are you okay, sweetie?' he asked, looking at her weary face.

'Mmm,' was all she muttered.

Kevin shot Edward a worried look, as Edward shrugged his shoulders in defeat.

'This came for you a few days ago, I signed for it.' He said handing her the envelope. 'Annie and I are going to leave now. We need to get to our families before lunch.'

'Thanks for everything,' Sarah said, looking down at the envelope and noticing the London return address. 'Merry Christmas! I will see you when I get back from London.'

'I will take care of everything for you, so no stressing about work while you're gone.'

'Thanks. I know I can count on you,' Sarah said feebly, getting up slightly to hug Kevin goodbye.

Kevin said goodbye to Edward, and whispered for him to take care of her, before going to fetch Annie so they could make the three hour trip back to Durban. He felt exhausted, but his exhaustion was clouded with worry for Sarah – she looked a mess.

Sarah looked down at the envelope in her lap as she carefully peeled it open. Pulling out the pages inside she went as cold as ice as the blood drained from her face. Tears began to seep through the cracks in her eyelids as her body came to terms with what lay inside.

Edward turned to see her face pale, and her cheeks wet with tears. Her body was rigid from stress and her hands clenched in tight fists of anger.

'What is it, Sarah?' he pleaded, taking the envelope from her, looking inside. 'Divorce papers?' he asked, looking up at her.

'I guess it's time I gave you an explanation,' Sarah muttered, her lips quivering as she spoke.

Edward poured her a cup of coffee and took a seat beside her. 'Whenever you're ready, princess. You are under no obligation to tell me anything.'

'I want to,' Sarah sighed, needing to allow the words to escape before they burst her bleeding heart.

Edward nodded quietly, studying her face, waiting for her to begin.

'Things have gone from bad to worse with Adam and me,' Sarah began. 'At first he was the husband I had always dreamt of: he was doting and affectionate, he would prance me around like his prized possession. But two years into our marriage I began to see a change in him. Suddenly he became frustrated with me; he seemed to treat me like I was his prison warden.'

Edward reached for her hand and held it softly as she continued.

'By the time Christopher was born I had almost given up on our marriage. I had been holding on to the idea of our perfect life together, instead of facing the reality that stared me in the face. But when Adam took one look at Christopher it was as if something in him shifted. Suddenly his glacial eyes towards me melted, and he was determined to make us a family.'

Edward nodded, seeing the way her lip quivered each time she mentioned Christopher's name.

'The first two years of Christopher's life, Adam was the perfect father: always home, playing with him, and taking us on family trips. He adored his son, he adored us, and I believed our lives were perfect.' Sarah took a sip of her coffee as she paused, thinking of how to get the words inside her out of her mouth. They had been trapped in there for so long, she had never told anyone the horror she had faced.

Edward noticed the agony it caused for her to describe each detail and he offered to help, 'Katy told me about Christopher's death. She said he died three months before you came to South Africa. She wasn't sure if that's why you chose to come here and she didn't want to ask why you would leave Adam behind?'

Sarah nodded. 'Yes and no,' she muttered. 'He passed away, but that wasn't what finally made me run away.'

'What happened?' Edward asked, wondering what could have been so terrible that in her state of mourning she had chosen to leave her husband and her family to come to South Africa. He had a feeling that she and Adam had gone their separate ways because she never wore her wedding ring and never spoke of him. In all her time here she had never offered them any explanation as to exactly what had happened.

'I was out on business the day Christopher drowned,' Sarah began again. 'I remember Adam calling me late in the afternoon, telling me I urgently needed to come home. When I arrived I saw the ambulance and police outside my home, and knew immediately something had happened to Christopher.' Sarah breathed in deeply and continued. 'Adam was standing inside with my sister, Lilly, and our parents. I screamed frantically and asked him what had happened and where Christopher was. He told me that the maid had been watching him and must have taken her eyes off him, because he had gone outside by the pool and had fallen in and drowned.'

'Oh Sarah,' Edward said tenderly, pulling his chair closer to hers, wiping the tears from her eyes.

'I ran outside to find the maid; the police were questioning her, but she just looked at me, bewilderment and shock in her eyes. She wasn't talking.' Sarah covered her face at the memory. 'Adam came and took me into the house, and got a doctor to give me a tranquilliser because I was hysterical.'

'That's only natural, princess,' Edward said, lifting her face towards him. 'Any mother would be that way if she found out her three year old little boy had just drowned, and the person she had trusted to look after him had neglected him.'

'That's just the problem,' Sarah's face hardened with anger. 'Two months after the funeral I was home and the maid came to the house for the first time since we fired her after

Christopher's death. She told me she had something to tell me: that she couldn't allow me to believe the lie anymore.'

Edward watched as Sarah's jaw clenched, and her hands squeezed him in what looked like hatred.

'She told me that she hadn't been looking after Christopher that day, that Adam was home and had told her rather to focus on cleaning the house, that he would take care of Christopher. She said she later heard a splash in the pool and ran outside to see what had happened, only to find Christopher's lifeless body floating inside.'

'So it was Adam who was responsible?' Edward asked in shock.

'Not just Adam,' Sarah paused. 'Adam and Lilly.'

Edward looked at Sarah, a sense of understanding washing over his face. 'They were having an affair? Your husband and your sister were having an affair?'

'Yes,' Sarah breathed, relieved to be finally saying it out aloud. 'And they were in the bedroom, having left Christopher in the lounge to play on his own with the sliding door that led to the pool wide open.'

'So Adam had blamed the whole thing on the maid to cover up his affair with Lilly?'

'I should have known, Edward, I should have known. But I always thought they were just close you know, like in a brother sisterly kind of way.'

'Shh,' Edward consoled, 'you couldn't have guessed they would both betray you in that way.'

Sarah put her head down and rubbed her temples, 'When I confronted Adam he was so nonchalant about it, blaming me, saying I was unable to meet his needs, that Lilly was more the woman he always wanted, and he didn't know how to leave me. Their affair started two years into our marriage and stopped after Christopher was born, only to start up again two years later.'

Edward shook his head, astounded by what he was hearing. He knew Lilly and Sarah had never been close. Lilly had always been a tormenting little sister to Sarah, constantly picking on her, and getting Sarah into trouble with her parents. She was spiteful and mean, and as a result Sarah had always clung to Katy more as a sibling. Sarah had tried numerous times over the years to form a bond with Lilly, but it seemed Lilly resented her. Sarah was more beautiful, more intelligent, with a radiant personality that won every man's heart. Lilly had always lived in her shadow, never able to be in a relationship, always envious of Sarah's uncanny ability to draw a crowd.

Sarah continued, 'He told me he wanted a divorce, that Christopher had been the only reason he hadn't divorced me sooner, and now that Christopher wasn't around any longer to bind us together he saw no point in keeping up his charade of loving me.'

'Oh Sarah, he didn't deserve you. He had to be cold and heartless not to love you, and to choose Lilly over you. The two of them are a match made in heaven. They are both cruel and selfish.'

'I know, I see that now, but it doesn't take the pain away. I thought for ten years I had the perfect life: an illustrious career, a doting husband and a son I adored more than life itself. Adam left me to grieve alone; he left me to face losing my son, our son, all on my own, as if I were a thorn in his side.

He was heartless to the anguish I was in over losing Christopher. I needed someone to hold my hand through the worst pain I had ever experienced, yet instead I had to learn to go through it on my own. Even though Christopher died because of Adams negligence, he seems completely unphased. His death still haunts me day and night, yet Adam has just continued with his life as if it never happened. He has never even taken responsibility for what happened.'

Edward's eyes filled with tears. He knew now why she had kept her heart so hidden. How could she ever trust again, when the past ten years she was living a lie? The man she had chosen to spend the rest of her life with had all along been sleeping with her sister, and her son whom she so loved had died so tragically at the hands of her husband and his lover – her very own sister. He too would have run away, he too would have not wanted to face the people who had caused so much pain.

'I packed up Christopher's clothes and toys, and put them in boxes in my parent's home. The only toy I didn't pack was his favourite giraffe. He couldn't sleep without his giraffe. So I took it and dug a hole next to his grave at the cemetery, and buried it next to him so he could sleep peacefully with his giraffe forever.'

Sarah sobbed, her mind envisioning her little boy lying fast asleep, looking so peaceful in the coffin. She had wanted to bring him back to life, she had wanted to hold him again, play with him again, tell him just how much Mommy loved him. She felt her life had ended that day. Her heart now lay in a cage, her body bleeding in anguish, and now she would have to get onto a plane and face the two people who had crushed her, who had stolen the only true thing in her life: her baby boy. Through their selfish needs she had lost her darling son. She didn't think she could do it, she didn't know how to face them.

Edward took her into his arms, and rocked her back and forth, her tears staining his shirt. Her strength astounded him. Despite all she had faced, she still had determined to start a new life, building it brick by brick, layer upon layer, in an attempt to salvage what was left.

'Please let me come with you to London; I don't want you facing them alone,' he pleaded, holding her tight.

'I need to do this on my own. I need to face them on my own so I know for sure I have the strength to survive this.'

Edward kissed her forehead gently. 'I understand,' he whispered, wiping her tears away. 'If you need me, just call and I will come running. I mean that, Sarah. I will do anything for you, anything.'

Sarah reached up and ran her fingers through his hair. 'I believe you,' she said, knowing he had never let her down before. 'I know I can count on you.'

Edward held her close, as she rested in his arms. He could only imagine the grief that swarmed her heart. She had lost three people the day Christopher died: her son, her husband and her sister. She must have felt so alone – he shuddered at the thought – and he wanted her to know she would never be alone again.

Edward took Sarah to her room, and sat with her until she fell asleep. Then he made breakfast for all the remaining guests and finally, once everyone had left, he woke her up and drove her to the airport. Watching her board the plane all alone made him feel so helpless; her body seemed so frail and limp. This was the saddest Christmas he had ever had. He knew this was the saddest Christmas she had ever had, and he decided that never again would he leave her alone on Christmas Day. Today would be the one and only time, because today she needed to say goodbye to her past so that she could heal and have a future. He thought of the giraffe she had on her bed, and how she clung to it that night he sat with her, realisations dawning on him like the rising of the sun. That was the only reminder she had of her little boy. He knew then what he needed to do for her, so she could have a piece of Christopher next to her forever.

He walked away, torn, heartbroken to let her leave, but hopeful of her return.

Chapter Twenty-Two

Sarah's eyes fluttered open heavily, startled by a peculiar sound somewhere in the distance. She stared around the room that was strewn with her bags and clothes, her mind steadily starting to recall her whereabouts.

She had arrived in London yesterday afternoon and the chauffeur service had brought her straight over to the Connaught Hotel. She was exhausted and had thrown herself onto the bed, falling fast asleep.

She stretched out in the bed, feeling her bare skin against the sheets. The sheets alone reminded her of where she was. The Italian linen and cashmere blankets felt exquisitely soft against her skin. 'I need to get up,' she thought lazily, realising her head felt like it had been run over by a truck dragging her down a gravel road.

The sound came again, as a voice bellowed out, 'Room service.' Sarah jumped out of bed and before she could throw on some clothes, a tiny woman stepped into her room staring wide-eyed at her half naked body.

'Oh, please forgive me. I called out and thought no one was in the room,' the maid stammered, running back out through the door without turning back or waiting for Sarah to respond.

Sarah threw herself back onto the bed, giggling at how ridiculous she must have looked in her underwear, with sleep still wound like crusted curtains around her eyes. She had pulled her clothes off the minute she had arrived yesterday, the thought of finding pyjamas in her suitcase too dreary an effort. Sleep beckoning her, she took the plunge in her underwear underneath the bed sheets.

Sarah looked around as she wriggled into the linen. She loved the Connaught Hotel. It was designed by the renowned designer Guy Oliver; he had a knack for creating beautiful tranquil spaces that oozed elegance. She had booked into the Deluxe King Room. To her right were two champagne wingback chairs set against the full length window overlooking Adam's Row. Above her was a modern painting in muted stripes set in a beautiful white frame. Her bed was full white with a champagne cashmere throw. It just exuded of contemporary sophisticated elegance.

'Shit,' she screamed, wondering what time it was. She grabbed her cell phone and saw three missed calls. With determined urgency she typed a message:

'Give me half an hour and I will be there. So sorry xx'

Throwing her feet off the bed onto the walnut parquet flooring, she rushed into the shower, allowing the warm water to wash away her sleep. For the life of her she couldn't understand why she hadn't woken up earlier. She had practically slept an entire day!

Wrapping herself in the oversized towel she rummaged through her bags and pulled on a skin tight pair of pale denim jeans and a white cashmere jersey. There was no time, she thought, checking her watch. Tying her wet hair into a messy bun she pulled on her tan stiletto boots and, grabbing her trench coat, she ran out of the door bracing herself against the cold winter chill as she made her way to Motcomb Street. She was late.

'Hello!' a ginger haired woman screamed with much excitement, grabbing a hold of Sarah and practically pushing her over.

'Hey there,' Sarah giggled, still freezing from the icy cold. 'So sorry I'm late, Jane. I must have overslept – jet lag or something.'

'I was worried you hadn't actually made it on to the flight back here,' Jane chuckled, showing Sarah to a seat and pushing over a steaming mug of hot chocolate.

Sarah took a sip, 'Mmm, how I miss our weekly trips to Rococo Chocolates,' she sighed, looking around at the familiar store. 'South Africa might have lions and rhinos but they sure don't have Rococo's hot chocolate.'

'I knew you would have missed this place. I took the liberty of buying you a box of truffles,' Jane said, tapping the box on the table, 'Thought you might need some chocolate to take the edge off.'

Sarah wrapped her hands around the warm hot chocolate, and looked into her eyes, 'I guess you've heard, huh?'

'Yup. Pretty much everyone knows now. I don't know why you couldn't tell me before you left?'

'Hey, I told you I was leaving the country; that's more than most people got.'

'You *had* to tell me you were leaving – I'm your personal assistant, remember? Who else would wrap up your business if I wasn't going to?' Jane asked wrinkling her round nose. 'Anyway, Adam and Lilly deserve each other; they are both two snobbish brats as far as I'm concerned.'

Sarah laughed, 'Excuse me! You were always the one telling me what a handsome husband I had!'

'Handsome … yes! Wonderful person …. hell, no!' Jane replied emphatically.

'Thanks, Jane, you're a good friend.'

'You are looking gorgeous, by the way. Very different from how I remember. Your hips are filling out those jeans in ways they never have before, and this hair!' Jane exclaimed as she twirled Sarah's curls around. 'I love it! Why didn't you wear your hair this way before? It was always pin-straight and lifeless.'

Sarah giggled, touching her curls self-consciously. ', Adam hated my curls. He would never allow me to leave the house in them. So I would iron them flat every day.'

'What torture. I don't know why you allowed that man to treat you like some prized possession to show off to his business partners. He will get a shock when he sees you now.'

'He will probably be glad he divorced me,' Sarah smiled weakly, her heart pinching at the thought.

'He would be mad to. You look better than you ever did. You've got curves you never had when you were always starving yourself to death. Your hair is amazing – adds so much character to your gorgeous face – and your skin is glowing without all those layers of make-up you always wore.'

Sarah looked down at the table, her voice suddenly serious. 'I feel more human now, Jane. No longer do I paint my face or do my hair to please Adam. Instead I live how I want to and the people around me love me for who I truly am. No pretentiousness, you know? It's as if the mask I wore all those years, trying to be the perfect wife, has finally been removed and I am beginning to love who I truly am. My identity is no longer found in Adam; I now have my own identity. I just wish Christopher was here so I could give him the best version of myself.'

'I can see that, and I love the new improved you. Christopher would have too, but he lived a full life filled with the love you poured on him,' Jane said squeezing Sarah's hands, 'It's the first time I've seen you so relaxed, in spite of the fact that your mother is sick and your ex-husband is a delightful pig!'

Sarah laughed so hard that she almost spat her mouthful of hot chocolate back into her mug, 'Delightful pig – mmm, I like that,' she sniggered. 'So how are things with you? Any man I should know about as yet?'

'Actually, now that you ask,' Jane teased playfully, a glimmer of mischief in her eyes, 'I have myself a chocolate covered hunk of a man.'

'You do!' Sarah exclaimed, 'Oh Jane, it's about time.'

'It's not cast in diamond rings as yet, but I would say it's pretty serious. He is naughty and playful, gorgeous as hell and oh so sexy!' Jane crooned, licking her lips at the thought. 'His body is a perfectly carved sculpture of chocolate muscles, each contour a new adventure I discover each and every day.'

'I take it the sex is good then,' Sarah giggled, reading between the lines.

'It's mind blowing,' Jane giggled excitedly. 'What about you, anyone special in your life?'

'Not really,' Sarah replied, 'I don't know if I will ever trust another man again.'

'Hey, don't make all men suffer just because of one man's indiscretions. There are still some good guys out there, you know. They may be rare, but they still exist.'

'Perhaps,' Sarah smiled wryly, an image of Edward appearing in her mind. 'For now, I've just got to get my life in order.'

Sarah heard the faint cries of her cell phone, reaching for it seconds too late as the incoming call cut off.

'Shit, that was my Dad. I had promised to call him as soon as I arrived, and I slept all day yesterday instead,' she muttered, feeling the vibration of an incoming message. 'Do you mind giving me a second to listen to the voicemail he left?' Sarah asked, as she rose from the table.

Jane shook her head, watching as Sarah walked out of the store. It had felt like years since she had last seen her, and yet in reality only six months had passed. But in terms of the change in Sarah, it was years. For so long she had watched as Sarah built her career, being a strong business woman, dominating the market with her signature design style and flair. Yet she had also witnessed her being a meek and mild wife, running after her husband, trying to please his every desire. Christopher had been the only solace in her life. He brought gusts of fresh air to her stale existence, and then suddenly the hope and love he brought was snatched away so tragically.

Jane burned with anger at the thought of what Adam had done to Sarah. She had always wondered why Lilly would always be at their home, hanging on Adam's every word, but at no point could she have dreamt they were having an affair for all those years. Jane felt her jaw clench. Sarah didn't deserve this. She was kind and loving, stunningly beautiful and charismatic. Any man would be a fool not to fall hopelessly in love with her.

Over the years there had been many men with whom Sarah worked who would run after her like puppy dogs, trailing after her scent, begging for one glance, one touch, yet she never seemed to notice them. Instead, all her time was dedicated to her husband, and then her son. She had no social life outside of them. Jane had become her only friend, only by default, because they worked together. Everyone else Sarah knew could only be described as acquaintances because she never had any time to commit to them in friendship. All her spare time went to her family.

Yet now, as Jane watched Sarah, she saw a new flower emerge: a woman who knew her purpose, who was comfortable in her own skin. She could see Sarah's face was still pained when she spoke of Christopher and Adam, yet behind the pain she could see flames of victory rising forth, determined to overcome the hurt, determined to rise above all life had thrown her. Hope glittered in Jane's heart at the sight of her friend's strength. Time was a healer, it surely was healing Sarah's pain, and from what she knew of Sarah's childhood, South Africa had always been her happy place. It was evident that something in South Africa was licking her wounds clean, giving them time to heal.

'Jane, I've got to go,' Sarah mumbled, running back into the store. 'My Dad said he was trying to reach me from last night to tell me my mother's surgery was moved up to today. It was meant to be the day after tomorrow, but the doctor wants to get it done today instead. I've got to get to the hospital; she is in theatre as we speak.'

'Let me drop you off there,' Jane said, grabbing her things.

'I feel so terrible,' Sarah said, tears muffling her words. 'I planned to go to the house to see her after I was done with you. She must have wondered why I didn't call. What if something happens to her, Jane?' Sarah's eyes were wide, stained red with tears.

'Your mom will be just fine; she is a fighter and so are you. Right now you are both fighting for your lives, and you are both going to win this battle!'

Jane grabbed Sarah around her waist and squeezed her tight, as they made their way out of their familiar chocolate store, into her car, headed for the hospital.

Jane dropped Sarah at the London Bridge Hospital, and begged to let her go inside with her, but Sarah refused obstinately, determined to face her family on her own.

She walked into the hospital, her mind swirling like a merry-go-round, mixing anxiety for her mother, anger and hatred for her sister with grief over the loss of her son and husband.. Taking a deep breath she made her way to the reception area.

'Hi, can I help you?' An oversized woman asked, sitting like a poached pear behind the reception desk.

'Umm, yes, I'm looking for my mother, Mrs. Lewis,' Sarah asked, politeness mixed with panic.

She watched as the chubby cheeked poached pear typed frantically on the computer, as if arm wrestling the keypad.

'She is still in surgery,' she said, reading from the screen. 'You will have to go and join the rest of the family in the waiting area,' she instructed, pointing towards a doorway a few feet away.

'Thanks,' Sarah muttered, wiping her sweating hands on her jeans.

She hadn't even had time to change, she thought, trying to picture the scene behind the door in the waiting area. She took a deep breath, in and out, in and out, as she moved her feet one step at a time towards the door, her throat constricting, suffocating her, strangling the air she tried to inhale.

'Come on, Sarah, you can do this. You are stronger now than you've ever been,' she told herself between gritted teeth. 'You are in control of your own happiness; they no longer control you.'

She ran her fingers over her hair, and straightened her back, lifting her chin, and holding her head up high. It was time to face whatever was before her. It was time to stand tall and no longer be the victim. They no longer had a hold on her. She had found her inner strength.

She took another step forward and opened the door; it was now or never.

Chapter Twenty-Three

Her feet stood still, frozen, as time seemed to come to an abrupt end. The sounds and chatter around her muffled as her eyes lost focus on all peripheries and saw only one thing: Adam.

He stood still a short distance down the passage, watching her enter the doorway, his feet moving in steady rhythm towards her. She panicked. She had thought she was ready for this moment but now, seeing him standing before her, she could feel her mending heart begin to crumble like a landslide.

She turned away frantic, her feet heading for the door, determined to get away from him as far away as she could. Suddenly she felt a hand on her shoulder – his hand. It could be no one else's. She knew his touch, this hand that had touched her for ten years. She inhaled his cologne and heard his voice: the one that had once melted her heart but now haunted her dreams.

'Sarah,' he whispered gruffly, 'please don't go.'

Sarah allowed him to turn her around so that her eyes looked straight up into his. For so long she had believed those jet black eyes were eyes of love, but now they were of stone.

'Hi,' she coughed, struggling to get the words out, trying to swallow the tears that threatened to expose her fragile heart.

'You look amazing,' he said, scanning her from head to toe, leaning in to kiss her lips.

She pulled back violently, 'Don't!' she grunted. 'Don't act like nothing has changed.'

He looked at her, startled by her sudden anger. Even when she had learnt about Lilly and him she had never shown anger. Instead she had left silently, her pain evident on her face; he had only ever seen pain on her face, never anger.

'Sorry,' he said pulling away, shoving his hands into his jeans pockets.

'Where is my father?' Sarah asked, trying to focus her energy on her reason for being here.

'He and Lilly are talking to the doctor. They should be back shortly.'

Sarah turned her back to him, the temptation to run her hands through his thick black hair being confused with her temptation to slap him hard across the face. Despite everything he was still handsome, and Sarah couldn't decide if that annoyed her or melted her heart. He had luscious thick hair that contrasted well against his tanned olive skin. His nose bent slightly to the right, but somehow it just complimented the strong angles of his jaw line. His lips were plump with a permanent crimson glow that would be the envy of any woman.

'Can we talk, please? Before they get back…' he pleaded urgently, blinking at her with his long eyelashes.

Sarah straightened her back and turned to face him, pulling out the envelope she still had in her bag.

'Here – your divorce papers, signed and delivered,' she said, handing him the envelope, grinding her teeth as she spoke.

'Sarah, I didn't want it to be this way. I'm sorry. I know I hurt you; I just didn't have a choice.'

'Didn't have a choice?' she snarled back at him. 'At which point did you not have a choice? The part where you cheated on me with my sister or the part where you left our son to drown in the pool while you screwed her in *our* bed?'

'Sarah, please. I am sorry. I never stopped loving you – it's just that with Lilly it's different, you know. It's like she gets me.'

'She gets you indeed! I see now how you are both selfish and self-centered, and neither of you have ever had any regard for my feelings, and you definitely had no love for Christopher!'

Sarah's eyes flashed like lightning, memories flooding her brain of times she had needed them both at different points in her life, and neither had ever been there for her, their own selfish needs always taking centre stage. She was always left out in the cold to fend for herself, yet they always demanded that she cater for their every whim and desire.

'Why did you have me followed, Adam? Why did you send some private investigator to find me in South Africa?'

'I was worried about you. No one knew where you were, and that silly little secretary of yours insisted on keeping her mouth shut. So I hired someone to find you. I couldn't move forward unless I knew where you were.'

'You mean you couldn't issue me with divorce papers unless you knew where I was?'

Adam looked away, quiet for a moment, words evading him. Never before had he seen Sarah so feisty.

'You're looking good,' he muttered eventually, staring back at her. "Really good. I can see South Africa has changed you. You seem different.'

Sarah watched as his eyes roamed her body from head to toe. She stood tall, allowing him to see that she had survived what life had thrown her; she had finished the race strong. She did not whimper and die in the corner he and Lilly had pushed her into, instead she rose above it, wiser and stronger than before. She felt a sense relief wash over her. He was no longer the monster she had thought, all because she no longer afforded him such power. From where she now stood, he looked like the puny college boy she had met more than ten years before, who, despite the wealth of his family had no direction and purpose for his life.

She had purpose, a new determined purpose to live and love and be free to enjoy all life had in store for her. She had been determined to finish strong, and she stood here now knowing she had accomplished just that. Now it was time to move forward, letting go of what was behind her. She would run life's race and allow joy and gladness to overtake her, and for love and peace to surround her. She knew now that what she once had with Adam was never true love, because love preferred someone else's needs above their own, and he had never done that for her.

She recalled what Katy had told her about John forgiving the man who murdered his brother, that he had forgiven him so that he could heal and live a better life. She turned to Adam, and with a new found sincerity and clarity, she spoke:

'I forgive you, Adam, for everything. I forgive you for cheating on me with my sister. I forgive you for the role you played in our son's death, and I forgive you for abandoning me to deal with losing him all on my own. Today I choose to forgive you, not because of who you are, but because of who I want to become. Forgiving you sets me free from the bondage of my past; it releases me into a new destiny.'

With that she turned and walked away, allowing her words to sink into his startled face. She sat down on a chair and waited to face whatever came next.

Adam and Sarah sat quietly together for what seemed like hours, neither saying a word. Sarah's mind moved forward from Adam, onto thoughts of her mother's health and wellbeing, yet Adam was unable to comprehend how just six months had turned Sarah from his wife who adored his every move, to a woman who so clearly flourished apart from him.

He had never expected to see this side of her. He had always imagined her cowering in one corner, pining after him, wishing he would come running back to her whilst he moved forward with his life. Her sudden boldness and disregard for him somehow made him want her back, and he realised for the first time how twisted he was.

He had never appreciated the unconditional love Sarah had lavished over him. Instead he chased after Lilly, who constantly toyed with his emotions. She made him well aware she could leave him in a heartbeat and never give him a second thought. He had given up true love from Sarah, for a disfunctional relationship with Lilly, and now it was too late. Now he knew Sarah would never give him a second chance, not after what he had put her through. He knew that Lilly had her claws so deep inside him she was now binding him to her forever – no matter what, he could never break free from her.

Remorse oozed through his pores like weeping sores. What he had done to Sarah was unforgiveable, yet she chose to forgive him. His head was so lost in Lilly's games that the death of their son had never reached his heart. Not once since Christopher drowned had he cried for him, or thought of him. Lilly had made it painfully clear they would never mention Sarah's or Christopher's name in her presence. She had kept him in a constant cat and mouse game since Christopher's death, so much so that he had never fully taken responsibility for it.

When Christopher had died Lilly filled his head with words of how this was all Sarah's fault: that if Sarah wasn't such a pathetic wife he would never have sought solace in Lilly's arms, and Christopher would never have died. She made him believe that Christopher's death was a blessing in disguise, because now they could be free to be together without Sarah always having a hold over him.

Adam shuddered as he realised just how cold Lilly was and how deeply rooted her hatred towards Sarah was. He had allowed Lilly to taint his love for Sarah, and to use him like a pawn to crush her in her own selfish desire to be the better sister. She had thought that if she could step into Sarah's life and take over it, that she would be better than Sarah in every way. Adam looked over at Sarah, her head in her hands. Despite all this she was now, and would always be, far better and more beautiful than Lilly could ever be. He had allowed Lilly to spin a web of deceit around him. Now he could never win Sarah back, and he could never get rid of Lilly. It was too late.

Chapter Twenty-Four

'Dad,' Sarah screamed running towards her father. She had been sitting with Adam for what felt like hours, yet had only been minutes, worrying about her mother, waiting to see her father.

'My angel,' Harry said, squeezing his daughter. 'It's so good to see you again – how I have missed you. Come, let's get a cup of tea.'

Harry put his arm over Sarah's shoulders to lead her away, but not quick enough to prevent her from catching a glimpse of Lilly coming up behind him. Sarah stopped, stunned by what she was looking at, the blood draining from her face. Harry took one look at her and pulled her quickly along.

'We will talk about it in the coffee shop, Sarah; I was hoping to be the first to tell you, before you had to see for yourself.'

They walked towards the door, which led out of the waiting area, in silence, shock rushing over Sarah like blades of sharpened glass.

'She is pregnant! Are you freaking kidding me? She is pregnant, Dad!' Sarah screamed, the door barely closed behind them. 'When did anyone plan on letting me know that?' she demanded, stopping abruptly and throwing her father's arm off her shoulders. 'I cannot believe you allowed me to walk right into seeing that with no mention of it before. What is she, like, five or six months pregnant?'

'Seven,' Harry said, trying to hold Sarah still, her body shaking from shock. 'Your mother and I planned on telling you when we saw you tonight; we did not know she would be rushed in for an earlier surgery.'

Sarah's eyes burned hot with tears. Christopher would have only been dead two months when Lilly had fallen pregnant with Adam's baby; she had wasted no time in replacing the child they had lost for one of her own.

'Sarah, please, let's go and sit in the coffee shop downstairs. We will talk about it there.'

She followed him mutely, her stomach suddenly convulsing in disgust, nausea submerging her, threatening to unravel every fibre of her being. Was Lilly truly so heartless that she could come in and steal her family away, and then re-create the life she once called her own?

Harry sat Sarah down at a table and motioned to the waiter to bring them a pot of tea.

'Sweetheart, I wanted to spare you this pain so desperately. What your sister has done to you is despicable. We always knew she was jealous of you, but we had no idea to what extent until we found out about the affair.'

'How did you find out, because *I* never told you?'

'When you left so abruptly we couldn't figure out what chased you away. Then a week after you had left Lilly packed her things and told us she was moving out. When we questioned her about where she was moving to she confessed the whole affair with Adam. She told us she was going to live with him.'

'In *my* house?'

'Yes,' Harry muttered, his face strained. The conflict in his heart was a perpetual battle. On one hand Lilly's behaviour was unforgivable, but she still was his daughter and he couldn't throw her aside. On the other hand Sarah's life had been stolen from her, from right under her nose, by her own flesh and blood. He felt like he was betraying Sarah by even talking to Lilly.

Sarah sat bewildered. Lilly had literally tried to just slot into her life. She was living in the house Sarah owned, Sarah designed: the house where Christopher had lived, and played, and showered her with love.

She had no intention of ever moving back into that house, and had signed it over to Adam in the divorce papers. She wasn't willing to go back to a place that would remind her of Adam's betrayal and her son's death. But the thought that Adam and Lilly were just going to start a whole new life, picking up from where she left off, stung every cell in her bleeding heart.

Sarah looked up and saw how these past few months had aged her father. His hair looked greyer than she remembered as it flopped across his forehead, and his dark brown eyes looked muddier. His chiselled face still held the rugged handsomeness it always had, but she noted the wrinkles around his eyes and forehead. He somehow looked as if life was drawing a map across his face, of all the mountains and valleys it had thrown his way. She reached for his hand.

'Dad, the reason I left is because I couldn't face them, but also because I didn't want you and Mom to feel you needed to choose which daughter to side with. Me leaving set you free from that. I don't expect you to turn your back on Lilly or your grandchild; I would never ask that of you.'

'I know, my angel, and that's what makes it even more testing. You have always been the loving and gentle one, while Lilly was always conniving and shrewd, and now you are the one suffering at her hand. I don't know how we brought up two completely different girls.'

'How Lilly turned out is no reflection on you as a father. She made her own choices in life to end up how she did. It's no fault of your own.'

The waiter came and set the tea pot and cups down before them, as Harry went over and hugged his daughter.

'I'm so sorry for what your sister has put you through. You deserve so much better.'

'Thanks, Dad,' Sarah said, squeezing him. 'Now no more talk of Lilly; I'm more interested in how Mom is doing. That's why I came back here in the first place, for her and no one else.'

Harry looked at his daughter as he took his seat, seeing her assured determination to be a survivor and not a victim. He was so proud of her. At least he had achieved one great thing in his life: Sarah. She truly was his greatest achievement. She had created an outstanding career for herself, but more importantly she had a heart of gold. Despite the fact that she had every reason to be bitter, she chose instead to rise on eagle's wings and soar above it all to victory. He felt his tight muscles unravel, knowing with uttermost certainty that she would get through this. She was a fighter, and she would finish stronger than she had begun.

'I spoke to the doctor. She is out of surgery now; he said the coronary artery bypass graft was successful. They have put her in the Cardiac Care Unit for now, waiting for the anaesthetic to wear off, and then we will be allowed in to see her.'

'Oh, thank God,' Sarah breathed easy, pouring tea for them both. 'What a relief. At least I've received some good news today.'

'Yes, it's a huge relief.'

'So how long will she need to be in hospital?'

'They say the duration all depends on the individual and how they are coping. Her surgeon said your mother has healthy heart muscle tissue and should be out of CCU hopefully in a day or two.'

'That's great, Dad! We can hopefully start the new year with Mom healthy. She is a fighter; I know she will pull through.'

'She is a fighter indeed, Sarah, and so are you.' Harry smiled warmly at her, his heart finally at ease; he had his wife and daughter safe and sound.

They made their way back to the waiting area once they had finished their tea. Sarah told her father all about South Africa, and how much it had changed since they had been there. He promised to visit once Sarah's mom was well enough to fly.

Sarah watched as Lilly clung onto Adam's arm the minute they walked through the door, as if staking one last claim on him to remind Sarah to back off. Sarah looked at Adam's embarrassed face as he turned his eyes away. She wondered whether he had wanted to tell her earlier about Lilly being pregnant, or if he was waiting for her to discover it on her own. Either way, she knew now, and it gave her one more reason to want to move forward with her life. It was pointless spending her days and nights with thoughts of them. The only memories she would treasure were her memories of Christopher. All other memories she would just as much rather forget.

The doctor came in and asked Harry to go in and see his wife first, before they were all allowed in. Sarah began walking towards Lilly just as she felt something grab a hold of her legs.

'Sarah!' she heard a familiar little boy's voice. She turned around to see Jamie staring up at her.

'Jamie! Sweetheart, what are you doing here?'

'We are here on holiday and Jamie hurt his arm so we came to the hospital to get it bandaged. Didn't we buddy?' Jake said, coming up behind Jamie.

'Yes, Dad,' Jamie beamed, clearly proud of his bandaged arm.

Sarah bent down to Jamie, as she hugged him. 'This is a lovely surprise! I hope your arm isn't too sore.'

'Nope! It's all better now,' Jamie grinned.

Sarah stood up and looked at Jake, 'It's good to see you. I'm sorry I never called. Things just got a little hectic.'

'I understand,' Jake said, leaning in to kiss Sarah on the cheek, 'Merry belated Christmas and all that,' he smiled at her. 'What are you doing here in London?'

'I should be asking you that?'

'We come up every year for Christmas – it's a tradition Jamie and I have had since he was a little boy. I try to give him the "white Christmas" he hears about in the Christmas carols.'

'Mmm, sounds like an awesome tradition,' Sarah smiled winking at Jamie.

'So, why are *you* here?' Jake frowned.

'Well, I'm actually from here,' Sarah tried to laugh. 'My Mom had to have bypass surgery, so I had to come up to be with her.'

'Will she be okay?'

'Yes, she just woke up; my dad is in with her now. Everything went well.'

Jake smiled warmly at Sarah, 'It's really good to see you again. You are looking well.'

'Thanks,' Sarah blushed, feeling the intensity of his gaze.

'Do you know why there are two people behind you staring at us and whispering?'

Sarah turned to where his gaze went, and laughed. 'That's Adam, the man who had me followed. He is my husband, well ex now. And the pregnant woman at his side is my sister Lilly, who is now seven months pregnant with his baby.'

'What!' Jake screamed, forgetting his manners to remain quiet in a hospital. 'Oh, what a bastard,' Jake said, his nostrils flaring as he clenched his fists, thinking of how he would like to punch him.

'Hey, you have been my knight in shining armour already. You protected me from my stalker. No need to punch Adam. Trust me, he will pay for a lifetime. The punishment of living with my sister for the rest of his life is far worse than any physical injury he could receive.'

Sarah touched Jake's arm to calm him down.

'If you ever change your mind, and want me to beat him to a pulp, I will gladly do it. No man treats you that way and gets away with it.'

'Thanks, Jake. You are one special man.'

'Not special enough to win your heart though?' he asked, eyebrows raised.

'Hey, now that you know what I've been through, do you blame me for not wanting to let love in again.'

Jake leaned in and kissed her forehead, before wrapping her in his arms. 'I understand,' he whispered into her hair. 'But if you change your mind I would welcome you with open arms.'

'I know,' Sarah smiled, letting him go. She saw her father motioning for her to go in to see her mother. 'I've got to go. I will see you back home?' she said looking at Jake and Jamie, realising for the first time she had referred to South Africa as her home. She kissed Jake on the cheek before bending down and hugging Jamie.

'See you soon, little man, and look after that arm now, okay?'

'I will, Sarah,' he grinned, wrapping his little arms around her neck.

Sarah smiled at them as she turned and followed Adam and Lilly in to see her mother.

Chapter Twenty-Five

Sarah eyes scanned her mother's face as she lay on the bed. Her face was a sickly ash grey, as if devoid of any colour or blood vessels. Her thin frame, a far cry from its former plump self, lay limply under the white sheet. Sarah walked in closer, taking in the sullen expression on her father's face as he held tightly onto her mother's weak hand. Lilly stood stone-faced in the far corner of the room, making no attempt to venture any closer to their mother's wrecked body.

'Mom,' Sarah whispered softly, breaking the silence in the room. She watched as her mother moved her head with calculated effort, until her red rimmed eyes met Sarah's.

'My beautiful baby girl,' Hannah smiled weakly, her lips dry and cracked as if mimicking the plains of the desert floor. 'It's so good to see you.'

'You're looking good, Mom,' Sarah lied, trying to remain upbeat in the wake of the operation.

'Mmm, as good as a wet straggly cat,' Hannah teased, the sight of Sarah's happy face stitching up her weary heart.

Sarah stood beside her father and held her mother's hand gently, grateful that, despite how she looked, her doctors were optimistic regarding her progress.

'You are looking good, baby girl; I can see the South African sun has kissed your skin with a golden glow.'

'Thanks, Mom. I feel good, especially now seeing you. I've missed you.'

'I've missed you too,' Hannah smiled, her tears springing forth like hot springs. 'How was Katy's wedding?'

'Oh Mom, it was beautiful. She was delighted with how everything turned out. She sends her love and so do her parents. They were sad you couldn't make it for the wedding.'

'Yes, I will have to come and visit you all as soon as I am well enough.'

'I'd like that, Mom.' Sarah smiled warmly, bending down and kissing her mother's cheek.

'Where is Lilly?' Hannah asked.

'I'm here,' Lilly said, moving into her mother's field of vision

'Oh, there you are. It's so lovely to have my two little angels in the same room together.'

Sarah turned and looked at Lilly. They had not said two words to each other since Sarah had arrived. Sarah watched as Lilly refused to return any eye contact, and instead smiled at their mother.

'I want you both to try to settle what has happened in both your hearts,' Hannah began. 'You are sisters, and if something happens to your dad or me, you two are the only family you have. We need peace, for our sakes as well as yours.'

Sarah squeezed her mother's hand, tears filling her eyes. Her mother was right; Lilly was the only other family she had and she needed peace between them as well. She knew she couldn't live this way any longer.

Sarah looked up to her baby sister, wondering what she had ever done to make her hate her so badly. Jealousy was one thing but Lilly had set out to destroy her life, even at the risk of destroying her own.

'Your mother's right,' Harry spoke up. 'We don't expect it to happen today, but at some point there needs to be love between you.'

'Listen, now is not the time to have this conversation. We came here to see you, Mother. This isn't a counselling session. If I'm going to be forced into some self-righteous lecture then I would rather leave,' Lilly spat hotly.

Sarah looked into her eyes – they burned like hot coals as she glared at Sarah and then at her parents.

'I will wait outside. Come on, Adam,' Lilly said, pulling Adam by the arm and walking out of the room.

'It's okay, Mom, don't worry about us,' Sarah said, seeing the pained look on her mother's face. 'Everything will come right in time, hopefully. Right now let's just focus on the most important thing and that is getting you better.'

Hannah nodded just as the nurse came in and asked them to leave so she could get some rest.

'I will come and see you tomorrow again, Mom, okay? I love you.'

'I love you too, Sarah.' Hannah replied feebly as they left the room.

Sarah saw Lilly seated in the waiting area as she came out from seeing her mother. Adam sat mutely at her side, his face sullen and strained. Sarah smiled slyly; she could just imagine the earful Lilly had given him once they had left her mother's room. She knew he had made a huge mistake choosing Lilly over her, and she felt he knew it too.

'Lilly, can we talk alone?' Sarah asked standing in front of her.

'Whatever you have to say to me can be said in front of Adam,' Lilly snubbed.

Sarah ignored her harsh tone and took a seat beside her, taking a deep breath to calm her violent heart.

'What's done is done,' Sarah began, trying to talk in a controlled tone. 'We can't change the past, but we can determine the future. What Mom said is true, we cannot live separate lives, we are intertwined by blood, and no matter what we will always be sisters.'

She watched Lilly's face for some reaction but got nothing, so she carried on. 'If a life with Adam is what makes you happy then go for it. I've moved on, and I see now that Adam never loved me,' she saw Adam move in his seat uncomfortably. 'Only you will know if he truly loves you, but for your sake I hope what you both share is true love.'

Sarah saw a flicker of fire in Lilly's eyes, and she continued before she had a chance to retaliate. 'I have forgiven Adam for what he has done to me, and likewise I choose to forgive you. Let's move on from here, please, Lilly; let us build a better future from that of our past.'

Lilly's head flung back in a roaring sarcastic laugh, which jolted Sarah; it was not the response she had expected.

'You forgive me?' Lilly scoffed. 'You forgive me? Oh please, Sarah, for once get off your moral high horse. I have done nothing to you – you have done it all to yourself. It's because of your inefficiencies that Adam ran into my arms, and it's because of your blinding trust that you didn't notice an affair right under your own nose. How pathetic can you be? Don't waste your forgiveness on me, I don't want it.'

Sarah felt the blood rush through her veins like hot volcanic lava. Lilly had some nerve talking to her that way; after everything she had done she still did not feel any remorse for her actions. She ground her teeth and clenched her fists, determined that she would move past this, Lilly would not cause her any more pain.

'I forgive you, Lilly, whether you accept it or not. I just hope someday you grow up and realise that this hatred you carry will only leave you brittle and alone.'

Lilly jumped up off her seat like a jumping jack sprung by bursting anger. Her face was tight, her expression loathsome.

'I don't need to sit and listen to you. Come on, Adam, let's go.' She pulled Adam by the arm in an attempt to carry him off, but instead he shrugged off her arm violently and turned to Sarah.

'I'm sorry for what I've done to you. I know I will regret it for the rest of my life. Please don't think I never loved you – I always did and I always will. I was just blinded by foolishness.'

Sarah nodded at him as Lilly grabbed his arm again and marched him down the passage. Her voice echoed though the silent hospital halls hurling insults at him as he walked beside her wimpishly, devoid of a backbone, a cowering reflection of what he once was.

She closed her eyes. If life had taught her anything, it was a vibrating knowledge that what you sow you will reap. She almost felt sorry for Adam. He had so easily succumbed to Lilly's manipulating controlling behaviour, and she feared for Lilly. In the wake of the crumbs of hate and disregard she left along life's journey, at some point she would reap its bitter reward. Lilly seemed to thrive on recklessness, and what she failed to comprehend was that, despite her best efforts to ruin Sarah's life, she had instead trapped herself in a loveless relationship. She failed to notice that the soon-to-be father of her child would resent her with the dawning of the knowledge that she had stolen from him the family he had once taken for granted. Forever Lilly and their child would stand as a monument testifying to the memory of Sarah and Christopher.

Sarah felt her father's arm around her. He had remained distant and silent watching in the shadows as Sarah had tried to reason with Lilly. He saw for himself her desire for reconciliation and Lilly's contrasting desire for discord.

'You have done your bit, my angel; there is nothing more you can do. It is for her to choose the path she walks upon: one of hate or one of love. For you, you have chosen wisely the path of love, as love heals all wounds.'

Sarah allowed her father's words to settle in the crevices of her mind. Every dark place that had plagued her all these months still threatened to surface. She knew she was still fighting for her life. She might be stronger now, but she knew she still needed to face the battlefield of her mind. Every thought that tried to trap her making her feel like a failure as a mother and as a wife, needed to be destroyed. It was one thing to think she had not failed, but it was another to believe it.

The darkness threatened to wrap itself like a smothering blanket in her mind. Her only solace was the knowledge that if she had come this far, and if she had faced those that had tried to destroy her, she could finally win this race and be victorious.

She shook her head in an attempt to clear her mind from the smog. Looking up she smiled at her father, allowing his dark brown eyes to provide the same comfort they always had when she was a child. When she had fallen and hurt herself, or when Lilly had teased and mocked her, his eyes had soothed her pain and calmed her fears. She couldn't understand why she had faced what she had in this life, but she knew one thing for certain – she was no longer obligated to beg for her sister's kindness or love. She was no longer obligated to have her be a part of her life. From this point on she would guard her heart. She would only allow those people into her heart and life who treasured the love she had inside. She would not subject herself any longer to people whose goal it was to trample her down.

'Come on, Dad. It's been a long day – how about we get some supper?' she smiled, standing up and reaching for her father's hand. 'Tomorrow is a new day, a fresh start.'

'It sure is, my angel. It sure is.'

She walked holding onto her father. He had always been like a tree, firmly rooted, unwavering. She was grateful to be by his side again. She was grateful she chose love over hate, because she could clearly see how each path led to such vastly different outcomes.

Chapter Twenty-Six

The car came to an abrupt halt as the driver stopped in front of Jane's apartment. Sarah handed him his money and stepped out onto the pavement. Despite it being New Year's Day the roads were buzzing with traffic, and Sarah had spent most of the morning shopping.

'What's in the bags?' Jane quizzed, kissing her on both cheeks, eyeing the bags in Sarah's hands.

'I did a little shopping for everyone back home,' Sarah smiled proudly, as Jane let her into her apartment.

Sarah had spent the entire morning in the Burlington Arcade looking through every store, trying to find the perfect gifts for Katy, John, Edward and Kevin. For Katy she had chosen an Eau de Parfum from Penhaligon's called Artemisia, which was a floral, fruity and sensual fragrance that she knew Katy would love. For the men, she decided on a gentlemen's grooming kit consisting of Endymion shaving cream and aftershave balm. She had always struggled to shop for men; it seemed the available options of things to purchase weren't as elaborate as they were for women.

'I hope there is something in there for me,' Jane teased, motioning for her to take a seat at the kitchen table.

'There sure is,' Sarah laughed, reaching in the bag and pulling out Jane's gift.

Jane took one look at the House of Cashmere logo on the bag, and threw Sarah a delighted smile as she opened it to find a baby blue cashmere silk crew neck sweater.

'Ooh, I love it,' Jane crooned, rubbing her hands and face all over the sweater. I will wear it tomorrow,' she beamed.

'I'm glad you like it,' Sarah chuckled, crumpling back into the chair looking at the piles of art books strewn all over the kitchen table. 'Mmm, I see you still have no shortage of books in here, hey?'

Jane giggled, 'You know me, ever the art history bookworm.'

Sarah smiled at her friend. It had been a long week. Her mother had been discharged from hospital, and she had spent every day since with them at their home. Despite their insistence for her to spend her remaining time there living with them, she chose not to, and instead remained at the Connaught Hotel. With Lilly and Adam living just down the street from her parents' home, she felt it too strange to be in such close proximity. It had been difficult enough having to pass by their home every day to visit her parents, and her heart still tugged as she remembered how, just a few months before, it had been *her* home, with Christopher running around joyfully inside. She was doing much better now emotionally with regards to everything, but she also knew to take things in stages.

She had spent a very quiet New Year's Eve at her parents' home last night. They had managed to fall asleep by ten o'clock, leaving her to see in the New Year on her own. Seeing her parents had given her the peace she needed to return to South Africa and truly make it her home. She had nothing left in London to come back for, and they had promised to visit her twice a year in South Africa, which were visits she knew she would cherish.

'Tea?' Jane asked, switching the kettle on.

'Oh yes, please. Some Earl Grey or chamomile if you have any.'

'Chamomile is the best I can do,' Jane laughed, reaching into the cupboard and wiggling the box in front of Sarah.

Sarah unzipped her jacket, suddenly warm in the well-heated apartment. She felt right at home with Jane as they had spent many nights here, planning and strategising for up and coming projects they were working on. Jane thrived on working in messy chaos, whereas Sarah preferred everything neat and organised. Jane had always insisted they work in her place, that way she didn't have to tiptoe around Sarah's immaculately neat home.

'So, how are things with the family?' Jane said, setting down the tea and biscuits.

'My parents are well. Mom is doing so much better now. Lilly still won't talk to me. In fact, because she knew I was at my parents' home all week, she refused to visit our mother at all.'

'She is only spiting herself. Her wretched personality will only get her so far in life before she has to own up to her faults.'

'I'm just so glad I'm leaving tomorrow – at least then my parents don't have to be in the middle of Lilly's feud with me.'

Jane eyed Sarah closely, sipping her tea noisily. 'How are you feeling about Adam and Lilly having a baby?'

'It's been heartbreaking to deal with. Them having a baby isn't what breaks my heart, rather it's the knowledge that Christopher's death seemingly had no impact on their lives. Adam adored his son, but somehow Lilly managed to turn his heart into stone.'

'Well, we all know what she is like. You just keep Christopher's memory alive, no matter what they do.'

'Oh I have,' Sarah beamed, biting into her biscuit, watching as the crumbs fell onto her saucer. 'I've designed a children's range of wallpapers and fabrics based on the giraffe Christopher loved as his toy. With every purchase I donate the profits to a children's charity. In that way he will forever be a part of my life.'

'That's awesome, Sarah,' Jane smiled, reaching over and squeezing Sarah's hand.

Sarah felt her phone vibrate in her jeans pocket. She pulled it out and checked her message.

'Happy New Year, princess. Hope this year is your fairytale year. We all miss you.'

Sarah smiled as she read Edward's words. She wondered who 'we all' referred to. She knew Katy and John were still on their honeymoon, so surely he couldn't mean them. Unless he was too shy to admit he was the one missing her.

Jane caught the smile on Sarah's lips. 'And who might that be? That message seems have lit up your face.'

'No one special,' Sarah shrugged, shoving the phone back into her pocket. 'Just Edward wishing me a happy New Year.'

'Ooh, is Edward the deliciously handsome brother of Katy you told me about?'

Sarah laughed. 'Yes, he is the handsome older brother. Did I really tell you that he was handsome?'

'Yes, you did!' Jane shrieked, laughing at how Sarah tried to hide her obvious weakness for Edward.

'Well, he is handsome,' Sarah smiled sheepishly, wondering why her cheeks suddenly felt hot.

'You're blushing,' Jane giggled, 'and don't tell me it's the heater in here making you hot.'

'Nope,' Sarah said, shaking her head violently. 'It's the tea,' she giggled.

Jane laughed, relieved to see that Sarah was so full of joy these last few days.

'So, are you missing him?' Jane's eyes gleamed mischievously.

'I'm missing all of them,' Sarah laughed, her heart telling her she missed Edward the most. 'Edward has promised to show me some mysterious painting he painted when I get back. I'm rather intrigued to find out what it may be.'

'Perhaps it's a painting of him standing in the nude, waiting to ravish you,' Jane giggled as Sarah's nose wrinkled at the thought of the image.

'I sure hope not! I wouldn't know where to put my face if I saw something like that.'

'Well, from what you've told me about him, he seems too sentimental to scare you off with a naked portrait.'

'Yes, I believe I don't need to worry about that.'

Sarah's mind drifted to Edward. What could he possibly have painted all that time ago when they were at Joseph's cottage? It almost seemed like a lifetime ago. So much of her life had changed since Christopher's death. She knew she had started developing feelings for Edward, but she still kept her heart in check. She would not allow any man to just walk in and rummage through her heart and tear down its treasures again. This time she wanted to know it was true, tried and tested love. Right now she didn't even know for sure how deep Edward's feelings for her went. She knew he cared for her, and would do anything for her, but maybe that was just a sense of loyalty from their childhood friendship. She couldn't allow her heart to pine for someone who might not love her. Quickly she suppressed whatever feelings tried to surface, and she turned again to Jane.

'I'm going to miss our chats at this kitchen table, friend. They have been therapeutic to me for many years.'

'They've been therapeutic to me too, Sarah,' Jane smiled warmly. 'I promise to visit though; maybe I could come there for Christmas this year. I would love a Christmas in summer. I've had it with these overrated winter Christmases.'

Sarah chuckled, 'It's a deal then. This Christmas it is. Maybe we could go on a safari in the Kruger National Park?'

'Sounds perfect!' Jane exclaimed, her ginger hair falling playfully around her face, lighting up her green eyes.

'Perhaps you could bring your chocolate drop with?' Sarah teased, referring to Jane's new boyfriend.

'More like chocolate chunk!' Jane giggled. 'I'm sorry you didn't get to meet him; time just wasn't on our side. But if all goes well he will definitely be coming along on our Christmas safari.'

'I look forward to that, my friend,' Sarah smiled. 'At least now you have a new holiday destination to come to.'

'You'd better believe it, and you'd better make sure you always have a spare room for me to stay in.'

'Even if I didn't have any spare place, I would gladly give up my bed for you,' Sarah smiled, grateful that, despite them now living on different continents, they were still both committed to preserving their friendship.

Leaving tomorrow would be bittersweet. On one hand she so looked forward to going back to her new life, and she had a feeling it would be a good life, but on the other hand she would miss the charms of London, her parents and Jane. She would also miss the knowledge of being close to the last place Christopher had been.

Her father had gone with her to Christopher's graveside. She had taken him roses and sat talking to him, telling him all about her new life. She knew he wasn't physically there, that his body lay lifeless beneath her feet, but in her heart she felt as if he heard her speak, as if he gave her his blessing to move forward. She promised to keep his memory alive in her always, and she knew she would never break that promise. He was her beloved son, her firstborn, and his loving spirit and joyful nature had defined her and changed her life from the moment he was born. Even though she had had only a few years on earth to share with him, she wouldn't trade those years for anything. The love he showed her daily had inspired her to be the best person she could be, and she would forever remember his smile, his smell and the way his face lit up when she came into the room. From this point forward she would live her life the way he lived, full of joyful energy. She would keep his spirit alive in her by celebrating life.

Chapter Twenty-Seven

Sarah checked her watch frantically. It was half past five. Yanking open the car door, she set her stilettoes down into the gravel of the parking lot, instantly regretting not obeying her instinct to keep flat shoes in the car. Things had been too darned busy to give into a nagging inclination to care for her already tired feet.

She locked the car, and marched rapidly through the parking lot, grinding her teeth as she walked, dreading the reality of the impact the gravel would have on her immaculate overpriced designer shoes. With each grinding step she could envision the stones wearing down at her heels.

Finally solid ground, she breathed, as her foot hit the paved pathway. She would never understand why they made gravel car parks! She made her way through the crowd as she entered uShaka Marine World. Kevin would be waiting and she knew she was late, but right now there was a more pressing matter to attend to.

Winding through throngs of tourists with the beat of the African drum somewhere in the distance, she wound along the village walk, barely taking in its thatched roofs and African curio shops. Finally she caught a glimpse of what she needed.

Darting into the beachwear store, she headed straight for the flip flops hanging against the wall. Damn, they only had bright yellow, but right now she couldn't be picky. Rummaging through the rack she found her size and headed for the till. The cashier gave her a puzzled look as she ripped off the tags even before handing over the money.

Pulling off her black stilettoes, she slipped her pale blue painted toenails into the yellow flip flops and breathed a sigh of relief. She saw out of the corner of her eye the cashier giving a hidden chuckle as she took in the sight. She knew the flip flops did not go with her formal black lace skin tight dress, nor did they do any justice to her perfectly shaped calf muscles, but right now her fashion sense was the last thing on her mind.

Throwing her high heels into her bag she walked slowly out of the store, head held high, and headed for the restaurant where Kevin was waiting.

It had been a long three weeks, with her fighting off jet lag and arranging the final finishes for the eco-friendly hotel she had helped design. Finally her range of eco-friendly wallpapers clung beautifully to the walls of the hotel, and the hotel and her innovative wallpapers had made the cover of *VISI Magazine*, which was an awesome achievement.

Today had been the hotel launch, and Sarah had spent the day schmoozing with the investors, smiling at the cameras and giving interviews. She was exhausted, but she had promised to take Kevin out for dinner, to thank him for his hard work and to make sure she was up to speed with everything in the business. He would be on leave for the next three weeks, and she wouldn't want to call him during his leave for any information.

Finally she saw the sign she was looking for, the summer sea breeze clinging humidly to her already perspiring skin. She felt as if she was playing dodgem cars, trying to bump and grind her way through the throngs of people walking in from every angle, most of them in their bikinis having spent the day either at the beach below or at the uShaka Wet & Wild waterpark. The sixteen hectare theme park seemed too small during these summer months, as people descended from all over South Africa and the world to soak up the Durban summer madness.

Sarah caught a glimpse of the sun beginning to descend as she made her way into Moyo restaurant.

Moyo had become Kevin's and her favourite spot to sit and strategise. It was an African-themed restaurant for sophisticated dining, yet its on-the-beach atmosphere gave it a more relaxed feel where you could sit and listen to live African music or watch Zulu dancing.

She scanned the tables for Kevin, catching a glimpse of him seated at a table overlooking the ocean.

'Oh Kev, I'm sorry to keep you waiting! That hotel launch took longer than expected, and I tried my best to sneak out as soon as no one was watching,' Sarah hurriedly spoke, bending down as Kevin kissed her cheek.

'No problem, sweets. I was enjoying the view too much to notice the time.'

Sarah sat down opposite him, throwing her bag on the mosaic Moroccan-style wrought iron table. Kevin caught a glimpse of her outfit.

'And this?' he said, swinging his arms up and down motioning towards her ensemble.

'Hey, my feet were sore, so I popped into the Billabong store and bought myself some flip flops. Don't worry, I didn't go to the launch like this,' she giggled, watching the corners of his mouth and eyes crinkle in amusement.

'Mmm, I would hope not! I was imagining seeing you on the front page of *VISI Magazine* in a killer black dress, only to see bright yellow flip flops below.'

'Hey, I'm an artist, so I could pull it off! We do get some artistic licence, you know. People seem to think being quirky makes you a better artist,' Sarah winked, knowing she was the least artistic in her dress sense.

'There is quirky and then there is bad taste,' Kevin laughed. 'Ooh, ooh, before I forget: your father called, he said he tried reaching you on your cell phone but you didn't answer. He has booked flights for your mother and himself – they arrive the end of next month.'

'Fabulous!' Sarah squealed.

Since she had come back to South Africa her mother had recovered marvellously well, and had insisted her father book them tickets to come and stay over for a month. She was so excited to show them her new home, and have them be a part of her life here. She knew their presence would put the final seal on making this place her home.

'Oh, and the other thing,' Kevin continued, reaching into his jacket pocket and pulling out a slightly crumpled envelope, 'Edward came and dropped this off for you. He said to tell you that if you want to see the painting you have to agree to what's inside.'

Sarah scrunched her nose as she looked at Kevin, his eyes sparkling. 'I take it from that look you already know what's inside?' she questioned.

'Hell, yes, and I think it's oh so fabulous! I would kill you if you don't go along with it.'

Sarah carefully peeled back the fold on the envelope, and pulled out the papers inside. A dried piece of lavender fell from the pages as she opened them, wondering with anticipated excitement what Edward was up to now.

'You have got to be joking!' Sarah exclaimed as she read the letter. 'Does he think I must drop everything just because he wants me to?' she giggled, trying to sound annoyed, but instead butterflies fluttered in her stomach.

'You'd better drop everything! This couldn't have come at a better time, Sarah; you need a break,' Kevin protested, watching her face closely.

Sarah read the letter again.

'Be at the harbour on Friday at two thirty in the afternoon. I've attached a list of things you need to pack for the five day trip. All will be revealed on the cruise to Mozambique and the Portuguese Islands.

Edward xx'

'He is taking me on a cruise for five days – all this to show me a painting?' Sarah mused, her heart beating faster, her mind racing. What would five days alone with Edward be like with just the two of them sailing into the sunset?

She giggled, as Kevin snatched the letter from her and started reading out the list of items she needed to pack. Her mind raced forward; it was Wednesday, and that only gave her one day to process it all. She hadn't seen Edward since she returned home, not even to give him the gift she had bought him. She had sent it instead via courier to his office. He had sent her a text to thank her and remind her that he would still show her the painting, but had made her promise to allow him to reveal it anyway he chose. Now she could see why he had forced her into the promise; he probably knew she would have tried to wangle her way out of it if she weren't bound by her word.

'Ooh, this is so romantic,' Kevin crooned, folding the letter and slipping it back into the envelope.

'Romantic? Oh please, Kev, don't get any bright ideas here. Edward and I are just friends,' Sarah emphasised, trying to convince herself.

'Mmm, just friends. Since when do friends surprise each other with cruises?'

'Maybe the painting is hanging on the ship, so he has no choice but to take me there.'

'I highly doubt that MSC cruises commissioned Edward to paint them a masterpiece in the middle of Joseph's cottage almost seven months ago,' Kevin chuckled, his eyebrow raised sarcastically. 'Just be open to the possibility, Sarah, that's all I'm saying.'

'I think I need to change the subject,' Sarah teased, snatching the envelope out of Kevin's hand. 'Where are these waiters when you need them!'

Kevin laughed heartily, as Sarah tried to cover her now blushing bright pink face with the metal bound menu. She deserved happiness, and he was thrilled to see such a dramatic change in her since she came back from London. It was as if chains that had held her hostage were broken there, and had set her free to truly move forward and find herself again.

The waitress came to take their order, as another waitress came to wash their hands in warm rose water and paint their face in white tribal Xhosa dots.

'Well, in an effort to abide by your sudden desire to change the subject, I have some news I've been bursting to tell you all week!'

'You do? Spill the beans!' Sarah giggled, sitting up straight in her chair, watching as Kevin suddenly cleared his throat as a gesture to make the grand announcement.

'I asked Annie to marry me,' he screamed, loud enough for the other patrons to turn and look at him.

'What!' Sarah shrieked, jumping off her chair and running over to hug Kevin. 'Why the heck didn't you say something sooner!' she said, slapping him on the arm.

'Well, I was waiting for the right moment. This week has been insanely busy.'

'Not busy enough for you not to tell me your big news! Oh Kev, I'm so happy for you guys! Annie is the sweetest; you two are perfect together. Details, please, I want all the details!' She giggled, sitting back down in her chair, and motioning to the waitress to bring over a bottle of champagne for them to celebrate.

'Well...' Kevin started, sitting up proudly, 'You know we've been together for what feels like forever, so I wanted it to be perfect but could never figure out just what to do.'

'Yes,' Sarah said excitedly, smacking her lips with excitement.

'We always used to drive past this house, and Annie would always mention how one day when we got married, she would love for us to live in a house like that one. She has been saying this for the last five or so years. Anyway... about two months back I saw the house go on sale and I immediately contacted the real estate agent and put in an offer to purchase it.'

'You did what?' Sarah screamed, clapping her hands. 'How exciting,'

'Excitement wasn't my initial feeling when it dawned on me the commitment I was about to make! But I knew I wanted to spend the rest of my life with Annie, and so giving her her dream home was all I could think about.'

'And so it should be.'

'Yes,' Kevin smiled broadly. 'The house was officially transferred into my name last week, so on Saturday I took her for a drive, and when we arrived at the house I took out the keys and let us inside.'

'Didn't she ask how you got the keys?'

'Yes, she did,' Kevin chuckled at the memory. 'I kept telling her to go inside, that I would tell her inside.' He paused, bouncing in his seat excitedly, 'As she entered the door, I had a huge sign hanging from the roof saying: *Welcome home, Annie. This house is ours if you will marry me?*'

'Oh Kevin, how romantic!' Sarah exclaimed.

'It truly was. The minute she saw the sign she screamed and spun around to look at me, and I was on one knee, ring in hand, asking her to marry me.'

'She said yes, of course,' Sarah giggled.

'How could she say no to me?' Kevin said, trying to sound as manly and important as possible.

'She must have gone crazy, knowing how she is!'

'She went ballistic! She jumped and screamed like a beach ball on steroids, running around the house, holding me and kissing me, and staring at the rather large one carat diamond on her finger.' Kevin beamed proudly.

'I can't believe you didn't tell me about this sooner, or even let me know you were planning all this.'

'I kind of needed to keep it secret for myself, because if I opened my mouth and told one person I was afraid I would slip and tell Annie, so I put a tight seal on my lips.'

The waitress came and set their food down in front of them, and poured them glasses of champagne. Sarah raised her glass to Kevin, 'To Kevin and Annie, may your lives overflow with abundant love, laughter and joy!'

'Thanks, sweets,' Kevin said shyly, clinking Sarah's glass.

'Anything you need for the wedding, just let me know. I'm there to help!'

'That's an offer I will gladly accept!' Kevin chuckled. He raised his glass once more, 'To a new year of adventure and love for both of us,' he smiled, winking at Sarah.

'I'll drink to that,' she giggled. 'Cheers.'

Sarah's heart swelled with joy for Kevin. He deserved to be happy, and she knew Annie made him happy in her own unique and adorable way. She couldn't imagine anyone more perfectly suited to Kevin than Annie. She was quirky and cute, constantly bubbly and happy, as if her heart was a joy factory. She had one more thing to look forward to this year, and that would be witnessing them walking down the aisle. She already had a feeling this would be a fabulous and amazing year.

Chapter Twenty-Eight

The sun streamed through her window. It was Thursday, and tomorrow she would be going on a cruise with Edward. She swung her feet off her bed and stopped herself. Was she mad? Going on a cruise with Edward! Was she really ready to embrace whatever that meant?

She allowed her toes to gently touch the ground, a smile somehow curling upon her lips, despite the apprehension in her heart.

Allowing the muscles in her legs to move, she stood up on her tippy toes, and made her way into the bathroom. Taking one look in the mirror she knew some grooming was required. A day at the hair salon was a definite must, with a new hair colour a possible option. Right now she wasn't sure what. Then her eyebrows needed to be waxed. She looked at them more closely and grimaced. How did she not notice the unruly hairs peeking out? The last three weeks had really been gruelling; she hadn't had time to go for her usual beauty salon treatments.

Grabbing her electric toothbrush, she slowly squeezed a pea-sized amount on the tip of the brush, as she brought it to her mouth. With the toothbrush on full speed, she allowed it to move merrily along her teeth, as she mentally went through the items Edward had put on the list. Adding to her mental list was what she knew she needed to get for herself.

Nerves and excitement fluttered around in her tummy, keeping her constantly on edge. The suspense he constantly seemed to have her in made her heart flutter all the more. Edward seemed to have turned a simple painting into an entire holiday aboard a cruise ship. She giggled silently to herself. What on earth did he have planned?

Sarah suddenly realised that she needed to get a move on. Her feet however seemed to match the daze engulfing her, as they moved to a slow rhythm beating to their own drum. Grabbing her towel, she threw it over the shower door and turned on the taps, allowing the warm water to soothe her muscles and reset her rhythm. It was ten o'clock. She needed to be at the salon by eleven and get a move on with this day.

Sarah parked her car in the Gateway shopping mall parking lot, and ran into the mall, mapping the familiar pathways to where her salon was situated on the ground floor.

The salon was full, as she saw Rocky, her hair stylist, waving at her.

'Hey, beautiful,' he smiled at her, motioning for her to sit in the chair. 'How was London?'

'As good as it could be under the circumstances,' Sarah smiled, trying to recall when she had told him she was going to London.

'I'm glad to have you back! Katy's been keeping me abreast of all the news, since I haven't seen your gorgeous face in ages' He smiled, having witnessed the confusion on her face.

Katy had been his client for years, and she had always spoken of her "sister" Sarah. She was everything Katy described and more. 'What are we doing with this hair today? Your usual trim?'

'Actually, I'm leaving for a cruise tomorrow, and was hoping to add some colour to my hair. What would you suggest?'

'To be honest, I love your hair the way it is. But if you really want to add some colour we can add some highlights just to give it some depth?'

'Okay, that sounds good, and then the usual trim.'

Rocky moved away from her to go and mix the colour and get the strips of foil to apply the highlights. Sarah's mind wandered back to her time in London. It had worked out to be a really therapeutic time for her, a time where she could feel that she could open her heart to love again.

When she had initially thought of going there she was so afraid. But now she knew it had brought the healing she so needed. The pain of Christopher's death hadn't gone away, but at least it felt a little more bearable now. No longer did it seem to entangle her every moment of the day. She knew she was keeping him forever alive in her heart with her collection, and it gave her a sense of comfort.

She watched as Rocky painted on the dye in pieces on her hair. Smiling to herself she began to relax, as his assistant handed her a steaming hot cappuccino. Its pleasant aroma wafted up her nose, reminding her she had forgotten to eat before she left home. She closed her eyes, knowing she would be here for a while.

By the time Sarah was done with her hair it was after two o'clock. She still needed to go and buy a swimsuit for the trip, as well as a few pairs of shorts.

She went up the escalator towards the food court, needing to quiet the rumblings in her stomach before proceeding with her shopping spree. Standing in the queue at Nandos she ordered her quarter chicken, chips and a roll, in extra hot peri peri flavour.

Smiling to herself as she collected the order, she meandered through the seating area, trying to find a seat where she could have a little space from the maddening crowd.

Suddenly she felt icy fingers on her shoulder as she took her seat, and a familiar voice resounded in her ear.

'Fancy seeing you here?'

Jasmine.

Sarah didn't even need to look up. She knew that chipper voice anywhere.

'Hi, Jas,' Sarah replied without turning around.

Jasmine came around and pulled out a chair at the table. Sitting down, she stared at Sarah for a while.

'It's been a long time,' Jasmine began.

'Yes it has, hey. Last time was up at the cottage.' Sarah looked up at her. She was as stunning as ever but her face scowled like a spoilt brat.

'How's Edward?' Jasmine enquired, her eyes becoming like slits.

'Fine, I guess.'

'Does he have another girlfriend?'

Sarah looked at her bewildered. Surely this beauty queen shouldn't be worried about her ex boyfriend's love life, when she had probably moved on herself already.

'Not that I know of, Jas. But that's none of my business, to be honest.'

'Sorry, Sarah. I don't mean to badger you about Edward. He just seemed to suddenly want to move on from me.' She swung her head to the left, and flicked her hair back. 'I'm not saying our relationship was perfect. To be honest, I never saw Edward as the serious type to propose or anything. But we were having fun, and I don't know why that suddenly wasn't enough for him anymore?'

Sarah took a sip of her mango juice, hoping it would quench the burn of the peri peri that now sauntered down her throat. From the way Edward had spoken at Katy's wedding, it sounded like he had left Jasmine for her. But she didn't know for sure, and definitely wasn't going to tell Jasmine that. She was still trying to figure out if Edward really cared for her, and if he did she definitely wasn't interested being with someone who wasn't the type to get serious. She had been through enough heartache.

The cruise started to seem like a bad idea. Was Edward of the idea that she would be his next fling? No! He definitely knew the pain she had been through. There is no way he would make a move on her if he wasn't serious.

Sarah caught herself imagining Edward kissing her. She squeezed her eyes shut to remove the image. Was she moving too fast, thinking Edward felt something for her that he actually didn't feel?

Looking back at Jasmine, she realised she hadn't responded to her.

'Jas, I suggest you move on. You are a pretty girl; I'm sure any man would have you in a heartbeat.'

Jasmine laughed sarcastically. 'Oh, don't get me wrong, Sarah. I've already moved on. I'm just trying to understand what went on in Edward's head that's all.'

Sarah shrugged her shoulders emphatically. 'Wish I knew. Sorry, Jas. If it's closure you want, I suggest you talk to him.'

Jasmine gave Sarah the most fake smile she had ever seen, and pushed her chair out and walked away without uttering another word.

Sarah breathed a sigh of relief as she took another mouthful of food. She hoped she was making the right decision going away with Edward.

Despite her brief encounter with Jasmine, she couldn't help but still feel excited about tomorrow.

Chapter Twenty-Nine

Sarah stared wide eyed at the magnificent *MSC Opera* ship docked before her. Its thirteen decks rose up gracing the Durban skyline, making her feel like a midget in comparison. The thought that this splendid hotel would float on water with her and over two thousand guests for the next five days, blew her mind. Sarah pondered the logistics of it all. The crew would need to have on board enough food for all passengers, and the ship would need to generate its own electricity for its entire two hundred and seventy-five metre length.

She looked around anxiously for Edward in the crowd. He had left her a text message to tell her to go ahead and board the ship without him. Why without him, she wondered? What was he up to?

She scanned the crowds again, hoping to see his familiar face. She felt a little daunted alone, surrounded by all these strangers, but was excited at what possibilities lay ahead.

Handing her boarding pass, luggage and passport to the crew member, she proceeded up the ramp to embark the ship. The sun beat boldly on her back, as excited travellers rushed past her, eager to get on board. She paused, and closed her eyes momentarily. She had never been on a ship of this magnitude before, and being here with Edward made it all the more enchanting.

The ship was magnificent! She took her key card from the woman at the reception on deck five, and made her way to the staircase to find her room on deck nine. Everything was opulent, sheer extravagance, in its art deco design.

Sarah allowed her feet to trail merrily on the carpeted floor in their geometric patterns, as her hand ran over the golden hand rails. She felt her thighs burn as she ascended the staircase, trying to dodge the scurrying passengers also eager to find their rooms. She felt no need to rush, instead her eyes scanned every nook and cranny for a glimpse of Edward. Meandering through the dimly lit passage ways, she finally found room nine hundred and twelve and inserted the keycard into the lock. The lock immediately clicked, signalling to her she was free to enter. With a pounding heart she swung open the door, half expecting to see Edward strewn on the bed.

Sarah laughed self-consciously, as her eyes immediately scanned the tiny ocean-view room. There was definitely no Edward in sight. She breathed a sigh of relief, yet felt a pang of disappointment pinch the corners of her heart.

The room was quaint; she took in its dimensions, estimating it was probably twenty metres square. Her critical designer eye immediately scanned each detail for any room for improvement. There was none. With this tiny space there was not much someone could do to make the space more functional. Her only criticism would be the bed linen, with its dull green duvet cover in a busy leaf pattern, matching the floral painting on the wall. She giggled to herself, looking at the fabric. She was glad she didn't design something so kitsch. Her ranges of fabrics were definitely trendier.

Putting her handbag on the bed, she noticed a note in Edward's handwriting.

'Welcome on board, princess.

Meet me on deck eleven with your life jacket, by the pool.

Edward xx'

Sarah looked around the room as she searched for where her life jacket might possibly be. It had a queen sized bed with side tables, with just enough space to move around the bed. There was a dressing table at a strange angle in the left corner, with a bar fridge and tiny television the size of a computer monitor on the right. She looked in the bathroom and gasped. How on earth would she fit in that tiny excuse for a shower? She giggled at the thought, imagining her daily fight with the shower curtain just to see who would get a splash of water first.

She heard a knock at the door and went to open it to find her luggage propped up against it. Pulling it in she felt the tug on her muscles. She had packed too much! But who could prepare for what you might need all the way out at sea.

The life jacket. She remembered. She pulled open the cupboard, taking in its limited dimensions, and noticed the bright red life jacket on the top shelf. Grabbing it, she bolted out of her cabin, hoping she would find the pool and Edward on deck eleven.

'What took you so long?' Edward smiled, leaning over and kissing Sarah on the cheek.

'I got so lost trying to navigate this ship. It's a nightmare!'

'Have you settled into your room okay? I'm in the room next door to you. So if you need anything just shout.'

'Thanks, Edward. And thanks for all this,' Sarah looked around, pointing at the ship, not sure what to say exactly. 'Doubt I could ever outdo this surprise.'

'It's not a competition. I wanted you to get to relax. No better place to relax than away from it all aboard a ship, out on the ocean.'

'That's for sure,' Sarah giggled, noticing how good he looked in his white shorts and blue striped v-neck t-shirt. She hadn't spoken to him since the day she had left for London, and right now that felt like a lifetime ago. Edward studied her face, noticing the change in her. There was a sense of peace that hadn't existed before.

'Seems the trip to London did you wonders?'

'Mmm, it did. I will tell you all about it later. So what's with the life jacket? New fashion statement?'

Edward chuckled, 'No, although it looks good on you. We have to do a safety drill before the ship sails. It's easier to be on the deck already, where your drill will take place when the siren goes, because everyone starts running to their cabins for their life jackets and it's a nightmare to get back up after they shut down the elevators.'

'Aah, I see you are quite the pro at this?' Sarah winked at Edward mischievously.

'A pro? No, but I have been on board this cruise before, in my younger days when I was looking for a five day party. But I'm all grown up now.' With that Edward stuck out his chest and stretched his muscular frame ever so tall for emphasis.

'All grown up? I think not,' Sarah quipped. ' When I look at you I feel like we are still children, running around your parents backyard.''

Edward's face suddenly grew serious and his voice husky, 'I hope by the end of this trip you see me for the man I truly am.' His eyes burnt with intensity as he took her hand and led her off to where they needed to have their safety drill, just as the drill siren sounded.

The drill was tedious and once it was over Sarah was relieved to be done with it. Edward took her life jacket to leave it in her cabin, while she waited for him on the viewing deck, waiting for the ship to leave the harbour.

The ship began to move just as Edward returned to her side, his digital camera in hand. 'I thought we could take pics to show everyone when we get back,' he said, pointing the camera at her. Click. 'Mmm, perfect!' he winked at her, as he grabbed her hand and ran with her to the other side of the ship. 'You will get the best view of the city from this side,' he smiled, leaning down behind Sarah and angling the camera in the perfect position to take a selfie. 'Smile and look like you are having the time of your life,' he teased, as he took the shot.

Sarah smiled up at him, his scent wafting up her nose. If only he knew that she *was* having the time of her life. She couldn't remember a happier moment.

They watched as the city of Durban diminished as they sailed away. The Durban skyline looking breathtaking against the afternoon sun, its high rise buildings and the Moses Mabhida stadium standing tall, making their statement and testifying to the beauty of the city.

Sarah breathed deeply as she stared at the Moses Mabhida stadium. Katy had taken her there when she had first landed. She couldn't have imagined that a few months later she would be sailing off into the sunset with Edward's arm gently slung around her.

The corners of Sarah's mouth curled up slightly, as she realised how Edward had seemed to have put his arm around her, so gently, almost hoping she didn't notice, but hoping she would noticed at the same time.

The crowd began cheering as the South African captain was airlifted by helicopter off the ship, headed back for dry land.

'So,' Edward began, 'how about we make use of those sexy shorts of yours by going and joining the party by the pool?'

Sarah blushed bright pink, 'Umm, I wouldn't call my shorts sexy, but okay,' she smiled shyly, hearing the music starting up on the pool deck.

They headed down to the deck and Edward ordered her a jungle juice cocktail at the bar. Before she would protest, one of the members of the crew grabbed her hand and pulled her into the centre of the deck. 'What's your name?' he whispered into her ear,

'Sarah,' she whispered back.

'Good afternoon, everyone, and welcome to the *MSC Opera*. My name is Charles and I am part of the Dream Team, your live entertainment on board!' His voice rang out as a roar and applause erupted on the ship. 'It's time to get this party started, and Sarah here has agreed to start it off with me!' With that he grabbed Sarah as the music started and he began to salsa with her. Her body took over, as it recalled all the steps she had learnt years before.

'Come along, everyone, join in the fun!' a lady called over the microphone, clearly also a member of the Dream Team. Sarah caught sight of Edward's amused look as he leant against the bar watching her dance. She giggled hysterically, finally unable to keep to the steps and prompting Charles to set her free. She scampered over to Edward, who grabbed her when she neared him, and continued to salsa with her.

'I didn't know you could dance like this, princess?'

'A girl has got to keep some secrets,' she giggled as he pulled her towards him just as the song ended. Breathless he let her go and handed her the cocktail.

'Thanks,' she smiled, still panting for breath, 'What a workout!'

They sat down at one of the tables beside the pool just as the music started up again, but this time there was a dance crew of ladies in sexy Spanish outfits dancing to the rhythm of the beat.

Edward pulled out a folded schedule from his pocket. 'There's lots to do on the ship. So we have to plan our time wisely to fit it all in,' he said seriously, his tone of voice giving away his undying excitement. 'The ship is headed to Barra Lodge and the Portuguese Islands. I've arranged for day trips once we anchor, so we can tour Inhambane in Mozambique.' He looked over at Sarah, 'Hope that is okay with you?'

'Yes, sure,' Sarah smiled, nervous and excited at the same time.

'Great! Now, for today we can just relax and tour the ship. Then this evening is dinner on deck five at the La Caravella restaurant at six o'clock. The dress code for tonight is casual Italian, so you have to wear green, white and red. Did you get the things on the list I gave you?'

'Yup, I did! 'Sarah smiled, now understanding the reason for the specifics on the list for her clothing. 'How about I meet you on deck five for dinner. There is something I need to sort out first, if that's okay with you?'

Edward gave her a puzzled look, but nodded in agreement. With that Sarah bounced off, grabbing a slice of pizza on the side bar as she moved towards the far end of the ship, headed for the reception desk on deck five. There was something she wanted to do for Edward tonight, and she would need some help arranging it. She crossed her fingers hoping the crew could help her.

Chapter Thirty

Sarah made her way to the restaurant. Her plan was in motion. She knew Edward probably thought she had forgotten, because she hadn't mentioned anything all day.

Her heart fluttered. Wiping her sweaty palms on her dress, she made her way to the head waiter to ask for where Edward was seated.

Edward beamed as Sarah walked towards him in her white summer dress, green and red chiffon scarf, and white sandals, her hair cascading down her shoulders, with a white rose pinned to the side. She was a vision of beauty, he thought, noticing for the first time the highlights in her hair.

He rose as she neared him and pulled the chair out for her, motioning for her to sit down. Sarah smiled up at him as she sat, taking in his full white shirt and pants, with a green, white and red woven belt.

The waiter caught her eye and gave her a thumbs up and wink to let her know the plan was in progress.

Sarah scanned the menu; each dish was in line with the Italian themed evening, from bruschetta to various pastas and tiramisu for dessert.

Their table had an ocean view, and they chatted as they watched the sun set over the water, changing the hue of the sky to different shades of orange and dark blues. The restaurant had a very opulent design, just like the rest of the ship, with gold detailing set against dark wood panelling, and lemon yellow tablecloths and chair upholstery. The down lights littered the ceiling – as they glowed brighter, the darker it became outside.

Edward watched Sarah's face light up as she described every detail she discovered on the ship. The glow of excitement made his heart explode with joy. He knew this was the best way he could spend time with her: here on the ocean, away from it all, just the two of them.

They were lulled into a comfortable silence as they enjoyed each course of the meal, their Polish waiters serving them with astounding efficiency and great enthusiasm.

Suddenly the silence was broken, as the waiters seemed to all line up and started singing excitedly in Italian. Edward couldn't understand the words, but he knew the tune of the song all too well. His eyes shot to Sarah, as he noticed she had been staring at him, her face beaming and eyes glistening with excitement.

'Sarah,' he began, as the line seemed to head straight towards him, all singing louder and more excitedly as they neared him.

She stood up and giggled, joining in on the parade, but singing to the tune in English. 'Happy birthday to you, happy birthday to you, happy birthday dear Edward, happy birthday to you!' She screamed at the last word, just as the waiters presented Edward with a cake brightly lit with candles.

Edward laughed loudly, as he took in a deep breath to blow them out.

'Wait, you need to make a wish,' Sarah screamed, over the cheers from the other passengers seated at the tables besides them.

'My wish has already come true,' Edward winked, as he leaned in and blew them out.

The waiters cheered and cut them slices of cake. Edward noticed one of the waiters leaving a gift on the table and smiling at Sarah.

'What's this?' Edward inquired.

'My gift to you. I had the waiters keep it here in the restaurant, so you didn't see me bring it in. Did you think I forgot today was your birthday?' she giggled, clearly amused that she managed to surprise him.

'I think even I forgot it was my birthday in my excitement to be on board the ship with you.'

Sarah looked at him seriously for a minute, as she took in his words.

'Open the gift!' she eventually exclaimed, waving her hands in excitement towards the gift.

Edward tore open the yellow wrapping paper, as the Michael Kors box was revealed beneath.

'What's this?' he asked, staring at the box.

'Umm, I think the plan is to open it to find out!' Sarah laughed, waiting to see his reaction as he opened it.

Edward gently lifted the lid to see the white gold watch tucked into the box.

'Sarah! This is beautiful!' He said, lifting the watch and turning it over.

He noticed the inscription on the back.

'Moments with you are always memorable. SL'

Sarah blushed as she saw the smile cover his face. Edward rose and came over to her. Leaning in to her he kissed her slowly and gently on her cheek, feeling them grow more pink beneath his lips.

'Thank you, princess,' he whispered in her ear. 'This is the best birthday I can ever remember, because I'm sharing this moment with you.'

Sarah felt her heart burst with joy. She couldn't think of any other place she would rather be.

Chapter Thirty-One

Sarah took one last look in the mirror, reapplying some lip gloss, and excitedly made her way to meet Edward for breakfast. They had sat in the Cotton Club listening to live music well into the early hours of the morning, as Sarah had filled Edward in on her trip to London

'Morning, princess,' Edward greeted, rising from the table as she was seated by the waiter.

'Morning,' Sarah said cheerfully.

'How did you sleep?'

'It took a while to adjust to the ship's constant rocking, but eventually I managed to fall asleep. And you?'

Edward motioned to the waiter to bring them some coffee, 'Sleeping was no problem, but that shower! OMG! Who designed that thing? Honestly, they forget real people have to fit in there.'

Sarah giggled, remembering her own fight with the shower curtain that morning. It was awful. Once she opened the tap, the shower curtain stuck to her wet body like glue, and she had to wrestle it to let her go, with barely enough place to turn around in the shower to wash herself.

Edward smiled down at her, as the waiter approached to take their orders.

'It's beautiful here,' Sarah whispered as the waiter left, smiling out at the view of the ocean. Edward watched as the sun's rays danced across her face, highlighting her beauty.

'It is,' he said, referring more to her than to the view. 'Have you got your costume on under there?' he asked, pointing to her dress.

'Yes,' she smiled shyly, noting how he looked at her.

The food arrived and they ate in a comfortable silence. After her evening sharing with him the highs and lows of her trip to London, she somehow felt more relaxed, as if she had offloaded her bleeding heart once and for all. She had told him about her past, now she wanted to focus on her future. Her future seemed as bright and beautiful as the sun rising over the horizon.

'So, what's the plan for today?' Sarah eventually asked, breaking the silence.

'Well, the ship is docked here in Mozambique, and we are going to do the tour of Inhambane today.'

'You mean I must get into that rubber dinghy and have it take me to shore? Edward, I'm petrified I will be eaten by sharks!'

Edward chuckled to himself. 'Do you really think I would bring you all this way to lose you to a shark?' His face a strange mix of sincerity and playfulness.

Sarah stared at him wide eyed. All she was thinking about was the rubber dinghy. She really wasn't the adventurous type, and for her a trip to shore on that counted as an adventure.

Sarah flung her legs into the water as instructed. They had just taken the rubber dinghy from the ship to the shoreline and her knuckles were as white as snow from holding on so tightly to Edward. Her heart still beat wildly at the memory of the boat being tossed in the waves, threatening to throw them all into the shark infested waters. Edward had laughed the entire time, as she screamed and shrieked as each wave crashed against them. The crew member walked her through the shallow waters from the boat until her feet touched the shoreline.

'Are you okay, princess?' Edward asked, still amused. Sarah looked at him crossly, folding her arms against her chest before breaking out in a relief of laughter. She had survived.

'There has got to be a better way to get from that ship to shore. Honestly! These rubber dinghies are not safe!'

'No one has died yet!' Edward chuckled, 'Come on, let's go find our tour guide.'

Edward grabbed her hand and they followed the crew members who ushered them to the correct line to stand in. There were many different tours going on, but they were in tour bus one. Their local tour guides name was Anesio, and he was born and bred in this region of Mozambique.

The day was splendid. Edward made sure not to leave Sarah's hand for a minute. They toured the local market in Inhambane, seeing how the makeshift tables were laden with the famous Mozambique prawns, different fruits from the region, as well as handcrafted arts and crafts.

Edward bought Sarah a handmade straw bag as a memento of the day, which she slung over her shoulder with pride. The area wasn't well developed and it was clear the locals lived in poverty, yet the smiles on their faces could light up an entire night's sky.

Sarah reflected how this proved that money was not a source of joy. It was contentment that brought about joy, as well as having the right people around you to remind you of the simple pleasures in life. She was so enchanted by the loving and caring nature of the people who, despite their lack of material wealth, seemed to have an internal wealth more valuable than anything she had ever seen.

After the town market, Anesio drove them all to the Hotel Casa Do Capitao. It was a beautiful quaint hotel with simplistic white and silver décor, set against the backdrop of the crystal clear ocean, flanked with palm trees.

Sarah and Edward sat by the infinity pool sipping on coconut milk, mesmerised by the tranquillity of the bright blue ocean, white sand, and peace that seemed to engulf the space. There was no city buzz or busyness from city life. Instead it was calm and serene, beckoning you to stay in this land and call it home.

Their lunch was served in the restaurant adjacent to the pool area. Sarah and Edward feasted on never-ending king size prawns, mussels, and various types of fish. The food was delicious, and was the perfect ending to their day of exploration.

They had spent the remainder of the afternoon swimming in the pool, basking in the sun and sipping on cocktails at the Casa Do Capitao Hotel..By the time they came back onto the ship they were exhausted..

Sarah grabbed Edward's hand and began jogging up the ramp as they embarked the ship.

'Come with me; I have a surprise for you.' Sarah smiled up at Edward, pulling him until he was near jogging.

'Where are we going to? I'm still soaking wet from swimming all day.'

'Don't worry, you won't need clothes where we are going,' she turned and winked at him as she ran ahead, forcing him to chase after her.

A few minutes later they stopped and Edward looked up at the sign, as Sarah went and chatted to someone at the desk. They were at the spa!

He could hear Sarah confirming the reservation for their full body massage, as two ladies came out and ushered them into the spa.

'What's all this?' he enquired.

'It's still part of your birthday surprise,' Sarah beamed.

'But my birthday was yesterday? And I'm the one who should be surprising you here,' he laughed, clearly enjoying all the surprises.

'It's going to be your birthday for as long as we are on this ship!' Sarah stated emphatically, before bursting into spouts of giggles.

The massage therapists seemed to turn to them and frown, which spurred on Sarah's giggling fit all the more as it dawned on her that she was supposed to be silent in the spa. Muffling her giggles, she realised she was laughing at her own attempt at a joke, which caused her to break out into another fit of laughter, provoking Edward to burst out laughing as well.

Eventually they managed to stifle their giggles long enough to look around. It was beautiful inside, with tranquil music playing softly in the distance and the breathtaking backdrop of the sun setting over the ocean coming through the glass wall in front of them. The bamboo flooring and cream coloured walls were a stark contrast to the art deco, brightly coloured design of the rest of the ship.

'Please take off all your clothes and wrap yourselves in the towels provided. Lie face down on the bed with your head through the hole,' the massage therapist instructed them, as they inhaled the scent of lavender and ylang ylang in the room.

Sarah looked shyly at Edward, and he realised she wasn't comfortable stripping in front of him.

Turning his back to her he began taking off his own clothes to allow her to feel more comfortable about taking hers off, without him gawking at her. He secretly longed to look at her, but he knew now was not the moment for that.

'You can look now,' he heard Sarah's muffled voice whisper. He had been standing staring at the wall, waiting for her to undress.

He turned around to see her lying face down on the bed, covered in a towel, with her head in the hole. He smiled to himself, as he saw her wriggle to get comfortable.

The massage therapists came in and began to massage the warm oil all over their bodies. Edward began to drift off into another place, as the scent of the aromatherapy oils engulfed him, and the soft chimes of the music allowed his mind to calm, his muscles to ease, and dreamland to approach as he floated off to sleep.

Sarah lay listening to the soft snores Edward made, and she smiled to herself. Never in her wildest dreams did she imagine she would be here lying with Edward. It amazed her that after all the pain she had been through in the past few

275

years, she could allow herself to relax once again, and be beside a man who knew how to respect her. She closed her eyes and allowed herself to be lulled into a deep relaxed sleep.

Chapter Thirty-Two

Sarah awoke in her cabin feeling as if she had won the lottery. The last 3 days had been amazing. She and Edward had spent the day before on the shoreline of the Portuguese Islands. The Dream Team had also been on the shore with them, and had entertained them with singing and dancing. They had a barbecue on the island under the thatched roof restaurant, feasting on grilled chops and prawns, with various salads provided by the ship's staff.

She and Edward had walked the makeshift market on the shoreline, where the locals sold different sarongs and bags. The brightly coloured fabrics decorated the skyline and gave Sarah new ideas of textile ranges she could launch.

Edward had held her hand all day and kept her close to his side, as they swam in the ocean and laughed until their stomachs hurt.

The evening had been spent watching a concert on the deck by the pool, sipping on cocktails that were poured into carved out pineapples, while they watched gymnasts do stunts on ropes to the sound of the music.

Sarah had danced until her thighs burned, sharpening her salsa skills under the African ocean sky. Today was their last full day on the ship; tomorrow they disembarked. Edward kept telling her he had a surprise for her today, she just didn't know what the surprise was. For now all she knew was that she needed to hop out of bed to do her daily dance with the shower curtain, before meeting Edward for breakfast at their favourite table overlooking the ocean on deck five.

'Good morning, beautiful,' Edward smiled as she walked towards him. The smell of bacon and eggs surrounded her nostrils, causing her tummy to growl in hunger.

'Good morning,' she replied, almost calling him handsome, but feeling shy to say so. He did look really handsome, however, in his plain white Lacoste golfer with beige shorts and white converse sand shoes. Her heart leapt as he rose and kissed her cheek before pulling out the chair and ushering for her to be seated.

The waiter came to take their order but Edward barely noticed, his eyes and mind were locked on her. Sarah stared right back at him, observing how his eyes twinkled as the sun beams bounced around the room.

'What's the plan for today?' Sarah blushed as she realised Edward was staring at her so intensely.

'Wouldn't you like to know,' he chuckled, but finally consented to offer up some sort of info. 'There are actually no plans – I lied,' he winked. 'We are just going to lounge around by the pool all day eating Nutella pancakes and sipping on some cocktails. Then it's off to bed for me. It's been a long three days.'

'Sounds perfect to me!' Sarah smiled, wondering what he had up his sleeve. She knew there was no way this was all he had planned, not after the way he kept telling her she would love the last day. She just had to wait and see. She had waited so long already.

They sat and ate their breakfast, reminiscing about all the lovely things they had done since embarking the ship. There really was loads to do: from watching all the shows, to relaxing at the poolside or gambling in the casino. Her favourite had been the evening shows. Each lounge on deck had different styles of music, and she and Edward would meander around listening to each performance, dancing until the early hours of the morning.

Time seemed to have gone so fast, yet it seemed to have stood still all at the same time. Being here with Edward made the rest of the world disappear. It was as if nothing else and no one else mattered. It was just the two of them getting to know each other better, and she felt herself fall head over heels in love with him. She could see he felt the same way – even though he didn't say it, he didn't have to. It was in the way he looked at her, studied her, every moment of every day. It was in the way his hand held the small of her back, or seemed to effortlessly fit into hers as he gently took hold of her hand. She felt at home with him, as if she had found the puzzle piece that fitted in perfectly with her. With all her imperfections he had stood by her side, and she knew she wanted to spend every waking moment with him.

She wondered silently if he would ever say out loud how he felt for her. She wished he would, because she wanted to tell him how she felt about him. She felt shy though. Edward had always been like her older brother. Yet somehow he had brought her healing and wholeness in a way that made him nothing like a brother, and she saw that now..

'Penny for your thoughts, princess?' Edward interrupted.

She looked up at him, her face suddenly bright red and embarrassed. If only he knew what she was thinking?

'Are you ready to go and relax by the pool?' he asked. 'I need to go and do something, so I will meet you up there a little later if that is fine with you?'

She looked up at him. A smile teased the corner of his mouth; she knew he was up to something.

'Mmm, what could you possibly be doing without me?' she teased.

He kissed her cheek as his eyes sparkled in surprise. 'Won't you have to wait and see!' With that he turned on his heel and strode off with purpose.

Sarah spent the morning on deck thirteen getting a sun tan at the solarium. Once she felt she had baked enough, she moved down to deck eleven to cool off in the pool before lounging at the poolside. Edward seemed to have been gone for a really long time, and when he eventually returned it was time for lunch. She wondered what he could possibly have done for so long! It was a ship, she thought to herself – not many places to go. Her mind couldn't help trying to figure out what he could be planning. She didn't think he was planning a massage – they had done that already. Perhaps he had bought her something in the Via Condotti shopping arcade on deck five? But surely that wouldn't have taken all morning to do?

She stared at him over lunch, hoping his eyes would give away the surprise. No luck there. His lips and eyes were sealed! She would just have to wait and see. Half the day was already gone; surely this surprise should be revealed shortly.

'Are you trying to figure out my surprise?' Edward smiled, noting her silence during lunch. He took her hand and led her back on the pool deck, ordering her an ice cream sundae from the stalls beside the pool.

'Umm, how did you know?' Sarah giggled, realising he had read her mind.

'I know you by now,' he laughed, handing her the ice cream sundae. 'What I will tell you is that after the ice cream, we will go back to your room, and all will be revealed there.'

Sarah's stomach suddenly flipped. *Go back to your room.* He had never come into her room since they had arrived here. He had constantly toyed with her: kissing her cheek; holding her hand; allowing his breath to brush against her neck as he held her close. All this without making any further advances. He would make her skin burn just by his close proximity, yet never make enough of a move to let her know exactly how he felt about her. Now he wanted to come to her room? Her cheeks burned. She didn't know what to expect or how she would react.

They sat in a strange silence as Sarah nervously ate her ice cream. Edward could sense her nervousness and he knew it was because of his statement. He needed to know if she would protest if he hinted about going to her room. Her lack of protest let him know that the plans he had for tonight should go off without a hitch. If she still saw him only as a brother, she would have laughingly questioned his statement to go to her room. The fact that she sat there all embarrassed showed him that she too felt more for him than just brotherly love.

He reached over and squeezed her hand reassuringly, letting her know he would never harm her. Then he picked her up and ran with her screaming as he threw her into the pool. As they came up for air, he pulled her close to him in the water and whispered in her ear, 'I only have the best in store for you, princess,' and with that he turned and dived back under the water, leaving her breathless at the sincerity of his words.

Chapter Thirty-Three

Sarah and Edward walked back to their cabins. He winked at her as he walked on past her door and let himself into his own room. His door clicked closed, and she realised he had not meant what she had thought earlier. Laughing self-consciously, she opened the door to her cabin and found a gift lying on her bed. She immediately knew it was from Edward, as it was wrapped in his signature white embossed wrapping paper, with red ribbon and a piece of lavender tucked in the bow. She smiled as she read the note on the box:

'Wear this for our date later tonight.

Meet me at seven pm on deck twelve in the ballroom.

Edward xx'

As she opened the box she saw a beautiful lavender evening gown folded neatly inside, and on top of it was a white gold necklace with a diamond pendant in the shape of a giraffe.

Her eyes immediately filled with tears as she realised just how thoughtful Edward was. She had told him what the giraffe meant to her before she returned to London and he had remembered. Now she could have part of Christopher forever with her. She opened the clasp and hung it around her neck.

She stared in the mirror. It was beautiful. A slow smile covered her face as excitement started to mount, anticipating what Edward had in store for their evening.

Eagerly she got showered and dressed, gently moving herself into this stunning evening gown. It was figure hugging with a sweetheart neckline and mermaid style bottom. It fitted her like a glove, as if it were specifically tailored for her. She applied her make-up, opting for a nude natural look, realising Edward hadn't actually seen her in make-up since she had returned to South Africa. She applied the nude pink eye shadow, making sure to highlight it with a pearl white complementary shade. For her cheeks she chose "Peach Wonder", and on her lips she glazed them in "Very Cherry" lip gloss. Twirling around in the tight space in her cabin, she gave herself one last look before heading out of the door to meet Edward. It was already seven o'clock.

Sarah opened the door to the ballroom and gasped. It looked beautiful. There were fairy lights dancing across the ceiling like a billion stars lighting up just for her, and an exquisite candlelit table set in the centre of the room. The room was huge but it felt so cosy, as there was a candlelit pathway leading from the door to the table. She noticed how the floor was covered in red rose petals, placed neatly to form heart shapes of different sizes Edward turned and caught his breath as he saw her. She took in his sturdy frame as he strode towards her with purpose in his black tuxedo. He was breathtaking.

'You look more than beautiful, princess," Edward whispered in the nape of her neck, as his lip brushed her cheek. 'I knew this dress was made for you the moment I laid eyes on it.'

Sarah touched the giraffe around her neck and blushed up at him.

'Thank you for the dress and the necklace,' she breathed, unable to say more, overwhelmed with emotion.

'You're welcome,' he said, holding the small of her back as he led her to the table to be seated. 'I want you to know that Christopher will always be a part of your life. He lives in your memories, and in your dreams, and now as a reminder on your necklace.'

Sarah smiled up at him, as she took her seat at the table. 'No one has understood just how significant this giraffe is but you.'

Edward leaned over and kissed the tip of her nose. 'You deserve happiness, Sarah,' he said, as he took his seat beside her. 'I will do everything I can to let you know that every day of your life.'

Sarah suddenly felt so shy and self-conscious. She had known Edward practically her whole life, yet this felt different. It felt as if it was the first time she laid eyes on him. His gaze burned her cheeks making her blush. Something had happened between them – her heart was racing wildly.

'I hope tonight is the start of new memories for you,' Edward began, as the waiter left with their orders. 'All of this is to show you what you mean to me!' His words burned with the same intensity as his eyes.

The stage beside the table suddenly lit up and a band began playing the song "Love of my life" by Brian McKnight.

'Would you like to dance?' Edward asked, his hand outstretched beside her. 'Do you remember this song?'

'How could I forget?' Sarah gasped, as she placed her hand in his and walked with him to the dance floor. 'We danced to this years ago before I moved to London, at a wedding our parents were invited to.'

Edward smiled at her, grateful that she remembered.

'You were the very first girl I've ever danced with. I was so nervous, but I asked you to dance anyway.' He leaned in and pulled her close inhaling the scent of her hair. 'Your hair still smells the same as it did then,' he breathed. 'The scent of lavender.'

Sarah touched her hair self-consciously, suddenly realising that all the gifts he had given her always had the piece of lavender in the wrapping. Even the book he gave her had the dried lavender.

'You mean…' she began.

He moved her back and looked deep into her eyes, 'I mean, I loved you then and I love you now. I love your perfect imperfections, from the freckle on your nose to the way your mouth curls to one side when you smile. I love the way your hair smells like lavender, and your eye twitches when you're mad. I love every part of you,' he finished.

'Oh Edward! If only I had known how you felt about me then!' she exclaimed.

'I was too much of a coward to tell you. I eventually plucked up the courage to tell you and bought you a book: the *Wuthering Heights* book. I knew you loved to read and wanted to give it to you and tell you how I felt about you, but then I found out your parents were taking you to live in London. It broke my heart. So I just kept the book, and never gave it to you.'

Sarah thought back to the *Wuthering Heights* book he had given her when she had moved into her new apartment. There had been two inscriptions in the book; the one was more faded and in a more immature handwriting than the other.

'This is my gift to you:
A constant reminder that death and life can never conquer love.'

And on the other page had been a neater newer inscription.

'May this book's words grace the shelves of your bookcase,
Adding to it a sense of nostalgia that nothing is forgotten.
Edward xx'

'Edward!' Sarah exclaimed. 'The book! The first inscription was written when I first moved to London?"

'Yes,' Edward smiled, seeing the light dawn in Sarah's eyes.

'The inscription written all those years ago is still so valid, not just to the plot of the book, but to the plot of our lives.'

'I know,' Edward nodded, 'I didn't know then that my inscription would actually be a telling tale of what our love had to conquer to get us to this point. From life moving you far away from me to the death of your son. My love still stands through all of that, princess, and I hope you feel the same way about me?'

'I do, Edward, I love you with my whole heart!'

With that, Edward leaned in, his lips finally meeting hers, as he passionately kissed her. His kiss sent shivers down her spine, as she melted in his strong embrace. He pulled away gently and sounded out the words to the Brian McKnight song playing in the background.

'You're more than wonderful, more than amazing, the irreplaceable love of my life,' and he leant in and kissed her again. This time the moment seemed to last forever.

When the song eventually came to an end, Edward led her back to the table and pulled out a gift from beneath it.

'More gifts?' Sarah beamed, feeling like the princess he always called her. She opened the white wrapping, smiling as she moved the lavender and red ribbon, realising how much care he had taken with every gift, to reference it back to the smell of her hair and the moment they had shared during their first dance.

As she pulled the wrapping back she realised it was a painting of the two of them kissing in the cottage in the Drakensburg.

'Edward! Is this the painting you did at Joseph's place that you never let me see?'

'Yup,' he beamed. 'I knew from that moment that I was never going to let you out of my sight again; I want you in my life every moment of every day, princess.' With that, Edward got on one knee and pulled a ring out of his pocket. 'Sarah Lewis, will you do me the honour of being my wife?'

Sarah gasped with pure joy, feeling as if she was floating outside of her own body, the gleam of the princess cut diamond sparkling in her eye.

'Oh course I will marry you, Edward!' Sarah exclaimed throwing her arms around his neck.

Edward slipped the ring on her finger and kissed her like she had never been kissed. She felt his intensity, felt his adoration, she felt the decades of love that had stood not just the test of time, but the test of heartbreak, loss, and oceans apart. It was something she had never experienced with anyone else. She pulled back and cupped Edward's face in her hands.

'You are home to me,' she whispered, and she kissed him again. Just a few months earlier Sarah could have never imagined her life would change so magnificently. Never in her wildest dreams did she think she would find true love after all her tragedy and loss. But here he was. He had been here all along; she had just never noticed him. And now she has been given a second chance to experience true love and to spend the rest of her life in the arms of the man she had belonged to all along: Edward!